POISON ROOT

by

BETH KREWSON CARTER

Charleston, SC
www.PalmettoPublishing.com

Poison Root

Paperback ISBN: 978-1-64990-816-2
eBook ISBN: 978-1-64990-815-5

TO GRAY
WITH LOVE

CHAPTER ONE

John Runar slapped his hands against the heavy wood and shoved the restroom door as it slammed against the back wall. He uttered a string of obscenities while his angry footsteps echoed across the tile floor.

In determined strides, he moved towards the row of sinks. His fingers quivered in a struggle to control his rage. With a scowl, he heaved his computer bag onto the narrow shelf above the faucets.

He stared at his own glowering reflection in the long rectangular mirror and dropped his arms onto the edge of the porcelain basin. Resentment made his eyes glow like onyx stones. Broad shoulder muscles bulged under his dress shirt as he started to ball his fists.

How had it all gone wrong? His work was supposed to be urgent, to add value. Creating a new product for the company was the first good thing he had done since his time in the Army. One revolutionary cellulose process could change the future for packaging and Delta Paper. Now everything that was truly important was going to be destroyed just because temptation struck. But then, hadn't he succumbed to temptation plenty in his lifetime?

Corporate America really fueled his contempt for unbridled profits, but he had to be honest with himself. *John Runar, you're no angel yourself*, he thought with a shake of his head.

The five o'clock shadow on his chin cast a sullen shadow across his face. He studied himself and tried to work through his still simmering fury. The situation was clearly out of control and was going to require drastic action.

Well, at least he could try to put a stop to all the madness. There had to be a way to make things better even if the solution required pain. The military taught him to take the hill regardless of the hardships. His next steps would just need to be calculated.

John shook his head at his reflection and averted his eyes. Staring at himself wouldn't solve this problem. The last thing he wanted was to lose his focus on the big picture even if he was a creature of habit when it came to his bathroom stops.

He moved away from the mirror and stomped around the corner. Rows of stalls lined both sides of the large bathroom. He stepped inside one and slid the latch in place. If he made this quick, then he could start working tonight. The first step in fixing the project would involve putting an end to all the egotistical jockeying within Delta Paper.

Without warning, the sound of unexpected movement came from an adjacent toilet. Facing the wall, John suddenly remembered his briefcase. The computer bag was unattended and out of his sight. He turned back to the door. With so much on his mind, it was no wonder that he was forgetting things, but keeping up with his one prized possession was important. The Tumi bag was the only luxury that he had afforded himself after his final overseas tour.

Before he could take a step, the stall door flew open with one powerful movement and a fist cut across his jaw. John staggered back, tripping over his own feet. His hands splayed out to break his fall.

"Jesus! What the hell?" he shouted as stars passed in front of his eyes.

Lurching out of the stall, he squared his shoulders, ready to fight. His heart was pounding in his ears as he turned towards the row of sinks. A broad forearm grabbed his neck from behind and tightened. Struggling, John dug his fingers into the cotton fabric that crushed his windpipe.

He knew the person behind him was tall with a powerful grip that came from raw emotion. Fighting to break free of the chokehold, he lifted his legs off the floor. Kicking frantically, he saw the wall just as his head plunged against it. He gasped before his face smashed again into the tiles. On the third slam, he heard a snap in his nose.

John crumpled to his knees. Blood dripped down his face, clouding his eyes with a warm red stream. A sharp heel kicked between his shoulder blades and shoved his torso into the lower corner. Instinctively, he covered his head with his hands. Combat training told him that the next blow would probably hit a kidney.

Gripping the sides of his ears, he shut his eyes and calculated the odds. What was the possibility of finding his balance from a fetal position? Could he get to his feet or was it better to play dead and wait for an escape?

Before a decision could be made, he sensed an abrupt shift in the room. Special Forces taught him to always know the position of your assailant. Now he heard pounding shoes near the sinks. The bathroom door banged shut.

Gasping for breath, John pulled himself to his knees. He wiped his eyes and tried to look around the room. His ears were ringing above the thumping in his chest. He tried to clear his head, but the floor swayed unevenly.

"What the hell?" he choked into the empty room.

He crawled around the corner on all fours and lunged towards the mirror. A moan escaped his panicked lips. The computer bag was gone. Pulling to his feet, he stumbled to the door. Whatever just happened wasn't a random assault. His attack might just be the first warning to keep silent. The blows were obviously a prologue—his own personal, painful message to heed. Trying to catch his breath, he paused as a thought raced through his mind. Was it possible that his liaison had been discovered? Maybe the beating was really about his relationship with Starla.

He opened the bathroom door and glanced into the vacant corridor. Only the dull hum from the glaring fluorescent lights in the ceiling greeted him. From where he stood, even the sounds of the mill outside the building were muted.

As he staggered down the desolate hallway, he looked over his shoulder. The front office was eerily quiet this late at night. He turned quickly into a small cubicle and waited. Without moving, his eyes scanned the nondescript shelves above the desk. He half smiled. His laptop and cell phone were right where he left them, hidden in a bookcase next to a series of bulky accounting manuals.

He stood still and listened carefully for strange noises. After a full minute of total silence, the computer went under his arm and the phone slid into his pocket. Squinting around the edge of the partition, John scrutinized every doorway along the hall. The entire floor was deserted. Quickly, he took off towards an exit sign.

Whoever took his briefcase wanted something; he was sure of it. There were far too many personal and professional secrets on his devices. All the information that he now possessed made him wary of doing anything too obvious. A feeling of ultimate triumph started to swell in his chest as he passed a cluster of silent workstations. He loved outfoxing opponents. Too bad the thief would get nothing more than a charger, a few pads of paper, and, of course, a really nice leather bag.

As he angrily stomped towards the back of the building, John realized one thing. His ambush was meant to create fear. The indigo sky beyond the glass doors made him straighten his back and set his jaw. Scare tactics never worked; he had far more courage than to surrender to intimidation.

Marching out into the night, his eyes narrowed in resolve. One way or another, he was going to stop his rivals, starting with the first one he could find.

CHAPTER TWO

John glanced out of the driver side window as his silver pickup truck roared to life. His clock on the dashboard read just past midnight; the third shift had started an hour earlier. He stepped on the accelerator as the paper mill became an illuminated consolidation of machinery in his rearview mirror.

Touching his lower lip, he winced in pain. With his hand on his face, he recognized the scent of his own blood mingled with the smell of sulfur that still clung to the fibers of his white cotton shirt.

"Damn it," he said, looking down at the skin on his thumb.

Blood smeared across his fingers and up his sleeve. In the dim glow of the F-150's odometer, he could see pits of crimson like tiny rivets spreading across his hand. All the injuries and his bloodied shirt would require an explanation at home. His wife always demanded answers even though any version of events he told her would inevitably contain a lie. His lip was starting to swell.

"John, what happened at work?" He could hear her voice in his head right now, perpetually anxious and ever so whiny. Leah continually asked questions that forced him to distort the truth.

Instinctively, he relocked his driver side door and scanned the industrial grounds. Cruising down the entrance road, the only light came from the guardhouse and the company signage along the main highway. His truck slowed down just long enough to appear nonchalant. Painfully pulling his lips into a tight line, he nodded sideways to the security officer, careful to keep only his profile visible.

The night watchman sat in a motionless stupor in the tiny security building. John eased his truck past the miniature shack that was only slightly larger than a child's playhouse. From his peripheral vision, he saw the monitor screen that displayed multiple small images of the entire facility.

John felt the guard watching him. He knew from experience that the man wore the same passionless stare that he bestowed upon the world. The expression of the ancient officer—a hard glare that accentuated his Seminole heritage—had earned him the nickname of "Chipper" from all the hourly employees.

Pulling up to the stop sign, John saw the familiar highway that ran like long black ribbons in either direction from the mill. He peered straight out of his windshield. Only the outline of scrubby trees, planted in neat rows, met his gaze. John stared into the timberlands, surveying the endless acres of conifers. The pine saplings were the one true constant in Southern Alabama. They crowded the rural terrain in the silver moonlight.

He patted his front shirt pocket as his truck eased to the left. After feeling the cell phone against his chest, his right hand automatically drifted down to the passenger seat, brushing along the edge of his laptop. In the dark, the electronics were strangely comforting. He ran a hand up and over his short brown hair and thought about the blows in the bathroom. The first move was a sucker punch, and true to form, was always followed by a beatdown. It was meant to make a point. His face felt sore, but he had endured worse in Afghanistan.

Picking up speed, he looked quickly over his shoulder. Delta Paper reigned as a single bright mountain of buildings, pipes, and industrial towers. The manufacturing facility dwarfed the entire landscape. Only the billowing steam from the process of pulping wood rose above the giant lights of the plant and drifted continuously towards the darkened heavens.

For the first time that night, he began to hesitate. Maybe going home was best. Starla would understand. After all, their relationship had grown from a one-time fling to a solid agreement. He could just call her on the Tracfone they bought together in Walmart.

Leah would have drifted off by now, curled up on her side with the small bedside lamp burning. At this hour, the kids would be asleep too. No one ever really questioned him when he came home late. He would have plenty of privacy to make any kind of call that he wanted.

In about a mile, the road would force him to make a choice. His lip was throbbing and part of him just wanted to crawl into his own bed. Perhaps he should try talking to Leah, to tell her what he had learned.

Driving along, he wondered if communication with his wife was even possible. In the last two years, the cracks in their marriage had widened. The constant bickering was like an angry ocean riptide between them. Reclaiming what they once shared seemed impossible. John shook his head as he realized the inevitable truth. Turning back the hands of time with Leah was as unlikely as pretending that everything he now knew could magically be erased. The past simply couldn't be restored. Some things were forever doomed.

The road split like the forked tongue of a snake. His subdivision rested a mile ahead on the left. The preferred group of small homes that managers seemed to overtake in Campton held no appeal for him tonight. The sleepy paved roads and unlit windows of his neighborhood would have to wait. He steered to the right.

He was heading to the trailer. His face was a mess, and he couldn't go home covered in blood. Besides, Starla should know what happened. Everything from the last few hours involved her, too.

Leaning over, he unbuckled his seatbelt and opened his glove compartment. He needed to know that she was alone, to make sure they could talk. His foot pressed the accelerator.

Plunging his hand into the open compartment, he only felt the plastic sleeve that held his maintenance records and truck registration. His pulse started to quicken. The second phone was always buried under a pair of old work gloves on the left. There was no way that anyone had been in his truck. Hadn't his side door been locked at the mill? But where was the darned thing?

With slightly frantic movements, his hand searched, tapping over every surface.

"Where the hell is it?" he asked out loud.

His arm dropped down to search the passenger seat. Jabbing on the interior light, his eyes darted between the asphalt in front of him and the truck floor.

The road curved ahead, the last spot for cell coverage. If he didn't find the phone soon, his only choice would be to pull onto the shoulder and search under the seat. He was still glancing down when the lights hit his eyes. Out of nowhere, bright beams of high wattage were coming straight towards him.

Gripping the steering wheel harder, he jerked the truck to the right. The tires rode over what felt like something hard and possibly sharp.

Before he could find the brakes, his vehicle sailed off the road. The boom made his ears ring as the trunk of a palmetto tree sliced the hood and shattered his windshield. He felt himself falling forward onto the dashboard as if in slow motion. For a split second, he realized that his thoughts were strangely calm.

The edge of sharp leather smacking his skull was followed by a sudden impact that raced through his body. He gasped for breath and everything went dark.

CHAPTER THREE

The tires made a surprising pop as they drove over the spike strip in the road. The burst of sound was startling, almost mesmerizing to him. From his car, he watched John Runar sail off the road. He only winced at the deafening boom of the truck as it folded around a thick tree and the horn began to sound. After a few seconds, the dull blare stopped.

From his position on the shoulder of the highway, he surveyed the scene without moving. Half expecting lights and sirens to follow the crash, he waited for the pavement to crowd with first responders, but the woods remained strangely quiet. In the moonlight, only the sound of the hissing motor filled the air. The usual chirp of the cicadas had fallen silent in the trees.

He slowly opened his car door and carefully started to move. His own breathing was labored in his ears as he walked onto the asphalt. Looking into the dense vegetation, he felt slightly lightheaded. The destruction was fantastic. His adrenaline started to course through his veins. Quickly, he pulled his spike strip off the road and stuffed it into his trunk.

Would John come hopping out of his seat ready to fight? He had wondered about the results of a truck careening into the forest. How bad would the injuries be? Causing a terrible crash was uncharted territory to him. The force of impact would total the vehicle, but full-scale carnage remained the desired outcome.

Approaching the edge of the woods, he was surprised by the stillness of the truck. The shadow of a figure slumped over the steering wheel made him pause. He pondered the odd angle of the body.

Why had it come to this? Why didn't people know their place, especially in situations beyond their understanding? John Runar had claimed to work for a higher purpose, but he never stopped his own bad behavior. Even when his actions hurt others, he never considered the implications. People could be such hypocrites.

With methodical steps, he made his way carefully through the sandy soil. His gloved hand gripped the driver's door for support as he looked inside the window. Digital numbers from the instrument panel cast flashing signals onto the console.

Collapsed forward into the deployed airbag, John Runar sprawled in the truck cab. His motionless torso, covered in blood, had twisted sideways. Facing the passenger seat, his body looked lifeless.

Savage fury filled his mind as he yanked open the driver side door. Two small interior lamps miraculously flickered and then illuminated. With a single punch, the bulbs were extinguished. No light was necessary for what was to come.

His hand grabbed John's hair and turned his head towards him. With a forearm under the limp neck, he held the mangled face upright.

"Runar, you knew that we weren't finished, but I'm done with you," he said with contempt.

The words sounded loud in his ears, making him angry. He didn't owe anyone an explanation. John had brought this on himself.

Throaty gags filled the cab as John rolled his head to the side. His eyes opened, but his stare wavered vacantly. Leather gloves reached for their target. John raised one hand to fend off his attacker, but strong fingers tightened their grip against his windpipe. After a minute, a dark stain spread across John's khaki clothed legs and the scent of warm urine filled the air. He studied the body when the shoulders began to slump to the side. The finality of death bolstered him.

In one movement, a small pen light began to sweep the truck. John's cell phone was pulled from his front shirt pocket. Wedged between the console and the passenger seat, the edge of a laptop protruded upward. He reached over the bloodied shirt and pulled the computer free.

Possessing both devices gave him a sense of relief. John had always claimed that he deliberately never backed up his files. Everything was supposedly saved only on a thumb drive in his office. Was that really true? If so, the external memory would have to be located, and soon.

He tried to think about every detail of the crash discovery. With the computer tucked under his arm, he stood next to the crumpled hood. Logic dictated that the accident had only taken seconds, but he felt like hours had elapsed.

With determined scrutiny, he started a deliberate slow-motion dance. Every surface was checked. Like a primordial urge, the desire to leave the woods finally made him retreat from the damage. On his way up the embankment, he used the edge of the laptop to scrape long swatches into the loosened soil. Footprints disappeared under the dirt.

He tossed the cell phone and computer onto the back seat of his sedan and smiled. The electronics looked like they belonged to him.

After a final survey of the accident, he started his car. Insects danced across the headlights as he pulled away and moved unnoticed down the empty highway.

Only after the road was left in total darkness did the cicadas start to sing again. Their chirping chorus, oblivious to the destruction that had invaded their habitat, continued with a steady rhythm. The night-time sounds of the forest grove were answered by one small human noise. Under the passenger seat, a mobile phone, the one clue that had been left behind, started to ring.

———

After driving for an hour, the sedan came to a crawl along a deserted two-lane bridge. Rolling close to the edge of the concrete railing, the car stopped. The moon cast the only light on the desolate landscape. Humidity made the car windows fog ever so slightly. The June night was still thick with heat when the driver side door opened.

Careful hands lifted the cell phone and laptop from the back seat. As they rested together on the highway, lighter fluid cascaded onto the devices. A match dropped on top. With a roar, the golden blaze danced as the plastic and glass began to melt into a pile of debris. He stood quietly, watching the dissolving components. Only the distant sounds of a train whistle and the rushing river pierced the quiet terrain.

His gloved hands grabbed the still smoldering mound and tossed it over the railing. Beneath the bridge, deep black water rushed like swift moving coffee. The remnants, fragments of minerals and synthetic layers, landed with a soft splash in the water and disappeared instantly, sinking as if nothing had ever entered the river at all.

He started his motor again. The headlights became tubular glowing fangs that cut a pathway on the empty road. He smiled to himself as the car disappeared into the mist.

CHAPTER FOUR

The police cruiser slowly eased along the side of the building and pulled into the vacant parking lot behind the store. Leaning slightly forward in his seat, Officer Hawkins peered first at the deserted loading area of the Dollar General Store and then out towards the edge of the trees beyond the pavement. At almost fifty, he had been on the job long enough to learn the value of observation. A single utility pole cast a bluish glow over the unlit business.

"We need to check the back door. The assistant manager called today and complained about some teenagers loitering around the entrances," Hawkins said to his partner. "Do you want to do the honors or shall I?"

"I'll get out and check. You keep your eyes open," Officer Landers replied as she looked up from her cell phone and unbuckled the seatbelt from around her heavyset frame.

Opening the car door, the policewoman walked slowly towards the large metal loading dock that lined the back of the business. Her eyes searched the empty lot as she pulled on the door handles until they rattled. Turning around, she shook her head and moved deliberately back towards the car.

"Locked up tighter than a drum," she confirmed, sliding into the passenger seat.

Hawkins merely nodded, still scanning the woods just beyond the parking lot. The light entering the car window made his crew cut appear silver and his ears large and wax colored. Landers reached for the can of Diet Coke in the cup holder and popped the tab.

"You still drinking that stuff?" Hawkins asked.

"Got to. I need it when I'm going to be up all night."

"Well, it's not good for you, you know," he said, in a tone he often used with his own children.

"Well, being up all night isn't good for me either, but I have to do it. Besides, if I don't drink some caffeine, I might fall asleep."

She settled into her seat and took a long sip of her soda before putting the can down. In boredom, she peered through the windshield. Silence settled over the car.

"Nothing ever happens out here at night anyway, so I have to stay awake the best way I know how," she added as she ran her hand through her short hair before resting her neck against the headrest. "God knows, Campton is one boring ass small town."

As the patrol car idled, a voice came over the radio of the cruiser.

"708, 711, and 714, respond to a traffic crash on the Mill Highway, just west of Delta Paper Company. Possible fatality. Medical has been dispatched."

The partners nodded to each other.

"This is Hawkins. We're on it, heading that way," he said into the hand piece.

Pulling her seatbelt over her chest, Landers straightened up as her eyes focused on the ebony shadows of the trees that lined the square pavement. The blue lights of the cruiser started to rhythmically rotate.

"And you were saying that nothing ever happens in Campton?" Hawkins asked as he circled the squad car around the back lot and picked up speed. "Well, let's just hope that this isn't as bad as it sounds."

———

Jasmine Landers studied the two-laned road and darkened landscape. For twenty minutes, her eyes had been sweeping the vast wooded terrain along the highway. In the path of the flashing blue lights of the police car, she spotted the silhouette at the exact moment that her partner raised a finger from his steering wheel. She watched the lone man stumble out from the scrub pines, his jeans damp from dew-covered honeysuckle vines. With wide eyes, he waved to the police.

Darrell Hawkins pulled his cruiser into the middle of the road. Both officers surveyed the figure in silence. After making quick eye contact with each other, they opened their patrol car doors and stepped into the muggy predawn air.

With deliberate strides, Hawkins moved towards the man in the grass. He slowly pulled his hand up to the black holster and rested his fingers over his gun. Landers stood by the car, studying the exchange, with her eyes covering her partner. She spoke into her shoulder radio as they watched the person on the embankment with concern and suspicion. Life mandated that any scene, at any time, could become dangerous.

"Sir, did you call about car trouble?" asked Hawkins as he stood in front of the disheveled man.

"Yeah, I called 9-1-1," the man said, a quiver in his voice.

"Are you hurt, sir?"

"Nah, it's not me," he said, turning around and pointing. "It's over there, in the woods, a truck...it's bad."

Like a well-orchestrated dance, Landers moved towards the man while her partner strode to the edge of the pavement.

"Were you in the car, sir?" she asked.

"No, I came around the curve on my way to work, and I saw it, well, the edge of it, and I stopped," he said gesturing to the truck and breathing heavily. His entire face glistened with sweat.

"What's your name, sir?" Hawkins inquired as he looked back at the man.

"Robbie, Robbie Dobbs. I work the day shift at Delta Paper. I was coming in early to have a meeting with the third shift manager in my area. I rounded the curve, and I could see the back of the flat bed in the trees."

More cobalt lights whirled into view. Policemen appeared and formed a human wall along the highway.

"Wait here," Hawkins said to Dobbs.

Pulling on plastic gloves, the partners moved towards the wreckage.

A heavyset policeman approached the shaken man as if on cue. "Talk to this other officer," Hawkins called over his shoulder to Dobbs. Repeated questions began again followed by carbon-copy answers.

Landers held a flashlight and watched as her partner carefully opened the driver side door to the truck. The body fell towards the passenger seat as soon as Hawkins touched the neck with his two fingers. He turned and shook his head.

"He's a mess," Hawkins said as he studied the figure in the bright glare of his own searchlight. "His face looks beat up, and he has odd marks on his neck, too."

"How long?" asked Landers.

"A couple of hours, but we'll let the paramedics confirm."

Hawkins backed up from the truck and squinted his eyes.

"Look at these tires," he said pointing his flashlight onto the hubcaps. "They've been shredded."

Landers bent down and studied the rubber wheels in front of her. "What do you think?" she asked.

"I think this is more than a simple wreck," he responded quietly. His gaze moved to the gathering sea of police forming on the highway as he lowered his voice. "I remember another case, years ago, where the tires were flattened like this. It was a big trial—ended up being drug related."

In the distance, a siren wailed, and red lights approached. The policemen scattered as an ambulance whipped to the edge of the asphalt.

"Over here," called Hawkins, waving his long arm to the paramedics. "Bring your headlights over here."

The ambulance bumped over the shoulder of the road until the bright front beams illuminated the twisted metal.

A first responder grabbed a medical bag and darted towards the truck as a second medic moved carefully behind the first.

Almost instinctively, quiet fell along the roadway. The line of law enforcement personnel exchanged concerned glances as they studied the accident in the early morning light.

Landers emerged from the edge of the bushes. She walked to the witness who was still talking to the same patrolman.

"Sir, I'm going to let you go with this officer over to his car. You'll need to give him all the information that you told me in a full statement."

As the two men headed towards the line of patrol cars, the remaining policemen moved expectantly towards the wreckage.

"What have you got?" asked a rookie cop as he craned his skinny neck towards the scene.

Hawkins and Landers shook their heads, their expressions sober.

"DOA," the paramedic called out from the side of the truck. "No pulse."

"Call the detectives," shouted Hawkins to the uniforms lining the highway.

"For a DOA?" asked the rookie.

"Yeah," replied Hawkins, "because this wasn't just a wreck, it was murder."

CHAPTER FIVE

The detectives pulled to a stop behind the line of patrol cars as pink light flooded the sky. The two seasoned investigators glanced at the crowd and then back at each other.

Early morning cases were either the beginning or the end of a shift, depending upon the current staffing schedule. The two detectives scanned the scene, trying to assess their first call of the day. As their car doors opened, the two bleary-eyed partners emerged to face a cluster of policemen in the middle of the highway. Lifting the yellow tape, the detectives lowered their shoulders and walked forward to the officers.

"What have you got? Who called this in for us?" asked Nick Simpson, the lead detective.

"I did," answered Sergeant Hawkins, stepping forward from the group.

The stocky lead detective walked ahead in a slow circle studying the accident before him. His hazel eyes narrowed as he looked at the road and the trajectory of the tire marks on the highway. His partner, Mia Lee, intensely scrutinized the topography.

"What makes you think this wasn't just a car wreck?" asked Detective Lee as she pulled a small notepad from the pocket of her pants.

"Several things are off on this one," replied Hawkins. "First, all the tires are completely flat, like they hit something altogether, but the road is clear. Second, his neck looks broken."

"Hawkins, isn't it?" asked Nick Simpson as he read the name badge on the older man's navy shirt to confirm his memory. "You know, people break their necks from trauma all the time. What makes you think this is any different?"

"Well, for one thing, this guy has a bruise on his neck, several of them, in fact. The paramedics said the pattern looked like a hand mark."

The detectives looked at each other and then towards the truck. They had learned to take the lead from first responders. What appeared to be only a tragic accident was starting to sound strange.

"What about ID? Who's the victim?" Simpson asked. He was already processing details, wondering if the name would be familiar on his mental radar.

"That's another thing," said Hawkins. "Just a wallet, no cell phone."

The detectives again glanced at each other. Who drove a fancy vehicle at night in rural Campton without a phone? They returned their scrutiny to the truck. The gray leather interior was visible even with the airbags resting inside like deflated marshmallows.

"I ran the plates just to be sure it matched the ID on the victim," said Officer Landers as she joined them. "The truck is registered to a John Runar. He lives on Live Oak Lane, which is in the Pineland subdivision, so I assume that he works at the mill since that neighborhood houses all the managers."

"I think I actually may know that name," said Lee as her dark eyes glanced up from her pad of paper. "Did you say Runar? I think his wife teaches school." Her lips pursed together in thought as she started to bob around other policemen to get a better look at the truck. "My kids had a reading specialist with the last name of Runar. I remember her from the teacher conferences last Spring." Lee bowed her black hair over her notes and wrote furiously.

"Well, there was something else odd," added Sergeant Hawkins. "We found a flip phone, like a cheap one, under the passenger seat."

"Any idea why a white guy in a fancy truck would have a Tracfone?" Nick Simpson asked both officers.

"I don't know," replied Hawkins as he studied the two detectives before him. "But I photographed and bagged it and left it on the passenger seat."

Pulling purple latex gloves from their back pockets, Simpson and Lee began to walk carefully towards the wreckage. Their eyes swept the entire forest as they paused to study the skid marks that left the road and trailed into the woods.

"Anything else you can add?" Detective Lee asked over her shoulder to Jasmine Landers.

"No, Hawkins pretty much covered it with you. But this is definitely more than a simple car wreck. Take a good look at those tires. They've been shredded."

The detectives squatted down to study the bottom of the vehicle as both police officers headed up the embankment.

"You not staying?" Simpson asked the pair.

"We can't. We have to tell the next of kin," said Officer Landers.

Hawkins stood on the asphalt and turned around to study the scene one last time. He caught Simpson's eye as he spoke. "You detectives aren't going to have it easy. You're going to have to figure out what a guy like John Runar's hiding."

CHAPTER SIX

Starla Pittman studied the dusky gray light seeping under the bedroom blinds as she moved her foot nervously back and forth under the covers. Her legs felt jittery in the warm room. She had been nervous for hours, even before the argument with Glen when he left for work last night. Now the crawling restlessness was starting to drive her crazy.

As her eyes moved upward to scrutinize the water-stained ceiling of her bedroom, Starla realized that it wasn't the summer heat or the marital tension in the trailer that gnawed at her. She knew what was wrong. Her hand reached out instinctively to cradle the phone that rested on the bedside table.

"Why haven't you called me?" she asked the blackened screen.

The words sounded too loud in the empty bedroom, so she dropped the telephone onto the crumpled sheets and reached again onto her side table. The pack was right where she had left them last night.

Her thumb lit the small flame as she held the cigarette in her mouth. Taking a deep drag, she tossed the lighter back towards the bedside lamp and furrowed her brow in concentration.

John had been clear, almost emphatic, about needing to talk to her when he called. Starla was actually driving home, wondering when they could be together next when her cell phone rang. John sounded serious, going so far as to ask about Glen to make sure that they would be alone. Even if it was after midnight, he said, there was something that he needed to tell her. He promised to come to the trailer. The whole conversation had replayed in her mind over and over as the hours slipped by with her waiting for the rumble of his approaching truck.

Starla smoked half of her Newport before she happened to glance at her husband's spot in the bed. For the first time that morning, she wondered if Glen even sensed a shift in their marriage these days. Of course, they fought plenty, but surely, he didn't know about John. She reached out to touch the empty spot on the mattress that they shared. If there had been any suspicions, anything at all, he would have confronted her, most likely with a smack or two. The one thing that everyone knew was that Glen never hesitated to use his fists, especially when he was angry or drinking.

Stretching out in the bed, she savored the taste of menthol. For the first time in hours, her legs finally started to relax. Starla rubbed her eyes, trying to savor the moment. She was smart enough to enjoy any morning solitude that came her way.

As she blew smoke rings towards the bedroom window, the light brightened into a whitish glare, heralding the arrival of another brutally hot day. She heard the dog bark outside and knew something else was predictable. As soon as her cigarette was finished, she would need to get up, feed Buster, and head to the mill.

Maybe John just got caught up at work last night. Her imagination often produced endless possibilities for his absences. Starla rarely wanted to envision him going home to his four-bedroom house in Pineland Estates. Ultimately, though, she knew they were just having a bit of fun.

She and John had talked about their arrangement countless times. Of course, they cared about each other, that was a given. From the start, John had been completely honest with her and admitted that he just felt hemmed in between Delta and his wife. He only stayed with her to prevent anything from jeopardizing the homelife of his children, which was understandable.

His anxiety was another separate issue. Starla figured out pretty quickly he also suffered incredible stress from his time in the military. His nightmares were continuous, even when they spent the entire night together.

She tapped her ash into a Pepsi can on her bedside table and shook her head. People might call her a lot of things, and they usually did, but Starla was no home wrecker. For God's sake, she was just trying to endure her own trapped marriage, maybe figure out what she really wanted in life. She took the last few puffs of her dwindling cigarette and brushed the blond hair out of her eyes. She and John were just two people looking for an escape. What was so wrong with a little fantasy, anyway?

Sometimes, Starla told herself that the situation could have been different if she and John had met in another time and place. From the first day he saw her, there was always a connection between the two of them, like an electric current that could spark and ignite at any moment. They could have enjoyed a real future under better circumstances.

But, in the end, the truth had a nasty way of rearing its ugly head. No matter what she pretended, if she was honest with herself, there was only one logical conclusion to their relationship. Starla would forever be just the daughter of a drunk redneck from Ocala and the Scotch-Irish woman who loved him. Her family tried to run away from their poverty but only made it as far as lower Alabama. She would have been poor no matter when or where she met John. He, on the other hand, couldn't fathom the destitution of her youth. His middle-class roots had afforded him millions of choices and options. Life for John was so totally different. His decisions could forever revolve around wants, not needs.

She finished her cigarette and dropped the butt in the soda can. Throwing off the cotton blanket and sheet, Starla sat on the edge of the bed. Even at dawn, her trailer held the heat of the morning like an oven that had been left on and forgotten.

She pulled on a light terrycloth robe and headed for the shower. Already, the thought of tepid water falling on her shoulders made her almost giddy. Standing under any water that hinted of coolness would be the most refreshed that she would feel all day.

"This bathroom is so small," she once told Glen. "I feel like I have to go outside to change my mind."

"Well, so sorry that it doesn't suit you, your highness," he retorted. "At least it's paid for, which is more than anything you had when we got together."

And it was true. Starla had still been living in her parents' shotgun house in Monroe County when they had their first date. The single bathroom home, complete with moldy walls, held all six members of her immediate family.

Now after five years of marriage, she and Glen owned a trailer with five acres of scrub pine land. The beat-up Camry that she drove was finally hers after the last payment four months ago. All in all, not too bad for a scrawny girl who grew up being called "poor white trash" by almost everyone in her backwater hometown.

Besides, she and Glen had jobs at the mill. He worked in the forestry division on a team that monitored the thirty thousand acres of managed woodlands for Delta Paper. The company had offered him one of the better jobs in the area after his short stint in the Navy. Starla only started as a temporary clerical hire four years ago, but now she had risen to the role of secretary in the front office. Although her official title read "administrative assistant" because that sounded more "team focused," the words really didn't matter to her. She was the right-hand aide to the plant manager. Of course, her trim figure only accented her office skills.

Their jobs were both good, complete with corporate benefits, which was more than Starla could have ever imagined as a little girl when her meals often came from food stamps. Every day, Glen had money in his wallet and so did she. All in all, the situation was a definite win, Starla thought as she threw her damp towel on the bed and opened her closet door.

As she pulled on her skirt that was just a bit tight in all the right places, Starla stood and looked at herself half dressed in the bedroom mirror. She thought again about where things stood in life as she reached for her lingerie. Of course, John Runar was just a fun diversion. He was married, and she was too. And Starla, more than anything, prided herself on being practical.

She hooked her bra, the soft tricot sliding across her fingertips. The feeling made her smile. These days, she got all her underwear from the Victoria Secret store in Mobile. John always gave her new things in bags so that Glen would think that she had purchased them herself. So far, the lie had worked every time. But then Glen never was one to pay much attention to the little things.

Slipping a beautiful camisole over her head, Starla delighted in the fact that the fabric felt like cream against her skin. She ran her hands over the delicate lace. Both she and Glen might have originated from the same world, but John had clearly opened her eyes to a few of the finer things in life.

In the closet, she reached for the lightest white blouse that hung among her work clothes. The day already felt like a scorcher. Besides, the top was the right choice to be both cool and yet reveal just a hint of cleavage.

Starla walked down the narrow hallway of the trailer towards the kitchen and the old white refrigerator against the far wall. With its dented door that hung slightly askew on rusty hinges, the appliance gave the entire end of the mobile home a tired feeling. Grabbing a Slim Fast and a loaf of bread, she headed for the door. Coffee was free at the mill and there was often some sort of food left in the breakroom.

As she opened the trailer door, Buster strained against his metal chain. Starla shook her head at the sight of the dog.

"Damn it, Glen," she muttered to herself. "We have five whole acres and you still tie up the dog whenever you leave?"

"Hang on, boy," Starla said, as she unchained him. "I've got your breakfast."

From a plastic bin, she filled the dog food bowl, followed by fresh water in a separate bucket from the hose in the grass.

"That should hold you for today," she told the dog. "I'll refill it tonight."

Once inside her small sedan, she let the air conditioner blast a semi-cool stream of relief over her head and shoulders. Patchy sunlight spilled in the windshield of her car as she eased down the single lane driveway. From the front seat of her Camry, she studied the dry foliage of her uncleared property. The woods already looked limp in the morning heat.

She eased her tires into the front yard of the three-room shack that sat forlornly on the property adjacent to their driveway. Without a sound, she left her car running and mounted the sagging front steps.

In one swift movement, she tied the bag of bread to the handle of the front door.

In her rear-view mirror, Starla scanned the darkened windows of the old house as she turned on the highway. The place looked deserted this early in the morning, but she knew the truth. She thought about the two children that lived there. She often saw them in the yard. Their thin faces haunted her whenever she drove by, reminding her of herself as a child.

Driving along, her thoughts returned again to John. No matter how hard she tried, her annoyance with him was clearly starting to grow. He had not even tried to call her once in the last twelve hours. It was one thing to be the object of flirtation and fun, but, at the very least, she deserved some respect. Starla looked out at the desolate landscape that bordered her small town. Maybe when she saw him today at the mill, she would just ignore his advances. Giving John Runar the cold shoulder might be a good taste of his own medicine.

Starla turned in at the large Delta Paper sign and was surprised to see a single police car parked off in the distance. Even on the long road that led to the front office, the black and white markings of the cruiser stood out against the brown bricks of the main building. Puzzled at the sight, Starla wondered what could possibly bring law enforcement onto mill property. Out of habit, she headed to the back parking lot. There was an unwritten rule that only visitors could use the dozen spots in front of the large business center.

Opening her car door, she noticed immediately how quiet the entire facility seemed. Although she could hear a few log trucks rumbling to the manufacturing gate by the woodyard, the parking lot was strangely devoid of people. Starla placed her sun reflector in her front windshield and looked around. The steam from the mill process still rose vertically to the sky, but the air felt strangely silent.

When she entered the back of the building, an eerie stillness met her at the door. Somewhere, a phone was ringing continuously. Starla was always one of the first to arrive, but now she saw only the backs of a few people huddled together at the far end of the hall.

Instinctively, she quickened her pace and turned to the left. When she opened the door to the plant manager's suite, Starla was surprised to see the rooms were illuminated. Turning on all the office equipment and lighting were tasks that she typically did at 7:30 a.m. when she arrived.

Behind Roger's closed office door, she already heard voices. Stealing a peek into the adjoining conference area, she saw that the room was empty and dark. Starla put her purse in the lowest drawer of her desk and sat down quickly. As she was logging on to her computer, the door behind her chair opened and an older policeman emerged.

"Thank you for the call," Roger McVann said seriously. "I'll let you know if I find out any additional information."

"I appreciate that," the older officer replied. "And I'll keep you informed as we learn more." The policeman flipped his small notepad closed and nodded at Starla before he silently left the room.

Roger McVann looked troubled. Somehow, Starla knew that awful news was about to be shared. "Starla, I need to talk to you," her boss began. "We've had a terrible tragedy at Delta Paper."

She felt her fingers freeze on the keyboard. In her four years at the mill, Starla never remembered the police being on Delta property. The situation had to be bad. She stared silently at Roger.

"We had an employee pass away last night. The police were here and reported there was a car wreck," he said sadly. His eyes were moist as he looked out the window to the side of her desk. He moved his gaze back to Starla's face. For a moment, she thought that her boss didn't resemble a plant manager—he only looked like a father who had lost his child.

"I'm sorry," he began. "It was John Runar. He's dead. I know that you two were friends. I'm sorry."

Starla heard a sharp cry—a screech like an animal in pain. Her mind couldn't process the loud wail, and she stared up at Roger, wanting the noise to stop. It would be a full minute before she realized the sound of agony was her own voice.

CHAPTER SEVEN

For several minutes, Starla gripped the porcelain sink in the ladies' room. Slowly, her shaking hands moved towards the faucet. A cold stream filled her cupped fingers as she brought her palms up to her face. The water mixed with her tears.

"No," she choked with a sob.

Starla dropped her hands and stared at her own reflection in the mirror. Her mind was filled with images of John. How could he be gone? How could this be happening? He had just called her last night. Didn't he need to tell her something? Maybe there was some mix-up. Maybe everyone thought that John was dead, but he wasn't. Looking at herself, she could almost see John's profile next to her bloated face.

Standing in the harsh light of the bathroom, she searched her shell-shocked eyes for answers, but her brain was numb. She was straining to think. The glaring overhead light combined with her own rapid breathing and made her feel like she was falling into a nightmare. Wet knuckles rubbed across her mouth. Her mascara was now gone. Starla grabbed two rough paper towels from the dispenser and tried to dry her hands. She needed to compose herself.

For the first time, she looked around the empty room, and felt gratitude for the momentary solace. Thank God nobody else was in the bathroom to witness her meltdown. She took deep breaths, try-ing to pull herself together before plastering her typical cool-eyed expression onto her face.

Starla reached for the handle of the bathroom door but then hesi-tated. Biting her lower lip, dread started to fill her stomach. How was she going to make it through the day at Delta? What was she go-ing to say to everyone? Standing there, the thought of facing the rest of the office staff and their inevitable comments started to make her panic. What would they say to her? How many of them knew about her relationship with John? Anxiety rose in her chest, but she squared her shoulders and straightened her skirt.

With weak legs, she headed down the hallway to her desk. As she passed a group of managers huddled together, their low voices seemed to follow her.

"Hey, Starla," one of the IT technicians called out behind her. "Did you hear about John Runar?"

Starla stopped in her tracks, turned, and stared at the assembly of questioning heads that peered towards her.

"Yes," she managed to say.

"You were friends, right? I mean I saw him up here talking to you," continued the young man.

Starla stared at them and felt her head nod slightly. From their inquisitive faces, she knew they had been talking about her. She won-dered what her empty expression told the office clique. Inside, her heart cracked like it was breaking into a million pieces.

"I'm sorry," continued the young man.

She merely looked at him. Her words felt blocked.

"I'm sorry," he repeated again, more gently.

Starla felt dazed as she shuffled back to the plant manager's suite. Sights and sounds swirled around her in a blur. Before she could reach her seat, the phone on her desk began to ring incessantly. With her mind in a fog, Starla sat down and reached for the receiver, oblivious to the name on the caller identification screen.

"Roger McVann's office," she said flatly.

"Starla," Glen was on the line. "What's going on at the mill? The news reports are all over some story about a guy that that was killed—some Delta manager. It's on the TV news, and my phone is blowing up about it."

Starla shut her eyes. The sound of Glen's voice made everything harder.

"Yes," she said shakily. "A manager named John Runar was killed in a car wreck. The police have already been here this morning."

"Was it a crash like the news said or a mill accident? Why were the police there?"

"They came to the front office to talk to management," she replied. Glancing over her shoulder, she noticed that the door to Roger's office was shut.

"Well, everybody's all over this story. It's on the morning news and everything. The reports make it sound like there was more to this guy's life than meets the eye."

Starla froze. There was something in Glen's voice that made her catch her breath. Was it just her imagination or was he being smug? For the first time, Starla felt a rise of fear in her chest. John's death and any investigation into his connections could unravel her life.

"I have to go," she told her husband.

Starla hung up the phone and reached for a tissue on her credenza. When she turned back around, a police officer was standing next to her desk, staring down at her.

CHAPTER EIGHT

Starla gave a startled jolt.

"Starla Pittman?" Detective Lee asked as she stared intently at the woman sitting before her.

"Yes."

"You're the administrative assistant to the plant manager?" Lee asked as she glanced at the nameplate on the front of the desk.

"Yes," Starla answered. "You, um, scared me. I didn't hear you." A forced smile contorted her face.

The detective looked impassively around the room as if she was studying every detail. Starla felt her own jaw tighten as she stared at the officer who returned her gaze with unsettling silence.

Starla dabbed her eyes with the tissue she held. "You'll have to excuse me. This has already been a really difficult morning."

"I'm Detective Lee. I'm with the Campton County Sheriff's Department. I'd like to ask you a few questions," she began.

The sunlight coming through the office window bounced off the metal shield that hung around the detective's neck from a beaded lanyard. Starla suddenly felt hot. Her palms started to sweat as she clutched the damp Kleenex.

"All right," she said. Her tongue tried to wet the inside of her mouth.

"A plant employee, Mr. John Runar, was killed last night in a car accident," said the detective calmly. "I was wondering what you could tell me about me about Mr. Runar?"

Starla swallowed. Her eyes darted around the room and she hesitated. "Well," she began quietly. "Mr. Runar was an employee here at Delta Paper. He was a manager."

She stopped, letting her voice trail off softly. The detective's unmoving stare gave her the feeling of being under surveillance, and perhaps trapped.

"Um, I don't really know what you are looking for," Starla said slowly. "Perhaps you might want to talk to Human Resources or the people in his department."

"And what department would that be?" asked the detective.

"Finishing," she replied quickly.

Lee looked surprised. "Do you know everyone's department right off the top of your head?"

"Well, it's a small mill," Starla answered briskly.

Detective Lee raised her eyebrows again in question.

"I mean, it isn't exactly small. It's just that we all know each other. We work together, like a family" she started to explain.

"Were you and Mr. Runar friends?" The question was smooth yet pointed.

"Well, yes," Starla said haltingly. "Of course, we were friends," she added nodding her head.

"Could you think of any reason that anyone would want to hurt him?"

Ideas, like shards of glass, cut through her mind. "Hurt him?" Starla asked, confused. "No, no. Why would anyone hurt him? He was a nice man."

The detective stood before her without speaking. She appeared ready to ask another question, but she hesitated.

"Here's my number," she said producing a card from her shirt pocket. "If you think of anything else about Mr. Runar, or anything that may have indicated a problem for him, please call the number listed."

Starla watched the detective walk noiselessly out of the plant manager's suite. Sitting at her desk, she exhaled slowly, trying to process what the detective had said.

John Runar had a number of problems, Starla thought ruefully as she looked into the empty hallway beyond her desk. As her fingers gripped the card, thoughts suddenly crowded together in her head. Fear started to churn in her stomach. She swallowed hard, tasting vomit somewhere in the back of her throat.

Starla's eyes grew misty again as a new reality pushed its way to the forefront of her mind. All the details of John Runar's life were going to come to light, she realized. Eventually, all the revelations would lead the police right back to her.

CHAPTER NINE

The patrol car slowly eased down the first azalea lined street of the Pineland Estates subdivision as lemon-colored hues of daylight covered the sky. In the cruiser, Sergeant Hawkins and his partner looked grimly at the Spanish moss covered live oak trees that dotted the manicured front lawns. The officers sat in silence. They dreaded the task at hand.

"What's the address again?" asked Hawkins as he drove uncharacteristically under the speed limit.

"624 Live Oak Lane," answered Landers. "I think it's the next left."

As the preferred housing for the mill management at Delta Paper, most of the homes appeared only slightly larger than the other residences in Campton, Alabama. The partners stared out of their windshield at the still darkened homes. Small town hierarchy dictated that the neighborhood, regardless of house size, was elite. Divisions within the mill town were strong and only managers and a handful of Campton professionals owned real estate on the quiet streets that they now traveled.

Turning the corner, a single salt box style colonial house appeared at the end of a street. Landers pointed at the corresponding numbers reflected on the side of a wrought iron mailbox that stood next to a driveway.

"This is it," Hawkins confirmed as he pulled in behind a darkened red minivan.

The two officers opened their car doors and noticed the intense quiet of the street. Except for the sound of birds in a nearby pine tree, the neighborhood was completely silent. Making eye contact over the roof of their car, they both moved toward the brick walkway and began to approach the house with heavy steps. Hawkins rang the doorbell and waited.

Through the glass front door, a single lamp inside wobbled as a terrier rounded the corner, bumping the small hall table. The barking was ear-splitting.

A little girl opened the door and stood blinking in the morning glare.

"Is your mother at home?" asked Hawkins, in a softened tone of voice.

Nodding her head, she scooped up the dog and disappeared. The two officers exchanged concerned glances.

"Yes?" A woman stood in the door frame. Her honey-colored hair was pulled into a disheveled ponytail and she wore a long white cotton robe.

"Mrs. Runar?" asked Officer Hawkins.

"Yes," she replied.

"Mrs. Leah Runar?"

"Yes, I'm Leah," she replied.

"Mrs. Runar, I'm Sergeant Hawkins and this is Officer Landers. I'm sorry to disturb you so early in the morning, but there has been an accident."

"Accident? What kind of accident?" she asked with panic in her voice. She stared at the officers on her doorstep with wide eyes.

"Mrs. Runar, we are sorry to tell you this, but there was an accident on the Mill Highway and your husband was involved."

"John?" Leah grew suddenly white.

"We're sorry to tell you that your husband was killed in what appears to be a one-vehicle car crash. His truck hit a tree off the road."

With a crying gasp, Leah stumbled backward as Landers moved forward, trying to steady her.

"Ma'am, we're truly sorry," said Landers, as she held the woman's arm in support. "May we come in?" she asked, with one foot already on the threshold of the door. Leah stepped to the side limply as the two officers entered the small foyer. She merely pointed to the room on the right.

Morning sunlight was just framing the edges of the drawn blinds that covered the bay window. The room was empty except for a large desk that took up a third of the floor and two chairs nestled in a corner that seemed to create a small conversation area. Landers guided Leah to one of the armchairs by the window as Hawkins followed.

"Ma'am," began Hawkins as he stood in front of her, "we're terribly sorry for your loss." There was a slight pause in his words. "But we do need to ask you some questions."

The little girl rounded the corner of the room still carrying the terrier. He growled in her arms at the sight of the officers.

"Mommy?" she asked.

"Sarah," said Leah with a shaky voice, "go into the kitchen. I'll be there in a minute." The woman looked at the officers and they nodded. The child stood there, as if trying to decide what to do. Without a word, she turned and disappeared around the corner.

"Would this be easier at the station?" Landers asked gently.

"No," she choked out. "No, I don't want to leave my children." The officers nodded.

"Mrs. Runar," began Hawkins, "was your husband supposed to be at home last night? What was his work schedule?"

"John..." said Leah as she swallowed and put her hand to her throat. "John was supposed to come home late last night. He had a late meeting at the mill, and I fell asleep."

"What time was his meeting?" asked Hawkins.

"I don't know," she hesitated. "Late, like after eight, maybe. I really don't know."

"Do you know who he was meeting? What were they discussing?"

"I really don't know. It was work stuff–a new project that he was leading...." Her voice trailed off to a whisper.

"And did you expect him to come home? Were you concerned when he didn't return?" Landers asked the question softly as she studied the woman. Her tone conveyed sensitivity, but she leaned forward to gauge a response. The question was absolutely critical.

"I expected him home, but I fell asleep." She looked up, her eyes pleading for understanding.

"In the middle of the night...when he wasn't home...did you try to call him?" Landers fumbled.

"I was asleep. I watched The Late Show in bed and slept with the TV on," she answered. "I didn't wake up until I heard the kids this morning."

The officers nodded.

"It was a car crash, you said?" Leah asked.

"Yes, ma'am," Hawkins affirmed. "It appears that his truck left the road and hit a tree."

"Was he alive? After he hit the tree?"

The officers exchanged quick glances with each other.

"Ma'am," said Hawkins, "it doesn't appear that he was alive for long." Leah started to sob into her hands. She wiped her face on her sleeve.

"Can we call someone for you?" asked Landers.

"No." She stood up and faced both officers. "I need to be with my children." Hawkins nodded at Landers and they moved slowly into the foyer.

"Ma'am," asked Hawkins as he stood at the door, "did your husband have a cell phone?"

"Of course," she answered. "He just got a new iPhone last month. Do you have it?"

"No, ma'am," answered Landers as she looked at her partner. "They're still cleaning up at the scene."

Leah nodded absentmindedly and opened the door.

"We are so sorry for your loss," Landers said over her shoulder. The door closed behind them and the officers stepped onto the brick walkway. They trudged in silence back to their car.

"What do you make of it?" asked Hawkins after closing his driver side door.

"Well, seems like several things were off there," replied Landers as she looked back thoughtfully at the quiet house. "Does anyone really sleep all night, oblivious to the fact that their spouse never comes home? And sleeping all night with the television on and never waking up until morning? I don't think so."

Hawkins turned the key in the ignition and nodded in agreement. "I thought the same thing. We are definitely going to need to talk to the detectives on this case. But the first question is why a guy with an iPhone even has a disposable phone? What was he using it to do?"

CHAPTER TEN

Nick Simpson stood in the doorway and surveyed the cramped office in front of him. Desks, one behind the other, almost filled the entire rectangular room. In confusion, he glanced at the nameplate on the open door and then back at the crowded arrangement. For a Human Resources department, the space was smaller than most single car garages.

Seated closest to the door, a plump, middle-aged woman looked up from the papers in her hands. Her surprise at the visitor made her push her sausage biscuit toward the edge of her cluttered workspace.

"May I help you?" she asked.

"Yes," he replied. "I'm looking for the Human Resources department."

"This is HR," she said.

"I'm Detective Simpson with the Campton County Sheriff's Department. I was directed to this office because of an accident this morning. The gentleman involved was John Runar, a Delta Paper employee."

At the far end of the room, another woman had risen from her chair and moved through the maze of furniture towards the visitor.

"I'm Carmen Thomas, the HR manager," she said extending her hand. Her skin was the color of cafe au lait and her hair was pulled tightly back with a clip. "Mr. McVann called and said that you would be stopping by. This is Anne Dowden." She motioned to the seated woman.

"I'm going to need to speak with Mr. Runar's co-workers as well as his boss. Also, anyone that Mr. Runar may have had daily interaction with at work will need to have a word with us."

"Of course, whatever you need. Mr. McVann informed us that you would need to speak to several people from the area where John worked. He was in the Finishing Department. Fortunately, most of the managers in that area are on the day shift."

Carmen Thomas stood before the detective. Her aqua suit stood out against the drab beige décor of the room. Nick noted her confidence. Her professional image seemed in contrast to her colleague. His gaze drifted down to the older woman at her desk. There was something about the plump figure and large eyeglasses of Anne Dowden that reminded him of a grandmother. With a quick sideways glance, he realized that his partner now stood behind him in the hallway.

"This is just so terrible," lamented Anne as she reached for a tissue. Her curly gray hair shook with sadness and she looked ready to cry. "Mr. Runar was such a nice man. This is just devastating to our mill community."

Simpson said nothing as he watched the older woman blow her nose into a tissue and roll her chair over to throw away the crumpled heap of limp paper. The trashcan was already overflowing.

"Detective," said Ms. Thomas, "we have you set up in a small conference room here in the front office building. It should allow you to speak to people one at a time or all together. Here, follow me, and I'll show you to the area you can use."

As the trio walked quietly down the carpeted hallway, heads of employees seemed to pop over partitions and emerge from doorways. With wide eyes, they studied the officers. Both detectives glanced at each other. A visit from investigators would undoubtedly be the subject of intense gossip.

"Here you go," Ms. Thomas announced as she reached for the light switch at the doorway. "This is our Forest Room."

The detectives stood before a boxy meeting space and stared at the massive table in front of them. With a top made from a single section of a huge cypress tree, the polished rings fanned out over the pedestal base in an amazing testimony to the power of nature. The overhead lights flickered against the knotty wall paneling of the room. The space felt like a salute to everything made from wood.

"Here is your first manager," announced Ms. Thomas as she looked down the hallway. "I'll leave you to it," she said as she moved away from the door.

From the end of the corridor, a man in his early thirties approached the detectives. The officers watched the impressive figure moving in long strides. Hearing protection hung limply around his neck and he placed a binder under his arm before removing his safety googles. With his hard hat sitting on his head and steel-toed boots laced up to his ankles, he appeared taller than either detective.

"I'm Ethan Weir," he said. "You must be the officers in charge of the Runar case."

"I'm Detective Simpson, and this is Detective Lee." Ethan extended his large outstretched hand to the pair and then removed his white safety hat. "We would like to ask you a few questions about John Runar," said Simpson, motioning towards the empty room. He followed the detectives inside, shutting the door behind him.

"Your name again? And how well did you know Mr. Runar?" asked Simpson as the group settled in their seats.

"My name is Weir, Ethan Weir, but you can call me Ethan. I'm John's boss, or I was John's boss, in a manner of speaking."

"Okay, Ethan, tell us about John Runar."

"Well, he's been at the mill for about, gosh, I would have to check his personnel records to be exact, but I'd say about five years. He was a veteran with an engineering degree from Auburn. He served in the Army, I think. He joined Delta right after exiting the military. His first couple of assignments were in different departments at the mill, but he has been in the Finishing Department for the last year."

"Were those normal lengths for assignments?" asked Detective Lee thoughtfully. "Was that an indicator that he struggled to find the right fit at work?"

"Well, assignment lengths can vary. John was working on a project that kept him in the Finishing Module this last year," explained Ethan.

"What kind of project?" asked Lee.

"John was testing a new process that promised to revolutionize packaging."

Both officers looked at each other.

"What do you mean 'revolutionize packaging'?" asked Nick Simpson as he studied the man before him. For the first time, the detective wondered if his own lack of understanding regarding the pulping process at Delta Paper would hinder the investigation.

"John was developing a finishing application that would allow cellulose based material to be used to create shelf stable packaging."

The detectives furrowed their brows. They glanced at each other again. Comprehending technical production terminology was proving to be a problem.

"We're not sure exactly what you mean," said Simpson. "Tell us, in plainer English, what you mean by that."

"John was working on creating a process that could produce a unique product," Ethan said, slowing down to choose his words carefully. "This product would let any item stay on a shelf, without refrigeration, and maintain freshness almost indefinitely."

"And this was an important project?" asked Lee, as she wrote on the pad of paper before her.

"Of course," Ethan answered. "It could be a game-changer in the industry. Delta Paper could lead the pack as far as creating a base material for a new class of packaging."

"And this would be used how?" asked Simpson.

"The applications are endless. Food could be shipped without the need for refrigeration. Developing countries could keep, ship and distribute food with ease. Products like this could change the way people are fed; it could change the way medicine is delivered. The applications are limitless." The detectives both wrote notes and looked up at the man in front of them.

"Well, that's quite a project. Were there patents involved?" asked Lee as she narrowed her eyes in thought.

"The patent for the pulping process was scheduled to start after John's testing was complete."

"And exactly how would he do this testing?"

"We have a lab here," added Ethan. "He worked between Finishing, which was his department, and the lab."

"Was this project going well? Was it progressing?" asked Lee.

"Yeah, he was really making headway. Delta is looking to roll out this product to our project customer that will then integrate it in the marketplace."

"It sounds like an important company initiative," said the Simpson. "So, where did Mr. Runar store the test results?"

"We are a fully integrated facility, but most of the time, he had things on his phone. He also used the mill computers."

"Did he always keep his phone with him?" asked Simpson slowly.

"Of course," Ethan answered. "He was fairly addicted to it, but I guess we all are," he said with a laugh.

The detectives shot a quick glance at each other.

"And Mr. Runar got along well with everyone?" asked Lee. There was hesitation, and the room grew quiet.

"If there's something that you want to say, this is a great time to say it. Every piece of information can be important," coaxed Detective Lee with a nod.

Ethan shifted in his chair and for the first time seemed to falter. "But it was just a terrible car wreck, right? I mean, that's what happened—that's what everyone is saying."

"It was a car wreck, and we are investigating, but we haven't ruled out anything," said Simpson looking carefully at the man before him. Ethan Weir's expression of concern seemed to highlight the gray hair that was just starting to grow from his temples.

There was silence again in the room.

"This really is the time to give us all the facts," added Lee as she leaned into the table. "If you have anything to add, this is the best time to share information."

"Then I guess you should know something," Ethan began. "Yesterday there was a terrible fight."

CHAPTER ELEVEN

"A fight? Do you mean an actual physical altercation?" asked Detective Lee.

"Well, yes," admitted Ethan as he rubbed his neck with his large hand. "John and another manager really got into it." The two detectives locked eyes.

"You saw this fight?" asked Simpson.

"Yes," confided Ethan. "I even had to separate them."

"And do you know the nature of this fight? Who was involved?" asked Lee evenly.

"It was John and Travis. Travis Hutson. He is the hourly supervisor in Finishing."

"Tell us more, Ethan. Was it work related? Or did they have a personal problem with each other?" inquired Simpson as he studied the man before him.

Ethan Weir sighed and sat back in his chair. He stretched out his long legs under the table and crossed his ankles.

"Travis and John didn't get along, sort of an oil and water combination. From day one, they always seemed at odds."

"What was the nature of the fight yesterday?" asked Lee calmly.

"Yesterday," said Ethan, "was just a continuation of months of tension. But it all started with the project."

"Not everyone was on board with the new packaging product?" asked Detective Simpson.

"It's cellulose grade that is being made here," corrected Ethan. "We don't make any finished products here at the mill. We are strictly taking raw materials and creating bales and rolls of pulp for customers. The project that John was leading already had a company lined up to create the packaging from the specific grade of cellulose that he had designed."

The detectives merely nodded.

"But, no," continued Ethan, "not everyone was on board. Travis saw the incredible investment in this project as a threat to our other established customers due to the large number of resources allocated for John's work. I also suspect there was some jealousy from Travis. John was a young manager with a college degree, and Travis is a seasoned hourly technician in a supervisory role. This project was likely to be a career builder for John."

Simpson had been writing quick notes and studying Ethan Weir. Questions now swirled through his mind.

"So, tell me, Ethan," he proceeded, "what was the fight like? Was it physical?"

"It didn't start out that way, but in the end, I had to pull Travis off John. They both took a couple of swings at each other."

Both detectives raised their eyebrows.

"Go on," coaxed Lee.

"Travis had blood on his shirt. They were both furious. Travis was really worked up and angry."

"Did they say anything to each other?" questioned Lee.

Ethan shot a quick glance at both detectives. He hesitated and continued. "Travis told John that he would pay for the fight and screwing up production."

"Was that all?"

"No," admitted Ethan. "John used every four-letter word and told him to go to hell. Then Travis looked him square in the eye and told John to watch his back because he was going to make him pay for being such a miserable company backstabber."

CHAPTER TWELVE

Steam rose from the paper cups in Nick Simpson's hands as his partner closed the door of the small meeting room. Both detectives moved to the large table, ready to compare notes before the next interview.

"So, what do you think?" Lee asked as she took a sip of the slightly stale coffee.

"I think we need to talk to Travis Hutson next," responded Simpson as he blew on the lip of his disposable mug.

"A fight and then an accident," commented Lee. "That's rarely a coincidence."

"I agree, but somehow I think that we're going to find out that there's a bit more to Mr. Runar than just a career at Delta Paper."

"Who would have ever thought that an industrial mill filled with manufacturing processes requiring technical skills and physical labor would have so much emotional drama?" asked Lee in amazement as she stared at the oily grounds in her cup.

There was a knock on the closed door and the detectives fell silent. "Come in," answered Simpson as both partners flipped their memo pads to clean sheets of paper and rose to their feet.

"Are you the ones that I need to talk to? I was sent up here by my area manager."

"Come in," Detective Simpson said to the short, stocky man in the doorway. "And what's your name?" he asked.

"I'm Travis Hutson. Mr. Weir said that you needed to talk to everyone from the Finishing Department and lab. He sent me up here first."

The detectives studied the man as he moved into the room. At just under six feet tall, Hutson had a broad chest and large arms that testified to a lifetime of physical labor. With straight dark hair, his deep brown eyes looked warily around the meeting space.

"We're detectives with the Campton County Sheriff's Department. I'm Detective Simpson, and this is Detective Lee."

"Have a seat," said Lee, motioning to the chair.

Hutson placed his phone face down on the wooden surface in front of him as he rested his arms on the table.

"We need to ask you some questions," began Simpson. "It's about John Runar. He was killed last night out on the Mill Highway."

Travis Hutson simply nodded and remained motionless.

"May we call you Travis?" asked Detective Lee.

"That's fine," he replied.

"Travis, tell us about your relationship with John Runar," started Detective Simpson with his eyes glued on the stoic man in front of him.

"John works, or I should say worked in Finishing. That's my department."

"And you got along well?" asked Simpson smoothly.

There was lull in the room. Travis Hutson stared at the detectives in front of him. "John and I had our differences," he said carefully.

"Tell us about that," said Lee lightly.

"We didn't see eye-to-eye, as you might say," Travis responded, his jaw muscles tensing with each word.

"Did you argue?" asked Detective Simpson.

There was a pause. Leaning back in his chair and folding his thick biceps across his chest, Travis calmly smiled and started to shake his head. "Oh, I get it. You heard about the fight. The one that John and I had yesterday."

"Was it a fight, Travis? Why don't you tell us about that?" continued Simpson.

"John just never quit. He also rarely listened," started Travis as he sat up straighter in his chair. "Whether he wanted to admit it or not, there's more going on at Delta than just his precious pet project." The two detectives only blinked.

"Do you know how many customers we have?" asked Travis hotly. Without waiting for an answer, he continued. "Let me tell you, we have over eighty different buyers for our pulp. All of them have standing orders. In any given week, we have bales and rolls leaving this mill by rail and truck for contracts that already exist," he almost shouted.

"That sounds profitable," commented Lee quietly as she surveyed the man at the table.

"Hell yes, it's profitable!" he answered. His voice had risen to a crescendo as the detectives merely looked at each other.

"And Mr. Runar didn't share your concern about your existing customers?" asked Detective Lee.

"No, he did not!" The words spat out of his mouth. "John didn't give a rat's ass about anything that wasn't his project. If it didn't concern his one customer and his possible new application for cellulose fibers, then he blew it off and ignored it." He stopped as his eyes flashed in anger at the two detectives. "You can't run a business that way," he added through clenched teeth.

"I see," said Detective Simpson calmly as he nodded in agreement. "And yesterday, Travis, is that what you argued about?"

"Hell yes! We had standing orders with customers waiting and John was directing everyone to stop so he could run more tests on his project batch of pulp on the drying machine."

The detectives sat calmly and waited.

"We were running out of time!" said Travis emphatically. "We had rail cars that were going to leave our facility that were not at capacity. He was being a prick, and he just wouldn't listen!"

Both detectives appeared to be writing notes. The conversation momentarily ceased. "Travis, who threw the first punch?" asked Lee as she looked up from her paper.

There was silence in the room.

"It was mutual," Travis finally said slowly.

"Mutual? No fight is ever really mutual, Travis. Someone always has to swing first," said Simpson.

There was another pause. Travis had a coldness in his expression.

"Sounds like maybe you hit him first," coaxed Simpson.

Travis turned his head to the shuttered windows and said nothing. He crossed his arms over his chest again.

"So where were you last night, Travis?" asked Detective Lee.

With a jerk of his head, his stare hardened again at the officers before him. "Oh no," Travis said deliberately. "No, you aren't going to pin his accident on me."

"So, where were you?" asked Lee again.

"I was home, for God's sake. I went to the house after the dayshift."

"Anyone with you, Travis?" inquired Detective Lee.

"No," he said pointedly. "I live alone."

Lee and Simpson wrote on their pads again and let a full half-minute elapse.

"No wife, Travis? No significant other? No kids?" asked Detective Simpson.

"I have kids—two sons. They live with their mother in Fairhope."

"So not one person can verify that you were at home last evening?" asked Detective Lee.

"No!" Travis snarled. "But I had nothing to do with anything that happened to that lying piece of shit!"

"And tell us Travis, why do you call him that? A lying piece of shit?" pressed Lee as she again scrutinized the man at the table.

"Because John Runar wasn't so great," Travis replied. "Yeah, I know he was a veteran and all, but he had plenty of dirty secrets. Check out his phone and you might just find out who he really was."

CHAPTER THIRTEEN

Detective Simpson pulled his Chevrolet Tahoe into an open spot in front of the Campton County station. Rising out of the sandy soil, the low precinct sat behind a landscape of boxwoods and pine trees. With glass doors and a flat roof, the beige stucco exterior was a dead giveaway to the institutional nature of the building. Opening their vehicle doors, the two detectives immediately felt the sticky heat of the late Alabama afternoon.

"Let's do a preliminary gathering of facts, and then we can call it a day," said Simpson as he walked through the double doors and into the air-conditioned lobby. "Your kids okay for another hour or two while we finish up here?" he asked.

Detective Lee looked up from her phone and nodded. "One of the benefits of living with my mother is that she can handle the children until I get home."

"Living with parents, I don't know—better you than me," Simpson joked.

With a nod to the front desk officer, the investigators moved to a back room. Their adjoining desks had been littered with papers in their absence.

"Would you look at this mountain of paperwork?" asked Lee. "We've been out in the field for most of one day, and I have more reports on my desk than ever."

"At least you got to check your email while we drove back. I bet my inbox is overflowing," replied Simpson wearily.

Lee moved to a large white board at the far end of the small office. She picked up an Expo marker and turned to her partner.

"I say we just get the basic facts up here while everything's fresh. The paperwork and emails can wait until we're done."

Simpson nodded in agreement as he settled in a chair and opened his notepad. John Runar's name covered the center of the board.

"I think we have to put Travis Hutson up here," said Lee as she started to jot words on the surface. "We know there was a fight and bad blood between the two. Also, he has no alibi for last night."

"Did anyone else strike you as a suspect? Anyone else that we interviewed at the mill?" asked Simpson.

Grabbing her notes, Lee flipped through the pages of her notebook. "Not really," she said. "Nobody jumps out at me from the managers that we talked to today."

"Put the phone information up there," added Simpson. "Everything that we know so far tells us that there are multiple phones, but one is missing."

Lee was still writing when the door opened. Simpson turned to the approaching police officer. "Hawkins, did you talk to Mr. Runar's widow?" asked the older detective.

"Yeah, that's what I came in here to discuss with you. Landers and I went out to the see the next of kin this morning," he said with a serious look and shake of his head.

"It never gets easier," assured Simpson with almost a paternal tone.

"No, it doesn't," agreed Hawkins. "The widow claims that she didn't know her husband failed to return home. She said that she slept with the television on until morning. I put everything in this report," he said handing the papers to Simpson. "But I do have more information that you need to know. Landers is checking out the credit cards of the late Mr. Runar, but we did get information back about the phone that we found at the scene."

"Okay," said Detective Lee as she capped her marker and placed it by the board. "What'd you learn?"

"The Tracfone primarily had calls made to one number. There were a few miscellaneous calls, but it was mostly used to contact one party."

"And?" Simpson asked.

"Well, it wasn't easy to trace. Evidently the party called was also a disposable number. But I went about it a couple of ways. Both phones were purchased at the same time from Walmart. It's a safe guess that Runar bought both phones simultaneously." Lee had moved to her desk to listen. "The number that John Runar called most often pinged off a cell tower in Broadax."

"That's out in the middle of nowhere," said Simpson as he furrowed his brow.

"True," said Hawkins with a smile, "but I did a bit of internet snooping."

"What did that tell you?" asked Lee as she propped her arm on the edge of her desk.

"It verified communication with another number that corresponds to the other phone he purchased. But John Runar's Tracfone also called a certain mill phone number repeatedly. We could figure out which line he called at Delta Paper, and on a hunch, we looked at county registration records to see if that same name lived in the Broadax area. There was a definite match."

"Who?" asked Simpson.

"It's out in the sticks, but one name stood out to us. It matched the office number at Delta Paper that Runar called. The line is listed as belonging to a secretary in the front building," said Hawkins. "Her name is Starla Pittman."

CHAPTER FOURTEEN

Starla Pittman slowly walked to her car. In the blazing late after-noon sun, the humidity in the air slapped her face like a wet cloth. She trudged along the parking lot struggling to breathe and feeling the heat of the asphalt right through the soles of her pumps. As she neared her hood, a slip of white paper on the windshield made her frown.

She opened her driver side door before reaching under the wipers. Carefully, she sat down on the sweltering cloth seat and started the engine. The black interior of the sedan radiated heat with the intensity of a furnace. She adjusted the vents to let the car cool down. The blasting air conditioner felt like a blow dryer.

Starla unfolded the paper and started to read. For a moment, she struggled to comprehend the words in front of her.

Forget what Runar told you. If you talk, you will be sorry.

Despite the heat, she felt a chill down her spine. The note slipped from her fingers and hit the floor mat by the console.

In one movement, Starla grabbed her keys from her ignition and staggered to her feet. She slammed the car door shut and put her hands on her knees. Her head was spinning as she gasped for air.

"Are you okay?" Starla looked up to see Ethan Weir taking long strides across the pavement. A look of concern covered his face.

With an inward groan, she tried to steady herself. Ethan Weir was one of the managers who always made a point of speaking to her. She straightened up to meet his troubled gaze, wishing that just for once he would walk by without being his usual polite self.

"I'm fine, just fine," she said, trying to smile.

Ethan stood beside her. His hard hat made him appear tall and solid, and he put a gentle hand on her back. "You look like you're going to faint," he said, ready to help her.

"No, I'm fine, really I am," she said. "I just…it was…oh, never mind."

"Are you going to be sick?"

"I just saw something…," her voice faded as she backed up against her car.

"You look like you've seen a ghost," he said, and then added apologetically, "Oh, sorry, poor choice of words after today." Starla pulled upright and cut her eyes at Ethan until he dropped his shoulders in embarrassment at his verbal blunder. "I'm sorry," he added sincerely. "I didn't mean to be insensitive. Do you want to come back inside the building where it's not so hot?"

Starla leaned against her window and remembered the note on the floor of the car. The last thing she wanted was anyone to see the weird message. "No, I'm fine, really I am," she said, smiling in determination. "It's just so hot, and this has been such a difficult day."

"You probably don't need to drive right now," continued Ethan. "Why don't you let me help you so you can get yourself collected back inside."

"No," she said more fiercely than she intended. "I'm good. I just need to get going."

"Are you sure?"

Starla furrowed her brow and scowled at Ethan. Why was it that whenever men decided to be chivalrous, the moment was inevitably inconvenient for her? "Yes, I'm sure," she said as she steadied her voice. She turned around and opened her car door quickly. Lowering herself onto the seat, she started the engine and pushed the button of her window part way. "Thanks, Ethan," she said, forcing herself to smile through the crack in the glass.

"Call me if you need anything."

"Yes, of course," she said as she rolled up her window.

Without waiting to fasten her seatbelt, she pulled forward and looped onto the outer lane of the parking lot. Only when she entered the long driveway leading out of the mill, did she look back at Ethan Weir. He was standing completely still, watching her go with a worried look on his face.

———

Starla pulled her Camry onto the unpaved road that bordered her property as the late afternoon sun beat mercilessly through the windshield. Her car had finally cooled down to a reasonable temperature, but now the harsh glare of the intense sunset made her eyes squint. She readjusted the air vents toward her damp skin.

Exhaustion settled across her neck and shoulders. The day had been both incredibly long and tremendously fast. Time had seemed to stand still whenever she tried to concentrate at her desk only to make Starla realize that the hours had somehow tumbled forward whenever she looked up at the clock.

John was dead. She knew that much was true. But the note on her car was terrifying. She bit her lip, trying to think. Everything felt like a bad dream. She wondered for a moment if grief had played some sort of trick on her. Grabbing the paper, she stared at the words. The message was still the same.

Pulling in front of the trailer, she put her car in park and let the motor run. Her head instinctively fell back on the headrest, and she shut her eyes as the cool air circulated over the front seats. For a full two minutes, she took long breaths in the quiet.

The banging on her car window made her jump.

"What are you doing?" Glen asked loud enough that she could hear him through the glass. Starla shoved the note into her purse and opened the car door. "What?" Glen asked, a hint of a sneer in his voice.

Getting to her feet, Starla turned to her husband. "We had a death at the mill today, okay?"

"Yeah, I heard, remember I called you about it," Glen said unemotionally. "Everyone from land management is talking about the guy. They said it was some manager down in the mill."

"Yes," Starla replied stiffly as she walked toward their mobile home. Glen followed her up to the wooden steps without saying a word. Starla entered the darkened trailer and put her purse on the kitchen table. She remembered the note tucked inside the flap. Hopefully, she could hide it when she had a private moment. In the kitchen, she realized that Glen continued to follow her. His close presence was unnerving.

"What?" Starla asked as she turned to face her husband.

Glen studied his wife but said nothing. He sauntered over to the refrigerator. "Got any beer?" he asked.

"I don't know," she answered in a tone of irritation.

"You know I like Budweiser," he said, staring at her.

"Glen, I've been at work," she said wearily. "Did you drink the last of it?"

"Well, there's no more, so I guess the answer is yes," he responded sarcastically.

Starla kicked off her shoes and rubbed her neck. Usually, she would be all about apologizing, afraid of what might come next, but now she just felt too exhausted. "I'll get some at the store," she promised and then added softly, "It was just a really bad day with everything at work."

Without warning, Glen stomped to the front door and grabbed his keys from the small table next to the sofa. "Where are you going?" asked Starla.

"Out for a beer and maybe some food since you don't have anything here. I don't have to be at work until later."

The front door slammed shut making the walls of the trailer shimmy violently. As Glen's truck roared to life, Starla sank onto the old recliner and listened to the sound of his vehicle as it faded down the long sandy driveway.

A feeling of relief washed over her as she sat in the living room. For a long minute, she rubbed her aching eyes in the silence. Her body felt spent. Without warning, a shrill ring startled her.

Rising on wobbly legs, Starla moved towards the kitchen table. Her fingers trembled as she reached for her smart phone. With relief, she noticed that the number was a local area code.

"Hello?" she said.

There was silence on the line followed by a muffled breathing.

"Keep quiet," a man's voice said.

Starla felt her knees buckle. "Who is this?"

For a moment, the silence caused her to wonder if the line was dead.

"Who is this?" she asked again, her voice incensed.

"I'll be watching you."

CHAPTER FIFTEEN

Starla leaned against the wall of her shower under a cascading stream of water. Her hand moved the circular knob of the faucet in slow motion. First, she started right with hot, scalding pellets that burned her skin only to deliberately push the lever to the left to deliver a blast of icy cold relief. Back and forth the temperature drifted as she felt the effects from her fingers to her body. Her mind was numb, but at least the changing deluge forced her to feel something.

Turning off the nozzle, she watched the water run in tiny rivers down the drain. Her shoulders ached with exhaustion as she wrung out her hair. Starla frowned as she stepped on the bathmat. The muscles in her lower back were finally unknotted, but now she had lost complete track of time. She jumped when she heard the sound; a persistent knocking came from the front door.

Starla listened for a moment in confusion. Had someone been at the door the whole time she was in the shower? What did Glen need? She thought about her husband as she threw a towel onto the sink. If he drove off in his truck to get beer, he had to have his keys. What could he have possibly forgotten?

"Hang on," she called. Pulling on a yellow terry cloth robe, Starla opened the bathroom door as steam billowed down the hallway like an overactive dragon.

She quickly glanced out the front window of the trailer. In the twilight, the empty patch of sandy grass where Glen usually parked his truck was empty, but a telltale white vehicle had taken its place.

"You've got to be kidding," Starla muttered under her breath as her stomach began to knot. She cracked the door open and forced a smile onto her face. "Yes?"

"Mrs. Pittman," began Nick Simpson as he flashed his badge. "I'm Detective Simpson, and this is Detective Lee, from the Campton County Sheriff's Department. We'd like to ask you a few questions."

"Well, I just got out of the shower," replied Starla. "I'm not really ready to…"

"This will only take a few minutes," added Detective Lee evenly. "It's about John Runar."

"It's just that this is not a good time." The two detectives remained immobile. Starla realized that even on the top step of her trailer, they were eye level with her.

"If you would prefer, we can do this down at the station," said Simpson flatly.

Starla stared at the officers who seemed to fill her doorway. They evidently weren't leaving. "Oh, all right!" she said with exasperation.

She angrily yanked open the door so that it slipped out of her grasp and bumped against a small table. Her eyes quickly scanned the yard for any sign of Glen's absent truck. "Well, since you put it that way, come on inside."

The detectives crossed the threshold as Starla pulled the short robe tighter around her waist.

"I did just get out of the shower," she repeated.

"This will only take a few minutes," stated Lee again.

Starla glared at the officers. "At least let me put on some clothes," she insisted. With annoyance, she pounded down the hallway and yanked on denim shorts and a tank top as she scanned the bedroom window for any sign of her husband. When she returned, the detectives were silently surveying her living room,

"May we sit down?" asked Lee. The detectives glanced at each other and took the three steps required to move in front of the sagging brown sofa. Without waiting for an answer, they lowered themselves in unison onto the lumpy cushions. Small notepads appeared in their hands. They moved their eyes across the room and then focused on the woman in front of them.

Letting out an indignant sigh, Starla took a seat on the edge of the plaid recliner and tightened both arms over her chest.

"We need to ask you a few questions about John Runar," began Detective Simpson.

Starla leaned forward and crossed her legs. Wet patches were spreading onto her shoulders from her damp hair. A lump in the back of her throat started to form even though she could feel her adrenaline rising.

"Yes, I assumed as much. You came by the front office this morning," she said with an edge in her voice as her eyes returned Detective Lee's stare.

"Mrs. Pittman," began Simpson. "May we call you Starla? You see, Starla, we need to know how well you knew the deceased."

"What is there to know? We both work at Delta. It's a small company," Starla answered, wondering if her words sounded defensive.

"Several hundred employees, really a thousand or more people working three shifts a day is hardly small," said Lee in a measured tone.

"Well, no, it's not really small," Starla retorted with a huff. "Not in that sense. It's just that we all know each other."

"Exactly how well did you know the deceased?" asked Detective Simpson in a more forceful tone this time.

Starla willed herself to remain silent and brushed back her wet hair nonchalantly, aware that the two officers were watching her with intensity. Returning their gaze, she felt her body involuntarily twitch as she leaned forward in her chair. Surely, they could see her damp cleavage from this angle. She wondered if that fact would excite either of them. With deliberate hesitation, she reached for the cigarettes and lighter on the tiny pedestal table next to her chair. Tapping the side of the pack, a Newport rose from the cellophane. As she put the long roll between her lips, the flame in her fingers had a slight tremble.

"What I mean is that we are all acquainted. Like a family, you know?"

"Phone records indicate that you and Mr. Runar enjoyed quite a close relationship," said Detective Lee without averting her scrutiny.

"Phone records?" asked Starla. She took a deep drag and forced a wide smile onto her face, then exhaled smoke in the direction of the officers.

"Yes, phone records," answered Lee evenly.

"I don't think that I ever called John, I mean Mr. Runar, on my cell phone," Starla responded with determination.

"We found Mr. Runar's Tracfone," said Simpson. "On it, we found multiple calls to you at all hours of the day and night."

Silence settled over the cramped living room. Starla reached up and placed two fingers around her cigarette and pulled the Newport from her mouth.

"And what makes you think that he was calling me?"

"We know that Mr. Runar bought two phones when he purchased the one we found. We have records that his calls were made to this area. We believe that he was calling you," pushed Simpson. The words hung in the air that had become thick with smoke. "Starla, we need to know exactly what relationship you had with John Runar."

"It was like I said," repeated Starla. "We were friends." She noticed her voice now seemed to quiver.

Detective Simpson leaned forward slightly. "Starla, you can either start talking to us or you can come down to the station."

Starla took another long drag of her cigarette and watched both detectives harden their eyes. Her stomach began to tighten. "What do you want to know?" she asked evenly.

"How long had you two been having an affair?" questioned Detective Simpson.

Starla threw her head back and laughed a single syllable. "Detectives, now you are really reaching. John and I were friends, just friends."

"How long, Starla? We want the truth," pressed Detective Lee.

"I don't know what you're talking about," Starla replied.

"Did you two argue? Was he going to leave his wife for you?" asked Simpson.

"This is ridiculous," Starla retorted as she tapped her ash into the dirty cup at her elbow.

"Where were you last night?" demanded Simpson.

"At home," Starla answered defensively.

"Can anyone verify that you were here?" questioned Simpson.

Starla's eyes went momentarily wide with surprise. "No!" she spat in anger.

"Not a husband at home?" asked Detective Lee.

"Glen works at Delta in the land management group. He was at work. There've been some kids that have been starting fires in the managed timberlands now that school is out for the summer. He was on patrol."

"So, let me get this straight," began Detective Lee slowly, "nobody can verify your whereabouts last night, and your husband just happened to be at work?"

"Yes," Starla answered through clenched teeth. "Glen was at work." The room grew quiet. Starla could feel her heart pounding in her chest. The questions were getting ridiculous. "Look, Glen was at work, and I was at home. End of story!" She smacked the lighter down on the table and scowled at the detectives.

"Did your husband know about the affair?" inquired Detective Simpson. "How did he feel about Mr. Runar?"

Starla said nothing. She glowered at the two detectives. "I think you should leave," she said coldly, rising to her feet. The detectives were motionless as Starla went to the door. Slowly, they stood.

"Starla, make this easy on yourself," offered Simpson. "Give us your disposable phone."

Reaching for the doorknob, Starla came to a halt. Facts raced through her brain. She knew her rights and turned to face the detectives. "I do believe," she said pointedly, "that you need a warrant if you intend to take anything from me."

Simpson took a step closer to the door, his expression serious. "Give us your disposable phone or we will pick up your husband tonight for an enlightening chat at the station. And after we talk to your husband, we will return with a warrant."

Starla seethed at the officers. She wanted to raise her voice but stopped. The air hissed from her throat. Glen knew nothing about John, but what if he were told by the police, especially after a few drinks? Starla bit her lower lip. She could almost feel her husband's provoked hands—the bruises that he would be sure to leave on her arms.

Stomping over to the kitchen chair, Starla grabbed her purse. Pulling it open, she unzipped a side pocket and dug her fingers into the hidden pouch. She held up a small phone.

"Happy?" she asked.

With three long strides, she crossed the room and smacked the phone into Detective Lee's open hand before flinging open the door.

"Get out," she commanded.

The officers moved towards the doorway.

"Don't leave town," leveled Detective Simpson as he stood on the threshold.

"I'm not leaving town!" Starla shot back at the pair. "Glen and I both have jobs and a home!"

Detective Simpson nodded to his partner before he spoke.

"Starla, this is a full investigation into the death of John Runar. And as of this minute, you're a key person of interest."

CHAPTER SIXTEEN

Ethan Weir took long strides around the floor of his department. With a cup of lukewarm coffee in his hand, he had already attended a forecasting meeting, checked his email, reviewed lab reports, and been up to the front office to discuss staffing. Even though his phone said that it was only a few minutes after nine, exhaustion was beginning to settle across his neck and shoulders. He had been at work for hours.

Through the glass windows of the control room, the dayshift sat monitoring the computer panels for the cutting machine that churned like a long, robust guillotine across the Finishing area. Ethan studied his team, aware that each worker looked spent. And why shouldn't they be exhausted? The morning was really only a continuation of the last twenty-four hours. Ever since John's accident was announced, not a single person, hourly or management, appeared to have been able to sleep.

"We have a plant meeting at ten," Ethan announced to the crew as he opened the door of the operations room. "It's in the conference hall. It's mandatory. Only the skeleton crew on the paper machines and the roll cutters can miss." Safety goggles nodded and workers mumbled to each other.

Ethan scanned the monitors from the doorway. His eyes automatically rose above the somber view of the team to the open deck, the last stage of the pulping process that towered above his employees. A humid fog engulfed the complex rows of screens and machinery that rolled out a continuous production line of pulpy cellulose on the second level of the plant. Ethan looked back at his workers with empathy. Since the news about the death of a fellow Delta employee, a sadness had settled a sadness over the group identical to the low hanging steam that rose from the pulp drying machine.

As he stood and watched the team at work, Ethan realized the only positive outcome from John Runar's death was that the usual distinction between technicians and supervisors had evaporated. In its place, a grim bond now united the entire staff.

"Do you know what the meeting is about?" asked Travis Hutson as he swiveled in his chair to face his boss.

Ethan studied his hourly supervisor. Of all the employees, Travis looked the worst. With a five o'clock shadow and a rumpled shirt, his puffy, bloodshot eyes seemed to rise from his sunken cheeks like two bulging disks.

"I'm not sure about everything," Ethan answered, "but I believe that the company will want to talk about John, his role, and then the staffing changes that we will have to make."

Travis merely nodded and turned back to his computer screen. His expression told Ethan that he was present in body only.

Shutting the door of the operations room, Ethan walked back towards his tiny office. As he approached his messy desk, he groaned. How had his usually neat tabletop become a sea of scattered papers in the one day since John's death was announced? Sinking into his tattered chair, he set his coffee cup on a thick pile of bills of lading and longed for a few moments of relative solitude. The morning had been tough, and the pending meeting would be tougher.

He moved his fingers instinctively towards his pounding temples. The aroma of the sulfur and wood compounds that clung to his hands made him wince. Between the harsh smells of the plant and the mess of his office, he felt overwhelmed.

Staring at the disarray in front of him, Ethan realized that calling his workspace an "office" was a gross exaggeration. A metal desk and a set of cracking leather chairs made up the sum total of his business furniture. His tiny space along the back wall of his department was separated from the noise and chaos of the mill by only a glass wall and an all-important air conditioner.

"All this glamour," he muttered to himself as he sat up and began creating stacks of papers. "Yes, this is why I busted my ass to get a chemical engineering degree."

The ringing of his cell phone made him jump. Blaring noise from the pulp cutters meant that every phone in the department stayed turned up to full volume. Ethan smiled as he recognized the caller.

"Weir," he answered.

"Ethan." He heard the smooth cadence on the other end of the line. "Hey man, it's Calvin."

"Hey, I was going to call you after the mill meeting," Ethan said. Without thinking, he started to smile. There was something about the velvet tone of the caller's voice that always made Ethan instantly imagine that he was talking to Marvin Gaye.

"Yeah, I guess we need to talk." There was a pause in the conversation, and Ethan could just imagine Calvin Jones searching for the right things to say. As one of only a handful of Black managers at the mill, Calvin was as careful in his speech as he was with his meticulous appearance.

Ethan looked out through his glass partition and gambled. Surely, Calvin had been informed about his new role. "It's probably best if you and I have some time together," he said.

"I agree."

A tiny, unwanted wave of envy nudged at Ethan as he held the phone. Did Calvin suspect that his pending assignment, sure to be announced in the plant conference hall within the hour, would leave Ethan once again feeling passed over for a special assignment?

"Why don't we have lunch together after the mill meeting?" offered Ethan, desperate to alleviate his guilt. "You can come to Finishing, and we can get something from the cafeteria or go into town."

"Lunch would be good," Calvin said.

Ethan looked over towards the edge of his desk. The lonely brown bag that his wife had packed earlier that morning sat forlornly crumpled. He quickly moved the lunch sack to the top of a filing cabinet behind his desk. Hopefully, Calvin didn't know about his frugal meal habits. The last thing he wanted was a ribbing.

"I take it that you already had a meeting this morning?" he asked.

"Yeah," Calvin confided. "Hackman came to see me, first thing. We talked about everything that had happened with John, and then we went up to McVann's office."

Ethan could just envision Bill Hackman heading deep into the plant to find Calvin. There was something about the way the assistant plant manager liked to trot off to do corporate bidding that reminded Ethan of a prancing bloodhound.

"So, Roger officially offered you Runar's role?"

"Yes," confirmed Calvin. "At first, I told him that I would need to think about it, but I'd pretty much decided to take the job before the meeting ended. The transfer will be considered a special assignment."

Ethan shook his head. Only Roger McVann could ask for sacrifices and teamwork on a half-finished project and get a commitment from any employee before the meeting was adjourned. As a plant manager, his art of persuasion was the stuff of leadership books.

"Well, I'm really glad that you would consider the role," said Ethan honestly. "It's a career building opportunity, although there will be quite a few challenges. John had the project in pretty good shape, I think. If the specs on the pulp can remain consistent, then I believe that we can really hit it out of the park for Delta."

"There's a lot that I'll need in order to get up to speed with where his testing stood. I need to really understand what his customers were looking for with this new cellulose grade."

Ethan nodded as he listened. Obviously, Calvin had already been thinking about what the job would entail.

"We can talk more at lunch," said Ethan. "But there are a few things that you need to know before you come to Finishing."

"Well, I imagine that there's a lot that I'll need to know before I head your way."

Narrowing his eyes, Ethan studied his department through the smudged glass partition in front of his desk. The dayshift moved as a synchronized ballet in the control room. Almost without thinking, his eyes settled on Travis.

"Not everyone in Finishing has always been thrilled with the possibilities of this project," he confided.

"I could have guessed that much," said Calvin in a knowing tone. "I suppose that I'll just have to win them all over with my exceptional personality."

Ethan smiled. Hearing optimism on the other end of the line was a good sign. "Just remember, Runar recorded most of the details of his project digitally, so getting into all of his results may take some time. I don't know if his devices have even been found. I'm also not sure, but I think most of his data was probably password protected."

"All right," said Calvin. "I may have to get IT to help me access everything."

Ethan swiveled his chair and stared at the empty desk and lab space that John Runar had once occupied on the production floor. Memories of private calls and computer screens that went dark whenever anyone approached replayed in his mind.

"I'll do anything to help you, but I didn't micromanage John," Ethan confided. "His work was controlled by Headquarters in Memphis, and he was not big on sharing. You'll have a challenge to pick up his work, but you can certainly handle it."

"So, what is the first thing that you think I need to do?"

"That's easy. The first thing you need is to know who John was communicating with on the project. I do know that there were people both inside and outside of Delta that he worked with on the results. You'll need to learn about the customers for his new grade."

"Do you have any idea who those contacts were?"

"Not a clue, beyond the folks at Headquarters," said Ethan.

Calvin sighed, and Ethan could just imagine him rubbing his neck under the perfectly starched collar of his designer shirt.

"I'll really need to get into his computer ASAP," he said thoughtfully.

"When you do, remember to look at everything. John was complicated."

"How do you mean complicated?"

Ethan took a deep breath as his fingers rubbed the bridge of his nose. Some of John's issues would need to be carefully shared over lunch. It was only fair.

"John Runar was an enigma," he said in a dropped voice. "He could be a determined leader and also be incredibly furtive. Let's just say that he did not always play well with others. When you get into his project, you're probably going to realize that not all things with John were always what they appeared to be."

CHAPTER SEVENTEEN

Nick Simpson eased his Chevy Tahoe into the driveway and stared out of his windshield at the house in front of him. In the morning light, he glanced sideways to his partner.

"Let's get the lay of the land with the widow," he said. "I want to probe for general information about the night of the accident. I also think that getting a feel for their relationship is important."

Lee nodded and closed the folder on her lap. Her eyes searched the front of the house.

"Hawkins said that something felt odd about the way Mrs. Runar said she slept all night and didn't know that her husband never made it home," she said.

In unison, the partners discreetly opened their car doors. They noiselessly made their way up the front steps. A knock on the wooden door started a dog barking from within the house. Simpson looked through the beveled glass panel and noticed the small foyer was dark.

"Yes?" A woman in gray loungewear opened the front door.

"Leah Runar?" asked Simpson.

"Yes," she said. Her face looked tired and worn. Without make-up, her eyes were puffy.

"Mrs. Runar, I'm Detective Simpson and this is Detective Lee with the Campton County Sheriff's Department. We're sorry to bother you, but we need to ask you a few questions."

Leah nodded. She looked blankly at both officers but then paused. "Don't I know you?" she asked Detective Lee.

"My son was at Campton Elementary last year. I think you were his reading teacher," she said. "Zack Lee? I don't know if you remember him."

"Oh, Zack," Leah said with a faint smile. "He always made me laugh."

"Mrs. Runar, may we come in?" asked Simpson. "We just need to ask you a few questions."

"All right," she said as she glanced over her shoulder. "My kids are still asleep. They had a hard time last night."

Leah opened the door and motioned to the darkened front room. The detectives walked towards the two armchairs.

"Would you like to sit down, Mrs. Runar?" asked Lee.

"I'll grab the desk chair—you two sit in the those," Leah said as her bare feet moved across the wood floor and a leather chair was rolled forward. She turned on the desk lamp before slumping into her seat.

"Mrs. Runar, we need to ask you some questions about the night of your husband's accident," began Lee. "What time was he supposed to come home that evening?"

"John told me that he had a late meeting at work. I don't really know—something about his new project. I wasn't really sure what time he would get here."

"When you went to sleep and he wasn't home, were you concerned? Did you try to call him?" asked Lee.

"I have allergies," Leah explained. "I think it's the pine pollen. So sometimes, I take an allergy medicine that makes me sleepy. I took some of my meds around eight, and then I went to watch television. I wasn't worried about John, because he liked to work late. He was sort of a night owl. I didn't call him because John never liked me to call him at work."

"Mrs. Runar," said Simpson. "Did you wake up at any point in the night and realize that he wasn't home?"

Leah looked down at her hands and played with her wedding band. "We have a downstairs guest room. When I'm really congested, I sleep in the guest bed. I slept in the extra bedroom that night because of the medication. Our bedroom is upstairs. I thought John was up there."

"Were you and your husband on good terms?" asked Simpson.

Leah looked up in surprise. "We were fine. John was a good father and a veteran."

The detectives nodded.

"Would it be possible for me to get his personal things?" Leah asked. "I'd like to have his wedding ring and his phone."

"I'm sure you'll get everything as soon as the investigation is finished," answered Lee smoothly.

Leah rubbed her hand across her face. "Is there anything else? I'd like to make some breakfast for when my kids wake up."

The detectives rose. Nick Simpson pulled a card from his shirt pocket. "Here's my card. Feel free to call me if you can think of anything else we should know."

As the partners walked down the front steps, they shot a sideways glance at each other.

"Well, what did you think?" asked Simpson after they were inside the car.

"Kind of convenient, isn't it?" responded Lee. "She just happens to sleep in another room the whole night that her husband is killed. She was also quick to claim that they were just another happy couple."

Simpson started the engine and looked back at the darkened house. "I thought the same thing, not to mention that she wants his phone. But her explanation is perfectly logical."

He backed out of the driveway and gave one final glimpse at the property. "What do you think the odds are that she didn't know about her husband's affair?" he asked.

"I thought she was a very sweet teacher when I met her last year," answered Lee, "but women always know. It's just a matter of how they decide to handle it."

CHAPTER EIGHTEEN

Mia Lee put the phone down and leaned back in her chair. She looked impassively over the photos of her children that lined the front of her desk and caught the eye of her partner.

"That was the coroner," she said. "They just finished the preliminary autopsy on John Runar."

"And?"

"He said the accident was severe. The truck tires were completely shredded which caused some of the trauma, but that the impact was not what killed him." Simpson pulled his eyes off his computer monitor with a questioning look.

"It's just as we thought," continued Lee. "The cause of death was a broken neck."

"And the marks that we saw at the scene? Everything on the neck and face?"

"The doc said that there was actually some facial bruising that happened before the accident. Eventually, he had blood pooling in his sinuses that had nothing to do the wreck."

"Really?"

"But everything else is just like we thought. The hand marks on the neck meant that another person was at the scene of the accident, and that someone snapped his neck."

Detective Simpson swiveled in his chair to face the whiteboard against the adjacent wall. He narrowed his eyes in thought.

"So, someone gifted John Runar with a few blows before his car wreck, eh? Enough to cause some blood in his cranium prior to ever getting into his truck. Makes me wonder about Travis Hutson..." he said slowly.

"They had a fight earlier that day," said Lee as she opened her notebook to review, "but it was Travis who got the bloody nose, not Runar."

Simpson pursed his lips together and faced his partner. "Let's recheck that detail," he said. "And let's give Starla Pittman more of a look. She's quite a little liar when it comes to information."

Detective Lee nodded as her pen slid across her pad. She looked up at the board and knitted her brow together. "I still feel like we're missing something. There're lots of pieces to this case, but something is still absent—something major."

"Agreed," said Simpson as he reached for a manila file and nodded. "But at least it's official now, just like we thought. John Runar was murdered."

———

The plastic blinds were shut against the onslaught of the afternoon sunlight when Starla unlocked the door to the trailer. Despite the dim interior, she could feel that the air beyond the doorway resembled a sweat box.

As she stood on the top step, she scanned the yard. The only sound came from Buster eating his dinner in the grass. He wagged his tail as he chewed from the bucket. Starla smiled. At least someone was happy at the end of a day, she thought.

Moving into the dim light of the living room, Starla could see the dirty dishes lining the counter by the sink. She looked at the mess and sighed. Glen was such a slob, she realized. He always left the kitchen full of unwashed pots and pans whenever he went to work.

She tossed her purse on the old recliner and thought about cleaning up behind him. Chores like that really didn't bother her. Just having him gone made the evening relaxing. A little housework was a fair price to pay for solitude.

Starla picked up the remote and turned on the television. The local news station blared a musical introduction to the six o'clock broadcast as she padded into the kitchen for a drink. The headline story made her stop. She turned and stared at the screen.

A picture of John filled her set. The anchorwoman was speaking as Starla moved back into the living room. Her legs suddenly felt weak.

"Delta Paper employee John Runar was found dead on the Mill Highway early Tuesday morning and his death has officially been ruled a homicide. Police are investigating the case. Anyone with information is asked to call the Campton County Sheriff's Department."

Starla crumpled onto the sofa and stared blankly. Images of the people she knew in Campton filled her mind. Rumors were running wild at the mill about John being murdered. Of course, she heard the vicious gossip, but how could it be true? The idea that anybody wanted to hurt John was ridiculous. People were just being cruel. Starla had angrily dismissed all the innuendo. Now her mouth felt dry.

In the quiet, she looked around the darkened trailer. If John was really killed, then why? A wave of nausea washed over her, and she rose to her feet. She bolted to the kitchen and leaned over the sink.

Hot tears blurred her vision. She missed him so much, and now she was frightened. Thinking about John being murdered was surreal. Starla gulped in air. Her world was falling apart.

Gripping the worn counter, she tried to steady herself. She opened her eyes and stared at the pile of used bowls and cups. Instinctively, the logical side of her brain started to work.

If someone murdered John and the police didn't know who it was, then only two questions remained: Why did they kill him, and who would be next?

CHAPTER NINETEEN

Ethan pulled out of his driveway in the early morning light and surveyed his peaceful neighborhood. A lone jogger waved at him. He was still smiling at the end of the road when he looked down at his dashboard. The constantly blinking numbers made him scowl.

Ever since he had purchased the used vehicle from a transferring manager, the flickering clock never stopped bothering him. The digital numbers on the dashboard of his Ford Explorer flashed 6:00 with annoying regularity.

"Well, the inside stinks like the mill and the clock doesn't work," his wife announced when she first inspected the car. Abbey's ponytail bobbed back and forth as she hopped from the front seat to allow their young son, Charlie, a chance to scramble behind the wheel for a pretend drive.

"Yeah, I know," explained Ethan. "But it's a mill car. The vehicle's just reliable transportation."

"Is this really what you want? Are you sure about this?" she asked as she scrutinized the dirty, faded exterior of the car.

"I think so. It'll be a good car to go to and from Delta."

"Well, I hope the AC works," she said.

"It's icy cold. I tested it."

Her arm looped through his waist, and she gave him a playful bump of her hip while Charlie climbed to the backseat. "Someday, Ethan, someday, you might just get more than a used car and life in a paper mill town," she gently teased him as she kissed his cheek and rested her hand on her second trimester belly.

Now against the tangerine sunrise, Ethan narrowed his eyes for the umpteenth time at the pulsating timepiece. On countless occasions, he had tried to reset the maddening numerals, but nothing worked. More than once, he contemplated taking his new purchase into the dealership in Mobile to get some relief from the unruly digits, but, inevitably, he always put off the appointment. Going to a mechanic would just be an admission. If Ethan actually scheduled and paid for a minor repair on his automobile, then he would be just another engineer who was ultimately thwarted by the computerized panel under the hood of his car. In the end, he made the decision to just live with the irritation.

Besides, he never needed the clock. Ethan was consistently punctual. At any moment, he could practically pinpoint the time of the day. The blazing sunrise that filled his windshield with hot glare this morning was a dead give-away that it was already past seven.

Ethan shifted uncomfortably in the blinding light and picked up speed. He felt a familiar fatigue in his lower back. He had been restless for most of last night. All the events of the past three days continually replayed in his mind as he rolled from one side of the bed to the other.

"Enough already," Abbey said when he threw off the covers for the third time. "Being uncomfortable is my department these days. What's the matter?"

"I think that I should tell someone," Ethan whispered.

"Tell them what?" she said sleepily.

"Tell about John Runar," he said in a low tone. He half expected his wife to laugh or at least to act like his older brother had done whenever Ethan was bothered by guilt as a child.

"You're such a Boy Scout!" It was the most familiar refrain from his childhood. Ethan could almost hear the taunting sibling words in his head. The jeer had always left him embarrassed. As soon as he spoke, he wondered if Abbey would find his thoughts funny.

"What exactly about John?" she asked, fully awake, her voice measured and caring.

Ethan rolled on his side to face her in the dark.

"John was having an affair. I know he was. He and Starla Pittman, you know, Roger McVann's secretary. Remember, I told you? They were having a thing," he said. The admission sounded silly when it came out of his mouth, but the thoughts behind the words were troubling.

"Okay," she said slowly, "and you think this is important?"

Ethan smiled at her question. Abbey sounded thoughtful, like she was trying to pick the ideas out of his head. Her concern made him realize how much he loved her.

"I don't know, maybe. It's just that the rumors going around the mill are that John was murdered," he said.

"Was he?"

"Nobody is saying much, except in gossip, which you know can be surprisingly accurate at the plant," he replied as he shifted to get comfortable next to her. "I must admit, a one-car crash out on the Mill Highway is weird. John could drive anything. I think he even drove a Humvee in the Army, and he was always in that big huge truck, which was more like a tank really. He never stopped bragging about the thing."

"It could have been a deer or something," she offered. "People swerve off the road all the time."

"Except that's not what folks are saying at work."

Abbey flipped her pillow over and yawned.

"How can they be sure?" she asked.

"Because one of the hourly guys in the Woodyard at Delta has a cousin that works in the county morgue. He said that it was murder—a broken neck with hand marks all over the body."

"Perhaps the marks came from a first responder."

"Everyone's saying that the crash wasn't that bad... that John would have certainly survived in that big truck... that he probably could have just walked out to the road."

"Okay, but didn't you already talk to the police when they came to the mill?"

"Yeah," Ethan admitted, "but it was right when I found out about John. I told them that there was tension between John and Travis, but I never said anything about the affair."

Abbey reached out to stroke his arm with her fingers. Her touch made him feel safe.

"Do you think it's really important?" she asked.

"Maybe not," acknowledged Ethan, "but, at a minimum, it feels like a fact they should know."

Her hand brushed his shoulder as she spoke. "You know, I taught with Leah the year before I had Charlie. I really hate this whole situation for her. If news about an affair comes out in this town...."

"That's why I'm wondering what to do."

"Well, if there's something to tell the police, then I think that it should come from you. After all, you were the manager in his department, and you can be discreet. Maybe you can stop the news before it gets to Leah."

Ethan nodded his head in agreement and studied the black silhouettes of the bedroom furniture along the wall. Abbey was right. If there was more that needed to be known about John and his relationships, then he should be the one to go and talk to the detectives. He shut his eyes and felt himself start to relax. Stretching out his long legs, he drifted into a peaceful sleep that lasted until the gray streaks of dawn glowed at his window.

But now as the sunlight pierced his vision, he wondered again if he was doing the right thing. Driving through town, his hesitation only increased when he saw the low stucco building on the horizon. With squad cars lined up in the parking lot, the police station seemed to broadcast the presence of law and order, making Ethan feel, once again, as if he had morphed into some sort of snitch.

Reluctantly, he pulled his car into the front lot and turned off the engine. For a full minute, he steadied his breathing and thought about what he wanted to say. Finally, opening the driver's door, he emerged into the thick, oppressive air. He straightened his shoulders with determination.

"Well, I'm here now," he muttered to himself.

Slowly, he approached the building. To his surprise, all the glass across the front of the station was tinted. The effect was unsettling, giving Ethan the sensation that he was staring into a pair of reflective sunglasses. He pulled open the heavy door and stepped inside.

Despite the glare of the fluorescent lights that hung from the ceiling, the temperature of the building felt delightfully chilled. Ethan could hear the hum of the massive air conditioners above the ringing telephones and muffled voices as he approached the front counter.

"May I help you?" An older policeman sat behind a tall desk. His bald head reflected the ceiling lights while a single eyebrow crossed his forehead like a hairy centipede.

"Yes," Ethan said, trying to smile, "I need to speak with the detectives, the ones handling the John Runar case. I think that one of them was Detective Simpson."

"Your name?" the officer asked blandly.

"It's Ethan Weir. They came to the mill, the two detectives. I spoke with them the day before yesterday," he said. A surprising feeling of nervousness caught in his throat.

The cool, gray eyes of the policeman behind the counter stared at Ethan. His hands steadily shuffled papers while his gaze remained fixed and penetrating. A ringing phone on the desk made Ethan jump.

"Have a seat," the officer said as he reached for the blaring landline. He motioned to hard plastic chairs that lined the walls along the front of the station. Ethan glanced over his shoulder. Every one of the seats looked like they were covered in a fine layer of grime.

Turning back to make eye contact, Ethan wanted to ask the policeman how long it would take to find the detectives. He could feel that it was almost half past seven, and while clocking into the plant like the hourly employees wasn't required, mornings were precious in his department. Early reports and shift changes were occurring while he was absent.

The officer had turned his attention to the papers in his hand and proceeded to speak in a series of one-word answers into the receiver. Ethan stood in front of him, aware that he was officially being ignored.

He turned around to look again at the dirty orange chairs and decided to forgo sitting. Moving toward the large tinted window, he pulled out his phone. At least he could do a bit of work and perhaps check the production results of the third shift while he waited to talk to the detectives.

"You wanted to see me?" Detective Lee asked as she stood beside the elevated front desk.

Ethan looked up from his phone. Dressed in pants and a light patterned shirt with the sleeves pushed to the elbows, the detective looked as if she had been working for hours.

"Yes, I'm Ethan Weir. You came to the mill two days ago and we spoke about John Runar."

"Of course, I remember. You were his boss."

"Well, in a manner of speaking, I'm the manager in Finishing, the area where he worked. John was really on special assignment in my department." The detective remained motionless while she studied Ethan.

The main door opened, and two policemen walked into the station with a handcuffed teenager between them. The youth had his head bowed, studying his feet, while the patrolmen sandwiched him as they pulled him along into the building.

"Is there somewhere that we could talk?" Ethan asked.

"Follow me," said Detective Lee.

Turning to the aisle beside the high counter, Ethan followed the officer as she navigated her way through a maze of desks into the center of a huge room.

"Have a seat," offered the detective when they reached a small cubicle.

Ethan moved towards the black padded chairs and looked around at the dingy, golden fabric walls of the partition. Except for the sleek computer resting on the metal desk, the work area retained a 1970's feel, strangely reminiscent of the mill.

Settling into a chair, Ethan marveled at the candid photographs that filled the entire back wall of the work area. The hundreds of diverse portraits amazed him. He surveyed the collage and guessed that they were probably pictures from cases that Detective Lee had solved. As his eyes drifted over the faces, Ethan wondered what it would be like to have resolved so many investigations and to have helped so many people. There must be satisfaction, he realized, by impacting such a large number of lives. Somehow, that thought made him simultaneously wonder about his own career. The paper industry was great, but hardly one that enabled him to point to a wall of aided people. The best thing Ethan ever got was an occasional email of thanks from a manufacturing customer.

"So, what was it that brought you in today?" asked the detective.

"There was something that I wanted to tell you about John Runar."

"All right," said Detective Lee. She reached for a small notepad while her eyes remained fixed on the man before her.

"John Runar was not always the most upstanding individual," Ethan said in hesitating words.

"Okay, exactly what do you mean?"

"John was having an affair," Ethan said quietly. "I figured out what was going on a few months ago. I didn't say anything the other day because I guess that I was in shock, you know, about his accident. But I thought about it after we spoke, and you said that I should contact you if there was anything else."

"I see," said Detective Lee in a calm voice. "Do you know who he was having an affair with?"

Ethan paused. Studying the expressionless detective made him question yet again if coming into talk to the police was the best strategy.

"John Runar was involved with Starla Pittman. She's a secretary up in the front office."

"And this had been going for a while, you said?"

"I have no idea. I found out about it a couple of months ago. Obviously, it wasn't the sort of thing that I would just bring up to John and Delta certainly takes a dim view of anything like this. I mean, the whole thing was really awkward. We all live in the same neighborhood, and I've known John and his wife, Leah, since he first joined Delta five years ago."

"Do you know if anyone else knew about this relationship?"

"I don't know. I mean, like I said, I didn't mention the situation," Ethan reiterated, immediately remembering the fact that he had told Abbey all about the affair. He studied the detective but decided to forgo mentioning that fact.

"I see."

"That wasn't the kind of information that really helps anyone, if you know what I mean. Delta has a strong policy against that sort of thing, especially between a manager like John and an administrative support person. Not to mention, John had a wife and kids and Starla is also married."

"I can understand that," said Detective Lee with a slight nod. "So, let me ask you a few questions."

"Sure."

"How well do you know Starla Pittman?"

"Well, she's the secretary to the plant manager. Obviously, if you want to get an audience with Roger McVann, it's always wise to go through Starla."

"What I mean is, what is Starla like? Was the attraction mutual?"

Ethan stared at the detective. He thought about the time that he rounded a corner by the conference room in the front office. John was in front of Starla, her back pressed up against a wall, their faces close. They had immediately moved away from each other.

"Yes," Ethan answered. "The attraction was mutual. But, like I said, they were both married, so I'm not sure that many people knew about the two of them."

The detective smiled slowly. "Well, you knew. Perhaps you weren't the only one."

For a moment, Ethan sat in stunned silence. Did other people know about the affair? Why had Ethan not heard rumors at the mill? He thought about the subtle tone of the detective's words. Maybe the police and the hierarchy at Delta already knew about John and Starla.

A memory of John's name and number flashing up on the caller ID bar of Roger McVann's phone one day during a meeting suddenly came back to him. Ethan had been surprised at the time that Roger didn't pick up the phone, but maybe he already knew that certain calls to the plant manager's suite were not for him.

The detective appeared to write notes but then inquisitively raised her eyes. "Was Starla happy with John? Do you think that she wanted him to leave his wife for her?"

"I can't really say what she wanted. She seemed to like the attention from John, but I don't know beyond that. John was happy with Leah and the kids. At least he seemed that way when I saw them together. Their kids play soccer, and our son just started, so I would see them at the ball field."

The detective was quiet for a moment.

"Ethan, let me ask you something. What about Starla's marriage? What can you tell me about that?"

Ethan looked at the detective. Should he tell her about the time that he went up to the front office and found Starla at her desk touching up her makeup, trying to cover a fading bruise on her chin? Ethan had recognized the mark. It was same kind that he had learned to hide when his own father got drunk.

"Starla probably isn't that happy," he admitted. "She's married to a guy that works in forestry. Glen is his name, but I don't really know him. I've only met him once or twice at Delta functions." He faltered on the last word before adding, "I don't think that he's that nice to her." The detective raised her eyebrows in question but remained silent.

"He knocks her around," Ethan confided. "I've seen the bruises."

The detective nodded quietly and wrote again on her pad.

"And what does her husband do for work exactly?"

"He works in the land management group at Delta, I believe. It's part of the forestry division."

"Is that a nine-to-five role?"

"It can be, but I think that he works the third shift. I've met him at a few company picnics, and he always said that he worked at night."

The detective looked puzzled. "Do they do forestry at night? That seems like a daytime job."

"Most of it is, but there are a few folks that work the back shifts."

"What do those shifts entail?"

"Usually, the second and third shifts involve more security work. They get out and patrol the land holdings and buildings to make sure that everything is secure, especially if there have been safety concerns."

The detective nodded again.

"Is there anything else you can tell me?" she asked.

"No," said Ethan. "I just thought about the situation with John and I thought you should know."

The officer nodded.

"If it's okay with you, I really need to be going. I'm already late for work."

Detective Lee reached across her desk and placed another card in Ethan's hand. He slipped the paper into his shirt pocket and rose to leave.

"Let me know if you think of anything else."

Ethan paused. "Delta Paper really is like a family. I'm hopeful that Leah and the kids will be okay. If there's any way that this piece of information about John's affair can be handled discreetly, I hope that you can."

The detective rose from her seat and studied the tall man before her. "We're conducting a full investigation here. I can't promise anything, but I do appreciate your talking to me. Feel free to call me if you think of anything else."

Ethan extended his hand as Detective Lee folded her notebook. "You must remember one thing," she said evenly returning his handshake. "In my experience, things have a way of coming out, even when people don't want them to. In the end, the truth rarely stays hidden for long."

CHAPTER TWENTY

"Here, I got you some mud," joked Nick Simpson as he handed a dingy ceramic coffee mug to his partner.

"Thanks," said Lee, taking the cup.

Both officers watched Ethan Weir make his way towards the front of the police station.

"Wasn't that the guy that we spoke to at the mill?" asked Simpson.

"Yeah," said Lee as she dropped the notebook onto her desk and took a quick sip from the steaming cup. "That was Ethan Weir."

"I saw him talking to you from the back room. He looked concerned, like he was in deep conversation with you, so I decided to just let the two of you talk."

"He came by to tell me that he knew that John and Starla Pittman were having an affair."

"Really?"

"He said that he thought about it after the interview and he felt that it might be important. He also seems to think that he was the only one that knew about the affair."

Simpson threw back his crew cut and laughed. "That would be a first. Did you tell him that affairs are like gossip? Everyone thinks that they are the only ones who know while the whole town is whispering behind their backs, especially in a small place like Campton."

Lee nodded and took another sip of her coffee. She winced at the contents and set the cup on the side of her desk.

"But," she confided, "he did tell me something interesting."

The older detective raised his eyebrows in question.

"He told me about Starla Pittman's husband, Glen. Seems he knocks her around a bit."

"Is that so?"

"Apparently, he's rough with her, bruises, that sort of thing. Mr. Weir said that he had even seen the evidence," Lee said, reading from the notes she was reviewing. "No wonder she gave up her Tracfone when you told her we would talk to her husband."

"Well, I think that it's time to talk to Starla and find out how physical this husband of hers could be. Maybe Mr. Pittman decided to deal with John Runar all by himself."

"There's something else," added Lee. "It seems that Glen Pittman also works a third shift job at Delta that involves security. According to Mr. Weir, the guy is out and about all night long keeping the timberlands under surveillance."

"What do you mean by out and about?"

"Evidently, Starla's husband patrols the land holdings of Delta Paper all night long—some sort of security surveillance."

"So, a job where he has the freedom to be anywhere in the dark?"

"Yep," said Lee with a nod of her head. She reached for her keys. "I think it's time we pay Starla and her husband a visit."

CHAPTER TWENTY-ONE

Starla looked up from her computer monitor and narrowed her eyes. Involuntarily, her fingers froze above the keyboard on her desk. What were they doing here? Why couldn't they just leave her alone?

From the doorway of the plant manager's suite, she watched the detectives methodically move toward her desk. Her stomach gave a sudden lurch.

"Yes?" she asked curtly.

"We need to ask you a few more questions," said Detective Lee with an unwavering gaze.

"I gathered as much."

The words spat out of her mouth, but she was through caring. This type of intrusion was unbelievable.

"Is there a place where we could talk?" asked Simpson.

Starla glanced quickly behind her. Roger's office door was shut so that he could take phone calls from Headquarters. She rose from her seat.

"Why don't we go down the hall? There's a work room that I think we can use."

The detectives followed Starla out into the main corridor of the building. As she passed the linear array of cubicles that inhabited the center of the floor, startled heads whipped around low walls to gawk at the police once again in the front office.

At the entrance to a small windowless room, Starla came to a stop. She flipped on the fluorescent lights and held the heavy wooden door indignantly for the officers. With an annoyed snort of exasperation, she quietly shut the door and stomped towards a large copier at the far end of the work area. When she turned around to the detectives, a cold stare covered her face.

"Look, I have a job here," she began. "I've seen the news reports on TV, and I know that John's death was a murder, but I don't know why you are back. I'm—"

"Starla, we need to ask you a few more questions about your relationship with John Runar," said Detective Simpson flatly. "How many people knew about your affair with him?"

Instantly, Starla moved closer and put her finger to her lips. "Shh," she whispered sharply. "Keep your voices down!"

She glared up at the older detective, aware that he was at least a foot taller than she was. The muscles in her jaw tightened. Anger made her boldly stand her ground.

"So, who knew about the two of you?"

Starla scowled at the detectives in front of her. She folded her arms across her low-cut top.

"Come on," she snarled. "I gave you my phone. Wasn't that enough? John and I were just having a bit of fun. It was an escape for both of us. I wasn't foolish enough to think that it would ever be any more than that, and neither was John."

She paused and took a deep breath before continuing. "For God's sake, he was married, and so am I."

"Very few women are content to just be the other woman," said Detective Simpson evenly, his eyes boring into the woman in front of him.

"Well, very few women are married when they start an affair, at least in a marriage that they don't want to rock."

"Did you want to rock your marriage?"

"Of course not!" she said with surprise.

"So how is your marriage?" Detective Lee asked. She had been watching Starla with quiet scrutiny. "Police records show that you called the authorities twice for domestic disturbances. It doesn't sound like your husband is all that great to you."

Starla eyed the two officers before locking her focus on Detective Lee. Would this woman even understand the first thing about her life? And what about marriage? Maybe, she would be painfully traditional, believing that men were inherently permitted their indiscretions just because they were male.

Starla studied Detective Lee. The solid and square officer, her black hair in a short bob, was obviously an emotionless female. With a face all but free of makeup and dressed only in pants and a simple blouse, the policewoman didn't even carry a handbag. For some reason, that fact alone seemed to answer Starla's questions.

"Glen has a temper, all right?"

"We've heard that he knocks you around. Is that what he does to you?" asked Lee.

Starla narrowed her eyes at the woman, giving up on the idea of making a connection with the officer. Sisterhood was clearly wasted on her.

"Well, you're the detective," she sneered. "Obviously, if my relationship at home had been great, then I wouldn't have been involved with someone else."

"What about your husband? Did he know what was going on with the two of you?" asked Simpson.

"Glen know about John? Absolutely not! If he'd suspected anything, then he would have confronted me."

"Is it possible that Glen did know and that he decided to take matters into his own hands?" asked Lee in a monotone voice that seemed to match her expressionless face.

"No!" Starla said emphatically. She took a deep breath, feeling her nostrils flare. This was ridiculous. The policewoman really was a bitch.

She dropped her voice. "Trust me, if Glen had suspected anything, I would have been the first to know. He wasn't one to hold back his emotions. And as you can tell from your records, he always showed me exactly how he felt," she added between clenched teeth.

"Tell me about his job," said the older detective.

"What about his job?"

"What exactly does Glen do for the land management group?"

Starla knitted her brow and shifted her weight from one foot to the other. She was unsure of where the two officers were going with their questions.

"Well, he works the third shift, doing security and surveillance for the forestry group."

"Security at night?" asked Simpson.

"He works on a skeleton crew that makes sure that the company land and timber holdings are safe and not disturbed."

"How does he do this, in the dark?" asked Lee.

"Well, there are cameras with night vision on them in different points–in different security areas all over the acreage that Delta owns. We even have drones that can fly over forestry areas. Glen monitors those cameras to make sure there are no disturbances out in the scrub pines."

"And if he sees a disturbance?" pressed Lee.

"He goes out and investigates what is going on," Starla said.

"So, all hours of the night, your husband is able to be out riding around to check on the land that Delta owns? Does he go out alone?"

Starla hesitated. She didn't like where the inquiry seemed to be heading or the skeptical tone of the probing, no-nonsense woman that acted like a terrier with a bone.

"Look, I don't know. I'm not with him at night, but he either goes with a team member or he checks things out on his own. It's his job."

"The night that John Runar was killed, your husband could have been out, riding around all by himself?"

"I don't like what you are implying," barked Starla, squaring her shoulders to match Detective Lee's sturdy build. "My husband was at work–work, okay–the night John had his accident."

The detectives looked at each other. Their impassive expressions suddenly made her nervous.

"Please," Starla begged, "leave my husband alone. Leave me alone. We had nothing to do with any of this. Whatever happened to John, it had nothing to do with us." She paused and dropped her voice. "If Glen learns about…about John, he might just kill me."

The room went silent and Detective Lee pulled a card from her pocket that she handed to Starla. "I'm sorry. You can call me if you need help, but there are no guarantees. We're going to find out what really happened to John Runar because this is a murder investigation."

CHAPTER TWENTY-TWO

Starla watched the detectives head out of the work room. Noiselessly, she shut the door behind them and started counting to one hundred as slowly as her trembling lips would allow. Somewhere around the double digits, she looked down at her hands. Nervous twitching was wreaking havoc on her fingers.

She shut her eyes and dropped her head onto the metal shelving against the wall. If only the minutes could somehow elongate before she had to emerge into the hallway. Absolutely no one at Delta needed to connect the dots and figure out that the police kept seeking her out for questions. Maybe they would just forget that she was the one leading the detectives through the building. Or maybe, they wouldn't ask her anything at all. Of course, her absence might be noticed if she was gone too long from her desk, but she could always bluff to co-workers with a vague retort about running executive errands. Right now, she just needed some distance between herself and the departing authorities. Besides, at the moment, she was afraid that her voice might crack if she had to talk to anyone in the office.

Slowly, Starla opened the work room door. Her head was pounding even though she was trying her best to be calm. With unsteady legs, she moved into the empty hallway. She dropped her gaze and walked hurriedly to the ladies' room, thinking about the detectives and their awful questions. How dare they imply that either she or Glen were involved with John's death. The whole thing was ludicrous. She had half a mind to complain about harassment.

As awful as the insinuations were, Starla knew that the two police officers were only half of her problem. John's death was the real devastation. Just thinking about the accident left her barely able to make it through the day. Then, before she even had a chance to process the loss, the weird note had appeared on her car followed by a threatening phone call.

The messages were the truly frightening part. What the hell did the warnings even mean? John had never told her anything except a few inside jokes about sex. The note told her not to talk, but talk about what? And how could she not speak with the police if they wanted to question her?

Ideas whiplashed in her brain as Starla slipped into the employee bathroom. Quickly, she glanced under each stall. The room was empty, making her utter a silent prayer of thanksgiving for her momentary privacy.

At the sink, cold water ran over her hands. She splashed her puffy face and almost felt lightheaded. The back of her hand ran over her eyes, removing what was left of her mascara.

How could this be happening? How could the police think that Glen had anything to do with John's death? And who in the hell was sending her these messages?

Starla stared at her reflection in the mirror. Dark circles were starting to rim her eyes. Big blotches covered her usually flawless cheeks. For a moment, she wondered who was looking back at her.

Trying to sleep since the police left her trailer two nights ago continued to be futile. Every time she closed her eyes, her mind would fall into a fitful dream that only ended when she awakened with a jerk. Now she looked away from her tired face.

She slumped in exhaustion, leaning on the edge of the porcelain sink. In the stillness of the empty room, her heart thumped in her ears.

"Get a grip," she muttered to herself as she raised her eyes to study her pale reflection. "You just need to think."

What was going to happen now? She needed to plan her next steps. Obviously, the police would question Glen.

Starla tried to imagine what her husband would say. How would he react when the authorities found him? Of course, the detectives would spill the beans about her affair with John. If they were going to try to figure out an alibi for him, then the police would inevitably reveal her affair.

She bit her lower lip. Thinking about Glen made Starla wince. She could only imagine his anger, his hands grabbing her, punishing her.

Maybe, she wouldn't go home. But what if the nosey detectives didn't go straight to Glen? How would she explain her absence from the trailer if she stayed out all night?

Starla turned off the dripping faucet and went to dry her hands. There had to be a way out of this mess. She was deep in thought as her eyes watched the rough roll of paper towels drop obediently out of the bottom of the motion activated towel dispenser. In a moment of rare clarity, she had an epiphany. If something as simple as sheets of cellulose could behave on cue, then certainly she could.

Starla straightened her posture. With determined steps, she moved into a bathroom stall and shut the door. From her pocket she pulled out the strange note that had been left on her car. She tore the paper into tiny pieces and flushed the soggy scraps down the toilet. Now the weird message was gone, and neither Glen nor the police would ever find it.

She slipped out of the stall and opened the bathroom door. If she calmly went back to work, then she could keep up appearances and buy herself some time. Her days at Delta always gave her a few hours to think. If any more questions came her way from co-workers, she could just lie.

Glen was the bigger problem at the moment. If she claimed to have a special project for Roger, she could text him that she was staying late at the office. His own shift schedule in the lands and timber group would have him working overtime this week. She suddenly remembered a motel on the edge of town that she and John had used. For a nice tip, the manager would probably let her have the room at the back of the building for a few nights. At least staying there would buy some time and distance from Glen's anger.

As she moved down the corridor towards her office, Starla thought about her situation. If she used her head and controlled her nerves, the details could probably be managed. After all, she was like a cat that could survive a terrible fall or a sudden fright. No matter what happened, she always landed on her feet. Now all that she needed was a longer-term plan.

"Starla, are you all right?"

Roger McVann stood in the reception area, near her desk, as Starla rounded the corner. A look of concern clouded his face.

"Yes, I'm fine," she said with a weak smile, taking her seat. "I just had to go the ladies' room."

"Are you sure?"

"I really am fine," Starla soothed. "I just didn't sleep well last night."

"Do you need to leave early?" Roger asked with genuine concern.

"No, no, I'm fine, really I am. I just need to get back to work."

"Well, you let me know if there's anything that I can do."

"I will," she said with a nod as she began to straighten the papers on her desk. "My phone has just been ringing off the hook, and I need to generate those reports for headquarters today. I'll have them on your desk in a bit."

"That's fine," said her boss. "I'm not in a rush. I actually thought that I'd go down into the mill. With everything that has happened, I thought it would be best if I took a stroll and made sure that everyone knows that my door is open to them."

"That's a wonderful idea," she agreed.

Starla's happy expression followed Roger as he put on his hard hat and strolled out of the door. She watched him go and let the smile slide from her face.

With her eyes continually checking the doorway, she quietly opened her lower desk drawer. Relief made her sigh when she found exactly what she wanted in the bottom of her purse.

In one quick movement, she opened the bottle. The small oval pill went on her tongue. She reached for the glass of water on the corner of her desk and took a quick sip. The Xanax went down her throat in a smooth gulp.

Her eyes looked up at the Delta Paper Company emblem on the wall opposite her desk. The wood carved image had the corporate name centered between a laboratory beaker and a pine tree. Her eyes focused on the small wording at the bottom of the seal: Nature enhanced through chemistry.

"Ain't that the truth," she muttered to herself.

CHAPTER TWENTY-THREE

Glen Pittman ran his hand through his rumpled hair as he turned on the television set. Squinting at the corner of the screen, he noticed the time. Having a new satellite dish on top of the trailer meant there would probably be something decent to watch, even in the daytime. Hopefully, the deluxe package that he purchased would have some sort of continuous boxing or wrestling matches on one of the sports stations.

He grinned as the first one hundred channels scrolled into view. There were so many options. He couldn't help but get excited. Man, the technology was awesome. A rugby game appeared on the screen in front of him. He studied the action for a moment. The European teams were new to him, but the field and plays seemed familiar. He tossed the remote control onto the sofa and went into the kitchen to find some breakfast.

Opening the door of the refrigerator, he snatched a plastic bottle of orange juice. He popped the top and took a long swig. He took another long drink before putting the container back next to his cans of beer.

He grabbed the milk, unscrewed the top, and took a suspicious sniff. A little past date, but the stuff looked fresh enough to him. He reached for a box of cereal from the top of the refrigerator and poured the brown flakes into a bowl on the counter. The game on the television set erupted in cheering. Glen looked up at the score as the milk started to pour.

"Damn it," he said. Cold liquid had sloshed onto his foot. He reached for the crumpled dish towel next to the stove just as the knocking started.

"Hang on," he called with annoyance.

Glen started swearing under his breath. He could just picture his neighbor, old man Jackson, from down the road. His ancient, dilapidated truck would probably need jumping off, and he never bothered to get his own cables. He yanked open the trailer door and squinted into the bright, glaring light.

"Glen Pittman?" asked Detective Simpson.

He looked at the officers in front of him in startled shock. What had he done that would make the police come to his trailer?

"Yeah," he said warily.

Badges were flashed. "I'm Detective Simpson, and this is Detective Lee from the Campton County Sheriff's Department. We'd like to ask you a few questions."

In the doorway, Glen felt the hot sun on his face. "Questions about what?"

"We need to speak to you about someone that we think you know. May we come in?" asked Detective Lee.

Glen stared back at the police. He started to rack his brain. Who did he know that had just gotten busted for drugs? His mind was blank. "Yeah, sure."

He opened the door and let the two detectives cross the threshold. Grabbing the remote control from the couch, he turned off the game which had started to crescendo in volume.

"May we have a seat?" Detective Lee asked.

The two officers dropped onto the sagging sofa in unison before they received a reply.

"Well, sure," Glen said with a slight shake of his head.

"Glen... may we call you Glen? We need to ask you a few questions about John Runar," began Detective Simpson.

Glen ran his hands through his hair. This certainly was not what he was expecting. He plopped down into the plaid recliner and rested his palms on his knees.

"John Runar?"

"Yes, Mr. Runar, the Delta Paper manager who was killed out on the Mill Highway. We need to know how well you knew the deceased."

Glen stared at the two detectives in bewilderment. "I didn't know him. I mean, I had met him once or twice at Delta picnics, but I didn't know him, not really."

The two detectives studied the man in front of them.

"I don't understand, did someone say that I knew him?" Glen asked.

The older detective spoke slowly. His gaze was penetrating. "Glen, we believe that your wife knew Mr. Runar very well—that they were, in fact, good friends."

"Starla?"

"Yes," Detective Simpson continued. "We believe that they might have been in a relationship." The words hung in the air. Glen felt his face go slack. He was suddenly speechless.

"Are you and your wife on good terms?" asked Detective Lee.

Glen made a sound like the air leaving his lungs. His eyes went wide, and, for a second, he felt like his whole world had suddenly shifted.

"I...I...Starla and I are okay," he managed to say.

"Glen, we know that you and your wife have really gotten into it. We know the police have been called more than once to your residence," said Lee.

"Is that what this is about? You think that just because Starla and I fought, that she had some sort of thing with John Runar?"

The detectives quietly watched the man sitting in front of them. They let the room fall silent.

"We have evidence," said the older detective, "that they were involved with each other. We need to know if you were aware of the relationship?"

Glen let his mouth fall open again. He blinked at officers before him. "No, no," he managed to say. "I, I, no, I didn't know anything."

"Glen, where were you on the night that Mr. Runar was killed?"

"The night?" Glen asked as he choked out the words from his dry throat. "I work nights. I was at work. I have worked every night except last night."

"Do you have the ability to leave your desk, to be mobile, when you are at work?"

Glen stared in disbelief. His head was starting to swim.

"I do security. I work with a group. We keep the Delta forest lands secure."

"Were you out by yourself the night Mr. Runar was killed?" Simpson asked.

Glen was stunned. Is this what the police thought? He tried desperately to remember on which day the accident occurred, but as he sat with the officers, the night shifts seem to run together in his mind.

"I was at work, with my group," he reiterated. "That's where I was." The room was still. The detectives stared at each other. As if on cue, they rose to leave.

"Glen, we are going to need to talk with the people that you worked with that night," said Detective Simpson.

"Look, I don't need any trouble at my job," Glen said, starting to feel his anger rise.

"And we don't want to make any trouble for anyone. But we're going to have to talk to your co-workers," said Detective Lee steadily.

"But I didn't do anything!"

"Then everything should check out for you. In the meantime, don't leave town," said the policewoman evenly.

"Leave town? Jesus, I have a job!" he shouted.

Detective Lee placed a card on the square end table.

"Here's our card," she said. "If you think of anything, you need to give us a call."

From the open doorway, hot air flooded the trailer. As Glen watched the detectives tromp down the wooden steps, he went over to the door and slammed it shut. In stunned silence, he walked to the kitchen. He gripped the edge of the stove and shut his eyes. Was it true? How could Starla have done that? Did she really have a thing going on with this dead guy? Had she fucked him just to get even for some of their fights?

He opened his eyes. A sick realization filled his mind. Was she trying to set him up? His eyes fell on the cereal bowl left on the counter. The neglected brown flakes had become a thick glue. In one swift movement, Glen picked up the bowl and smashed it onto the worn vinyl floor.

"That bitch," he said. "I'm going to kill her!"

CHAPTER TWENTY-FOUR

The patrol car pulled away from the trailer and bumped down the long sandy driveway. Both detectives sat without speaking until the thick foliage of overgrown palmetto fronds and scrub pines that lined the property covered their windshield.

"Well, what did you think?" asked Simpson.

"He seemed genuinely shocked to learn about his wife and John Runar," answered Lee as she steered the car over the unpaved road.

"Yeah, I thought so too."

Lee adjusted her sunglasses as the white glare of noontime dabbled through the windows of the squad car. Ideas and questions bounced through her mind as she navigated the ruts before her.

"We're going to have to check out his whereabouts on the night of the murder, but my gut says that he didn't have anything to do with it," she added.

"I had the same feeling, but my experience also tells me that when love triangles are part of the picture, the suspects are always involved, in one way or another, with the murder." The detectives were quiet for another minute. The ringing of a cell phone reverberated through the car.

"Simpson," Nick spoke into the phone. A voice on the other end fired words in rapid succession. "I see. What day will that occur?" he asked.

Lee gave a questioning glance to her partner as she pulled past a battered, leaning mailbox and onto the highway.

"Yep. I've got that information. Thanks," Simpson said as he hung up the call.

"What was that?" she asked.

"That was the morgue about John Runar. They have released the body to the funeral home. They think the services are scheduled for next week, most likely on Thursday or Friday."

"So, are you thinking what I'm thinking in terms of the funeral?"

"Absolutely," agreed Simpson. "We definitely need to observe. This case is just beginning, and we need to see who shows up and who doesn't."

The older detective picked up his file from the console and started making notes as the cruiser slowed down for a curve in the road.

"So, do you think that Starla Pittman did it?" asked Lee.

"I don't know. She's scrappy enough, but she is also pretty small. Whoever broke John Runar's neck was strong, with large hands."

"Let's go back to the station and review everything before we talk to anyone else. I just still feel like we're missing something," she said.

"Agreed."

"Should we tell Starla that her husband now knows about her affair?" asked Lee as she propped her hair behind her ear, a gesture that she only did when she worried.

"I don't want to tip our hand on anything. Besides, like I said, Starla Pittman is tough. I'm sure that she can take care of herself."

"Okay, but if she calls me, and if he is beating her, then I'm going to personally get her out of that house."

"Lee, you are one fine cop," said Simpson with a laugh. "You really care about everyone, even the likes of a little tramp like Starla Pittman. Did you see how flip she was with you when we went to Delta Paper earlier? I'm not really sure that she even deserves great treatment."

"Well, what can I say? I'm a sucker for the abused," she admitted with a shrug. "Even when I don't actually like someone, my protective instincts start to kick into gear."

"Do your kids know how much you care about the people in this rural paradise? Do they have any idea what a softie you really are inside?" teased Simpson.

Detective Lee stepped on the accelerator and shook her head. "My kids are young," she confided. "To them and to most of the world, I'm just a small-town Tiger Mom, out to compel them to do their best, ready to ride their backsides if they don't give their schoolwork the finest effort that they can. My children still think that I get the monsters out from under their beds at night. They have no idea how much I worry about everyone."

"So, you need to tell them sometimes—let them know how you handle the public. They'd be proud."

"Maybe when they're older," she said thoughtfully. "But right now, it's better for me to keep my cases to myself. Especially when real life involves getting the actual murdering monsters out of Campton."

CHAPTER TWENTY-FIVE

Ethan stood in front of the bathroom mirror and ripped his tie off for the third time. Lines of sweat cascaded down the sides of his face.

"It's too damn hot for this," he said angrily.

"What's wrong?"

Abbey appeared at his side in her black maternity dress. She pushed the back of the pearl studs into her earlobes and studied her husband.

"I hate this," Ethan complained. "It's too damn hot. Hell, I'm too damn hot to wear this tight tie."

"Let me see," Abbey said soothingly. "Turn to me. I think that you're just tying it too tight."

She gently took the two pieces of silk from the shirt collar and started to carefully work. Ethan surveyed his wife.

"You look nice," he said. He hoped his tone would suffice for an apology.

"Well, it's a black maternity dress. Hard to go wrong with that one," she said as she finished knotting his tie. She glanced at her side profile in the mirror and smoothed the fabric that flowed from her round figure. "Hard to go right with a dress like this either," she said with a small laugh.

Ethan smiled. Abbey could always find the bright side to anything. Her sunny outlook was one of many things that he loved about her.

When they were first married, Ethan found his wife's optimism almost grating. Abbey excelled at finding the silver lining to any problem. If he was honest, Ethan couldn't stand blind positivity. What kind of person in their right mind ever wanted to choose cheerfulness in the face of difficulty?

Ethan had a naturally different mindset. Whenever he encountered trouble, whether at work or home, he based his actions and words on data. He often told himself that his direct confrontations were a by-product of his technical education. And who wasn't to be congratulated for being clear and concise? Didn't the world need more rational people? Of course, if he were truly honest, his blunt reactions sometimes only furthered problems and miscommunications, especially at the mill.

At some point, Ethan finally started to watch his wife. He came to appreciate her ability to rise above most momentary annoyances. The realization took years, but he eventually came to see that Abbey was actually masterful, and that what she really possessed was considerable mental toughness.

A ringing of the front doorbell snapped him back to the moment.

"That's Madison, from next door," Abbey said. "She's out of school, so I asked her to watch Charlie. I'll get the door; you finish getting ready."

Ethan looked back in the mirror and frowned. The tie looked fine, but he hated wearing formal clothes. It was so much easier to just wear a cotton shirt and put on a hard hat. He stuck his fingers into his collar and tried vainly to give his neck more room. The fabric was useless. Every part of the choking neckband felt like a vice grip at his chin.

He reached onto the vanity to get a handkerchief for his pocket. That was when the whole thing hit him. He really wasn't upset by the dressy clothes or even the hot weather. What Ethan truly hated was funerals.

Standing in the bathroom he ran his fingers across the folded white linen square. Suddenly, he was thirteen years old again, dressing for his own father's funeral. He had put a handkerchief in his pocket on that day as well. For some reason, he felt the need to be prepared. The decision was just the sort of thing that his brothers used to tease him about at home.

When he sat in the church that day, Ethan watched almost his entire small North Carolina town parade through the doors. He shook hands with people and went through the motions. None of the neighbors who came to the service that day had talked about how drunk his father got, about how he often hit Ethan's mother or his family. Everyone just said they were sorry that the old man wrapped his car around a tree one night. They were too polite to mention his father's blood alcohol level. Ethan always wondered if maybe they were just more than a bit relieved to get a drunk driver off the roads for good.

By the time that Ethan went home, he had a disdain for all funerals. He also ended the day with a completely dry handkerchief.

"I love it!" Ethan heard Charlie's words followed by a squeal that echoed through the house.

"What do you say to Madison?" From the bedroom door, Ethan could see Abbey in the foyer, prompting their son.

"Thanks, Madi. Silly Putty is my best favorite!"

Madison started to laugh as Ethan joined them. Abbey smiled and ran her hands through her son's blond curls.

"Just keep it out of his hair," Abbey warned. "We had an accident with Silly Putty right before Easter, and his hair is still growing out on one side."

"No problem, Mrs. Weir," Madison assured her.

"Okay, emergency numbers are on the fridge. We are at the Methodist church. We should be back in about two hours, but you never can tell with these things," she added.

"Bye, Mom," Charlie said, busy studying the plastic egg in his hands.

Ethan handed Abbey her black handbag from the living room chair.

"Oh, and not more than two fruit snacks. He'll eat the whole box if you let him," Abbey instructed.

Ethan had his hand on his wife's arm. He was trying to guide her to the back door.

"We're making a run for it," he said over his shoulder to Madison.

"Drive carefully. We'll be fine."

Ethan pulled the door closed behind his wife and walked outside to the carport. The afternoon humidity made his skin instantly feel wet. As he held the passenger door for Abbey, Ethan could feel his shirt start to stick to his back.

"Let's get some air going," Abbey said as she slid inside, and Ethan settled behind the wheel.

The red minivan eased out of the Pine Acres subdivision while Abbey looked out of the passenger window from behind her large sunglasses. She turned to Ethan.

"I know that you hate memorial services and I know that these things bring back lots of bad memories, but you're really doing a good thing by attending." She let the words settle between them before continuing. "And you know that Leah needs our support."

"I agree," Ethan said quietly. The Campton square and small downtown came into view.

"I also know that things weren't always easy with John in the department," Abbey added. "I know that he made things a bit of a zoo for you," she said, hesitating before adding gently, "and I know that you had really wanted his assignment."

Ethan's face was stoic as he steered the car towards the white church on the corner. His wife knew him so well.

"It wasn't the assignment per se. You know I like running the Finishing Department," he admitted, "but John's role was the sort of thing that could open doors. He was getting noticed at Headquarters."

"Do you think John and Leah were in line for a transfer?" Abbey asked.

"If John had delivered clear results for Delta, he was probably in line for a promotion," confided Ethan. "Getting that type of attention would have easily meant relocation. He could have been in Memphis within a year."

"You do good work," Abbey said as she looked over at her husband. "The company will notice you, too."

Ethan pulled into a parking spot and turned off the engine.

"One can only hope," he said ruefully as he unbuckled his seatbelt. "But what do they always say, good guys finish last?"

"Well, you're a good guy and you do work in Finishing, but in my book, you'll always be first," she said.

Ethan opened his car door and looked up at the church steeple. "Well, given that we're here for a funeral, and it's not my own, then I'll take that endorsement and consider myself lucky for today."

———

From a side street, Starla Pittman sat tapping her steering wheel as she watched Delta Paper employees slowly approach the church. With her car motor still running, she bit her lip in thought. Maybe coming to John's funeral wasn't such a great idea. How would people react when they saw her attending the service? Her sweaty palms dropped down to smooth the nonexistent wrinkles out of her tight black shirt. She let out a frustrated sigh. All she wanted was a chance to pay her respects. She tried to settle her nerves with some deep breaths, but fear gnawed at the pit of her stomach. Why couldn't she just get up the courage to open her car door and join the swelling crowd? Suddenly, her throat tightened.

"Oh, hell no," she muttered. The two detectives emerged from their police cruiser on the corner and began to mill along the edge of a large group of mourners.

From behind her sunglasses, Starla automatically scanned her rear-view mirror. She desperately wanted to go to John's memorial but the last thing she needed was a scene. Shifting around in her seat, she checked the traffic. Her car made a quick U-turn.

She drove two blocks towards the town square before spotting a long alley that curved back in the direction of the church. Starla whipped her car into an empty parking space and waited for five minutes. If she could just delay her entrance until most of the people were seated, then possibly they wouldn't notice her. She balled her fists and tried to make her heart stop racing in her chest. All she wanted was a chance to say good-bye to John. She smoothed her hair and checked her lipstick. With a final determined scowl in the mirror, she squared her shoulders and opened her car door.

Starla lowered her head as she walked briskly down the narrow alley. There had to be a way to sneak inside the building. If she was lucky, she could find an unlocked door near the church sanctuary.

Surely there would be a hidden spot where she could see, or at least hear, the beautiful things that would be said about John.

She was still lost in thought when she rounded the side of an old building and saw them. Two boys were standing over what appeared to be a pile of old clothes. They turned at the sound of her footsteps, their faces defiant. Instantly, something about their expressions seemed wrong to her. Starla narrowed her eyes when she noticed that the pile of clothes on the ground started to move.

"What are you doing?" she asked suspiciously.

"Nothin'," sneered the older teenager.

Starla approached the pair and realized that the figure on the ground was a man. His jaundiced face looked haggard to the point that she could not have guessed his age. He struggled to sit up even as his thin hand grabbed the edge of his tattered coat to pull the dirty fabric around his thin frame.

"Leave him alone," Starla commanded. The force of her words sounded loud in her ears. The teenagers turned to her with a snicker. She realized that they were exactly her height.

"Make me," taunted the older youth.

Starla stood her ground as she silently calculated her odds of winning a fight against both of them. One of the unexpected benefits of her redneck upbringing was her ability to land a jab that could make any male wince. She paused, realizing the importance of her next move. The two boys looked like over-privileged punks. As her gaze settled on their insolent faces, she recognized something familiar about their dark curly hair. Memories of political advertisements flooded her brain. Effortlessly, it clicked.

"Leave him alone, or I'll call your father," she leveled.

A flicker of fear washed across both sets of their eyes. Starla smiled inwardly. She felt her resolve increase.

"I'm one of the top executives at Delta Paper and I'm sure your father, the mayor, would love a phone call from me. I'd be happy to inform him about what you are really doing," she lied.

The boys shot each other a sideways glance.

"Go," she commanded.

"Whatever," the older youth said as they both turned to go down the alley. "'Til next time, old man," he called over his shoulder.

Starla watched the two teenagers saunter towards the church. She let out a loud sigh of relief as they disappeared into a crowded parking lot.

"Thank you," the man said as he tried to rise.

"Here, let me help you," offered Starla, as she extended her hand. The man had a questioning look in his eyes as he took her arm. "Are you all right?" she asked.

"Yeah, thanks," he said, straightening his limp clothes. "You really knew how to handle those boys," he added with admiration.

Starla merely shrugged.

"That was sort of amazing. You're kind of like some sort of one-woman cavalry, aren't you?" he asked.

Starla met his gaze with surprise. John had always used that word—cavalry—when he described his own deployment missions. He often said that helping villagers in need made him a better person. She felt a lump in her throat.

"Well, thanks again," the man said as he started to limp away towards the town square. Starla watched him quicken his pace. Instinctively, she realized that he was afraid the boys would return.

"Wait," she called.

The man turned to her. Starla made an instant decision. She knew the best way to honor John.

"Can I buy you lunch?" she offered.

The man stopped and stared at her in disbelief. Starla could tell he was wondering if this was some sort of trick.

"There's a great place on the square. They have the best hamburgers. Would you join me? My treat."

A slow smile spread across his face. Missing teeth protruded from his shrunken gums. He nodded.

Starla returned the smile. For the first time that day, a feeling of peace settled over her.

"So, tell me your name," she said as she joined him.

———

A line of people snaked through the church vestibule. Ethan followed Abbey into the tight crowd and inched his way towards the sanctuary doors. A heavy smell of perfume filled the air from the dozens of large floral wreaths resting against metal tripod stands lining the walls. The warm air resembled a green house.

Inside the church, the old pine pews held the first mourners. Ethan led his wife to the outer aisle and found a seat on the far end of a row.

"I think this is a good place," he said in a hushed tone.

They slid into their seats as the organ started to play. Delta Paper employees and neighbors began a slow trickle into the historic chapel. Ethan looked over his shoulder to see the ushers placing folding chairs along the back wall.

Out of the corner of his eye, he caught sight of the two detectives that had been at the plant. They were in the back corner, almost hidden by the swelling crowd.

"I have to pee," Abbey whispered.

Ethan looked at his wife with a questioning glance.

"Sorry," she said. "It's crowded in there," she continued as she patted her front. "There's not much room for a bladder and a growing mini-me."

Ethan stood up, and his wife rose behind him.

"Wait here. I'll be right back—just hold our seats."

"No," he said, "I'm coming with you. We'll just get seats in a few minutes."

Back in the narthex, Abbey quietly spoke to an older lady who pointed and nodded. "Just down there, honey. The hallway wraps around."

Ethan and Abbey followed the dim corridor that seemed to zigzag away from the front of the church. Dark, empty rooms lined the vacant hallway. After several turns, the noise from the funeral crowd had become a distant hum.

Looking around, Ethan realized that there was no way that Abbey needed to be alone in an unfamiliar, poorly lit building. A worn sign for the ladies' room came into view.

"I'll wait right here," he said.

Abbey pushed open the heavy wooden door and turned on the light, leaving Ethan alone in the gloomy corridor. He pulled out his phone to check for any messages.

Voices drifted towards Ethan from a room at the end of the hallway. He looked up from his screen as a door opened up ahead and light spilled onto the floor. Leah Runar's southern drawl floated from the open space. She sounded engaged in conversation. Ethan listened and realized that John's family was probably gathered in preparation for the service.

To his relief, Leah started to laugh. At least she sounded all right, Ethan thought. There was nothing worse than attending a funeral with sobbing family members that might start wailing at any moment. Those kinds of emotional displays always left him uncomfortable.

Ethan watched as Leah strolled out of the room with a man at her side. He guided her with his hand on her shoulder. The short, muscular man had his back turned, but Ethan squinted his eyes to get a better view. There was something familiar about him. Why was he so recognizable? The strong profile of the man's face jogged Ethan's memory.

Suddenly, the pieces went together. The guy was Carlos Silva, Charlie's soccer coach. Abbey had introduced him to Ethan this past spring when they had signed up their son to play on a fall team.

In the dim hallway, Carlos brought his hand gently down Leah's back. With his olive-colored thumb, he stroked her spine in one long movement. She turned to him and whispered.

Ethan watched the two of them in surprise. Had Carlos Silva really run his hand all the way down Leah's back? The gesture was casual, but so slow. The caress was the same lingering touch that he often did with Abbey.

With a fluid movement, Carlos dropped his hand to his side as Leah moved back into the brightly lit room. As if on cue, Carlos turned around slowly and looked over his shoulder. From the end of the corridor, he caught Ethan's eye. His face tightened into a dark glower.

Ethan returned the stare, startled by the expression of hostility. Carlos turned and followed Leah into the room, shutting the door with a bang. Confused, Ethan stood in the empty hallway. Something about the whole interaction was wrong.

Carlos Silva looked more than angry, Ethan realized. There was something about his scowl that was intent on conveying some sort of message. Ethan stood there and realized that he had understood the interaction perfectly. It was an undeniable warning.

CHAPTER TWENTY-SIX

Ethan pulled his seatbelt across his chest and started the car engine. He said nothing as the minivan pulled away from the curb.

"Ugh," Abbey complained as she adjusted the air vents. "I'm melting! It's bad enough to be pregnant in the summer, but this heat is killing me!" Ethan stared forward in silence.

"Are you going to talk to me?" she asked. "I know that you hate these sorts of things, but you haven't said a word to me since we sat down in the church."

"I know," he said. "Sorry."

"I thought that it was actually better than most funerals. Leah actually looked okay, and the service was fairly short," Abbey began.

Ethan peered through the windows of the car—his expression hard.

"What?" Abbey asked with a hint of exasperation.

Ethan hesitated. Telling his wife what he witnessed, just putting the scene into words, was awkward. Would she even understand?

"I saw something," Ethan said quietly.

"Okay, what did you see?"

He paused again, running his hand across the back of his neck, deep in thought. With a heavy sigh, he began.

"While I was waiting for you in the hallway—when you went to the bathroom—I saw the room where the family was gathered before the service."

"Okay," she prompted.

"I saw Leah come out of the room with a man. They stood together in the hallway."

"Alright, they were probably put there before the service."

"The man that she was with, the one I saw, was Charlie's soccer coach, Carlos Silva. He stood next to her and ran his hand down her back."

"What do you mean, ran his hand down her back?"

Ethan shot his wife a knowing glance.

"I mean, ran his hand all the way down her back like I do with you. You know, when my fingers go all the way down your spine."

Abbey knitted her brow in thought. "Maybe he was just patting her back, you know, and his hand fell down to her lower back."

"No, this was intentional," Ethan asserted. "Trust me, this move was intimate. And after he did it, Leah whispered something to him."

"I don't know, Eth," she said, kicking the shoes off her swollen feet. "People hug each other at these sorts of things. Some people are just the touchy type. Isn't Carlos from Brazil? Maybe it's just a cultural thing for him."

"No, touching like that is different. There was something familiar between the two of them. It was definitely more than a friendly move."

Abbey was quiet behind her sunglasses.

"I know what I saw," he said firmly.

"But didn't you say the whole family was right there? Would he have been stroking her like that in front of her kids and her parents?"

"This was outside of a room. They thought they were alone for a moment, but I was at the end of the hallway. I saw them. And then Carlos realized that I was there, and he gave me quite a look."

"What kind of a look?"

Ethan pulled the car onto their tranquil street and shot a knowing eyeful at his wife. "I mean a look—like he was pissed off that I had seen him."

Abbey bit her lower lip and then turned to Ethan. "So, what are you going to do?" she asked.

He looked out of the windshield that was fully dotted with dead bugs and studied the live oak trees covered in Spanish moss in his neighbor's yard.

"I don't know," he admitted.

"Well, if you think that you saw something or know something, then you should probably say something."

Ethan nodded his head. He was coming to the same conclusion.

"That's what I'm thinking, but I need to turn it over in my head some more. I mean, I'm still looking for a logical reason why he would run his hand down her back and then give me some sort of killer stare."

He eased the minivan into the carport of their small ranch house that looked peaceful and familiar. Abbey reached out and touched his arm. When Ethan turned to her, she had a look of genuine concern on her face.

"John Runar was murdered, Ethan. Everyone's talking about what happened, and tongues are wagging all over this small town. I've heard at least four theories for his death and there have been no arrests made yet."

Ethan nodded in agreement.

"Please," she continued. "We have a family. If you saw something, then you have to say something. That's always what the police say."

Ethan turned off the engine.

"I know," he said. "That's what I keep telling myself."

"And, no matter what, you have to be careful," she said, her hand still on his arm. "For all of us."

CHAPTER TWENTY-SEVEN

"So, what would make these pulp bales uneven as they come off the finishing line?"

Ethan watched the two summer interns that stood in front of him. A look of confusion clouded their faces as they studied at the computer panels in the Finishing control room.

"Misalignment on the paper machine?" answered Daniel Matthews tentatively as he pushed his clear plastic safety glasses into place on the bridge of his nose.

"Okay, it's possible," coaxed Ethan. "But what else? What would be another reason?"

"Maybe something with the knives that cut the bales?" tried Hayley Schaffer squinting her eyes in thought as she studied the bound pulp through the glass.

"Yes," Ethan agreed. "Those are two possibilities, but in a situation where bales come off the line that clearly don't meet specs, you need to go where?"

Ethan held the control room door open for the students as they walked into the production area. He motioned to his office and the three of them made their way towards the back of the mill. Shutting his door behind the students, Ethan placed his reports on his desk and turned to the young people. He could almost see their mental wheels turning, searching for answers.

"Look, here's what I'm saying. Learning to think through all the possibilities of production problems is important," Ethan said encouragingly. "So, who do you need to communicate with when you see problems on the Finishing end?"

He waited. Ever since Ethan had first agreed to be an industry trainer, he realized that teachable moments like this were the key to success.

"Um...," Hayley wavered as she bit her lower lip in thought. Daniel remained silent as he shifted his weight from one steel-toed boot to the other and put a hand in the front pocket of his khakis.

"Okay, these are tough questions, but here's the thing," Ethan said as he propped onto the edge of his desk. "You have to learn to talk to the folk's upstairs, and I don't mean heaven."

Hayley and Daniel both smiled and started to nod.

"Talk to the people in Pulp Drying," Ethan said as he pointed to the elevated area of the mill above the Finishing Department. "Communication up and down the line is critical. If you can't readily see the problem in your department, then you have to step back and look at the whole process."

The two interns nodded and made notes on their phones.

"So, here's what I want," said Ethan. "I want you both to follow production, start to finish, taking a day in each department. I want you to really understand what you are seeing and next week—let's say Thursday—you email me and give me a list of process problems that you noticed and a variety of solutions for each issue that you identify."

The students nodded as their fingers flew across their screens.

"How many problems and solutions do you want?" Daniel asked when he raised his eyes from his phone.

Ethan looked at both of them and thought about the assignment. He wanted them to learn, but he also didn't want pages of extra work in his inbox.

"Let's say that you will identify three problems per department and three solutions per problem."

"Okay," Hayley said as she typed without ceasing.

"Oh, and work together," added Ethan. "That's how team collaboration happens in a real industrial setting. Also, joint effort is code for the fact that you will each have three different problems per department, and then both of you will have three different answers for each issue identified."

A unified groan from the pair made Ethan smile slightly. He caught the pained look they exchanged.

"It's not that bad," he consoled. "Look at this assignment as a chance to move all around the mill."

"Gee, thanks," said Daniel with a weak smile.

Ethan chuckled, remembering his own days of student work.

"Just be glad that I didn't give you all the dirty work in each department to do," he reminded them.

"Thanks Mr. Weir—I mean, Ethan. We'll get right on it," assured Hayley.

"And don't forget that tomorrow we'll spend time in the woodlands so you can get a firsthand view of our timber management," added Ethan.

Still furiously typing, the students opened his office door and scurried across the department floor, their shoulders practically touching. Ethan watched them go, remembering his own early training at Delta Paper. Understanding the journey from tree to pulp and all the problems of production would keep them busy for several days. He rose from the edge of his desk and settled into his chair. His smile slowly started to vanish.

Why did he always feel so old when he worked with college interns these days? It was bad enough to have to realize how much technology had changed in the ten years since he graduated from engineering school, but now he had young people constantly trying to call him by his last name. And why did they look younger each year? If he hadn't known better, Hayley could have been Charlie's babysitter, and Daniel looked just like the kid that cut his grass.

Ethan scratched his chin in thought. Instructing students was starting to affirm his not-so-young-anymore status. These days, the task of teaching was feeling more and more like a ringing endorsement for his own middle management slump.

"If only I could be paid like a big shot with some actual career climbing, then being old would be great," he muttered to himself.

"Hey, Ethan, my friend!" Through the glass partition of his office, Ethan looked up and saw Jerry Hillar trot in a bow-legged strut across the production floor.

"Was that the young intern named Hayley that just walked out of Finishing?" he asked breathlessly at Ethan's doorway.

Jerry quickly looked over his shoulder to make sure that they were alone. "Did you see her guns?" he asked in a dropped tone as he gestured on his own chest. "God, she is hot!"

Ethan shook his head and felt himself cringe inwardly; Jerry was nothing if not predictable.

"Yes, that's Hayley Shaffer," Ethan confirmed. "She and Daniel Matthews are the two pulp and paper students from North Carolina State who are here for the summer."

"And you get to train her? You lucky dog! What I wouldn't give for an opportunity to have her in my lab..." Jerry said wistfully as his voice faded. He leaned onto the edge of Ethan's desk. "We might actually get to try some unsafe lab maneuvers, if you know what I mean."

Ethan reclined in his chair and sighed as he surveyed the man in front of him. At just under six feet, Jerry Hillar's graying red hair appeared to sprout from the edges of his hard hat. Famous for his quick laugh, his work as the laboratory manager was known to be accurate and fast. Unfortunately, he was even quicker to be off color.

Out of habit, Ethan peered out into his department to make sure they were actually alone. Talking to Jerry always resembled a walk through a landmine of innuendo.

"Sorry, my friend," Ethan reminded him, "but they are my interns this summer, and I'm tasked with protecting them from the likes of you. Besides, you're married, remember? Your daughter babysits for my son."

Ever since Jerry's wife had become Abbey's best friend in Campton, the families were often together socially. Ethan swiveled his chair to face his visitor. He wanted to change the direction of the conversation. Depending on the day, Jerry could be either entertaining or excessive. Jerry craned his thick neck to look back into the mill before edging closer to Ethan.

"It's all right. Beverly and I have come to an arrangement," he said in a naughty tone.

"You and Beverly have an arrangement? Let me guess, she will knock you upside the head if you do anything wrong? I have seen your wife when she is angry, and it's not pretty."

"Beverly told me that I can always look at the menu, I just have to eat at home," he said with a nod.

"Well, what you suggested in your lab is a lot more than 'looking at the menu,' and besides, I think that Hayley and Daniel are dating."

Jerry plopped down in a black chair next to Ethan's desk and leaned back, lacing his fingers behind his scuffed hard hat.

"What does that young buck have that I don't, anyway?" he asked thoughtfully.

"Are you kidding me? How about youth? Or how about his washboard abs? Or, I don't know, maybe a future without Beverly coming after you with a meat clever," answered Ethan.

"These young girls today, they don't know what it is to have a date with the Great Jerry Hillar," he boasted as he patted his blue golf shirt that stretched tightly across his bulging stomach.

Ethan threw his head back in laughter. "Jerry, let's be clear, the only thing a date with an intern will get you is a charge of sexual harassment."

Jerry shrugged. "A guy can dream, can't he?"

"As long as it's only dreaming," Ethan agreed.

Jerry raised his eyebrows and laughed wickedly. Ethan rolled his eyes to stifle a chuckle.

"Do I need to enroll you in another sensitivity training?" Ethan asked half seriously, trying in vain to redeem their conversation.

"Training, smaining," Jerry replied. "I attend all that crap when Delta gives it. The only problem is that all that gender awareness rigmarole ignores my own unique male approach to life. That stuff just kills me with political correctness."

Ethan leaned on his elbows and observed his co-worker. On a hunch, he decided to try a different approach.

"Well, let me ask you this, Jerry. You and I go to church together. When I see you at worship, what are your prayers about on any given Sunday morning?"

Jerry pushed his palms together towards the ceiling. "Deliver me from temptation," he said in mock seriousness. Ethan rolled his eyes again. Talking to Jerry had an amusing futility to it. He rose to his feet.

"Well, on that note, I have to go," Ethan said.

"Have to go? But I came in here to see if you wanted to come with me to the cafeteria. It's Monday, my man," Jerry said as he hoisted his girth out of the chair and grinned. "And you know what that means, right? It's chili dog day!"

Ethan struggled to hold a neutral expression. Watching Jerry Hillar eat any food, especially hot dogs, was akin to watching a sloppy Saint Bernard wolf down a bowl of dog food.

"I can't today. I have an appointment in town."

"But you never leave the mill," said Jerry in surprise. "You always pack your lunch or do some other type of frugal bullshit."

"Well, today," Ethan said as he grabbed his keys and phone. "I have to go to town."

"Okay, well, gosh," Jerry said with surprise. "I guess that I'll just have to go eat chili dogs and check out the hot young engineers without you."

The two men walked in silence across the loud production floor as Jerry's short legs tried to match Ethan's long strides.

"Sorry that I'm missing chili dog day," Ethan offered as they approached the front gate of the plant.

"It's okay," Jerry said with a slight air of disappointment.

"Hey, what about Calvin? He's working the lab this week with his special assignment, right? Maybe he would want to join you."

"He's actually going to meet me in the cafeteria in fifteen minutes," Jerry said as he checked his phone. "I just thought we could all eat together."

Ethan glanced sideways at Jerry and had an instant mental image of the lunch he was missing. A trio of men sitting in the mill cafeteria could easily be construed as some sort of three-way 'bromance.' Inevitably, Jerry's slightly yellow buck teeth would mow through his usual two loaded hot dogs as he eyed every female employed by Delta Paper. Only when his golf shirt resembled a roadmap of his culinary adventure would they return to work. The entire meal was destined to resemble a rowdy middle school lunch table. It was enough to make Ethan relieved to be absent.

"Maybe we can do it next week," Ethan suggested.

"It's a date," Jerry said as he headed off towards the plant dining room.

Ethan turned to the parking lot and thought about his pending appointment. The hot asphalt under his work boots only added to the discomfort that he started to feel as he walked to his car. He was going to the police. Detective Lee had suggested that they should meet when he called her.

He unlocked the door of his Explorer and felt the oven-like temperature of the interior smack him in the face. Looking back at the plant entrance, Ethan almost wished for a moment that he was sitting with Jerry. At least at work the difference between what was truly hazardous and what was just outrageous was usually clear.

Ethan started the engine and maneuvered slowly down the long industrial driveway. Talking to the authorities was the right thing to do. He and Abbey had talked about it for two days. The police needed to know what he saw at John Runar's funeral.

Turning onto the highway, Ethan looked back over his shoulder at Delta Paper. The huge complex was a modern-day engineering marvel. With all the chemicals and processes working around the clock, safe production happened every day, thanks to strict protocols.

If only real life was so well defined, Ethan thought, as he set his jaw and grimly stepped on the accelerator. Bad things might happen in manufacturing, but the real problems in life usually centered on whatever secrets people created.

CHAPTER TWENTY-EIGHT

Ethan spotted the low stucco building of the Campton Country Sheriff's Department just as his air conditioning was starting to completely cool his car. For a moment, he contemplated just riding past the unattractive, beige headquarters and simply making a loop through the woods back to the mill. He dreaded talking to the detectives. The way they looked at him made him feel like a specimen under a microscope.

Last night, he had rehearsed exactly what he would say by practicing in the shower. He tried to plan out his speech, but the words always ended up sounding silly, almost like some sort of gossiping.

Empty parking spots lined the front of the station. Ethan pulled in and, for a full minute, he looked through the windshield at his scratched car hood that was covered in mill ash. Snippets of phrases raced through his mind. He adjusted the rear-view mirror to coach himself with his delivery.

"It was an intimate touch." The sentence was the only one that he could recall, and the words made him shutter.

"I sound like some sort of feminine hygiene commercial," he muttered to himself with a scowl.

Grabbing his phone, he opened his car door.

"Here goes nothing," he grumbled.

Approaching the tinted front door, he caught a glimpse of his own reflection. Like an overgrown do-gooder, Ethan noted his single-minded pace and frowning expression. God, did he really look that determined? Was he just a Johnny-on-the-spot Bozo to the rest of the world?

The same bald officer that he remembered from his first visit was still behind the desk when Ethan opened the main door. Hunkered down over stacks of papers, his head glistened with perspiration from the glaring overhead light.

For a moment, Ethan wondered what it would be like to see all of humanity walk through the doors of a police station every day. An endless parade of the daily population of Campton would inevitably heighten the senses of observation for anyone. With a smile, he approached the policeman.

"Hello, I'm Ethan Weir. I have an appointment with Detective Lee."

"Okay. Does she know you're coming by today?" the man asked, barely looking up from his mound of paperwork.

"Yes," Ethan said slowly, trying to catch the man's eye. "I have an appointment."

"Wait over there," he said with a jab of his thumb.

Ethan moved over to the same grimy orange molded chairs that he had seen on his first visit. As before, he decided to forgo sitting. His phone pinged, and Ethan reached into his pocket, grateful for the distraction. No sooner had he started to read his text messages than he heard footsteps behind him.

"Mr. Weir, right?"

Detective Lee, her hair in a clip, stood behind him, wearing pants and a white shirt.

"Yes."

"Good to see you again," she said holding out her hand.

Ethan extended his arm and noted the cool politeness of her demeanor. Her expression was almost impossible to read, making him wonder if having a poker face was a job requirement for being a detective.

"Why don't you follow me?" Passing the cubicles of his first visit, Ethan was led to a small, well-lit corner room.

"Have a seat," she said, pointing to a nondescript, padded chair. Ethan sat down and looked around as the policewoman settled herself behind a steel table. To his surprise, a small camera, mounted to the ceiling, blinked with a steady red flash.

"You have a camera in here?" Ethan asked, somewhat shocked. He stared at the detective and felt the nerves in his stomach tighten. This was only supposed to be a simple chat. It was bad enough to have to tell the detective what he saw, but he had no idea that their conversation would be recorded.

Maybe coming to the station was a huge mistake.

"The camera is standard," Detective Lee said nonchalantly. "We get a lot of people that come by to talk about cases we work on. The cameras help us to keep everything straight."

Ethan gave a slight nod and wished for the umpteenth time that he was back at the mill, or some other place, or anywhere besides an interview room with a detective.

"Okay," began Lee as she crossed her legs and opened a pad of paper, "when you called, I think you said you had some other things to tell me about the John Runar case?"

"Yes," began Ethan with hesitation, "but maybe it's not that important."

"Why don't you let me be the judge of that? Just tell me what you know."

Ethan faltered. His mouth had gone dry.

"No details are too small," Detective Lee said with encouragement.

Ethan ran his hand through the back of his short sandy hair and wondered where to start.

"Sometimes," continued the detective, "it's the small bits of information that really move a case along."

"Okay," began Ethan, trying to forget about the recording camera. "I saw something at John's funeral that was really surprising to me."

Detective Lee held her pen in mid-air and looked slightly surprised to Ethan, as if she had not expected the conversation to center on the memorial service.

"Go on," she said.

"I accompanied my wife to the restroom before the service started, and I saw something with the family, really with Leah, John's wife."

"What did you see?" Lee asked steadily.

"I saw Leah Runar come out of a room with someone. I was down a hallway. The lights weren't on where I stood, but I could see the area ahead of me because it was pretty bright. Leah came out of the room with a man that I didn't immediately recognize. As he turned in the light, I was able to see his face."

"Who was it?"

"It was Carlos Silva. I recognized him because he runs the soccer program in town, and my wife just signed my son up to play in the fall."

"Okay," the detective said slowly. "So, you saw this man, Carlos Silva, come out of a room with John Runar's widow?"

Ethan met the detective's gaze. He realized that she was trying to follow the story.

"He came out of the room with Leah. They acted like they thought they were alone. Then he ran his hand down her back."

"Ran his hand down her back?"

"Yes, with his thumb," Ethan said. He raised his hand and made a sweeping motion to show the detective. There was a pause as the policewoman simply looked at him. "It was an intimate gesture," Ethan told her, trying to describe what he saw.

The detective merely gave a slight nod. Ethan could feel the color rise in his face. His explanation had indeed sounded like some sort of maxi pad commercial.

"So, let me get this straight," Detective Lee reiterated. "You are at John Runar's funeral, down a darkened hallway, and you see this man, Carlos Silva, run his thumb down Leah Runar's back?"

"Yes."

"Couldn't it have been some sort of hug?"

"This wasn't a hug," insisted Ethan. "It was something more, something, well, intimate." He paused and then added, "It was the way a man touches a woman when they are a couple."

The detective dropped her eyes, wrote on her pad, and looked up. "Anything else?"

"Well, after he ran his hand down her back, she leaned into him and whispered something and walked back into the room. Then Carlos Silva turned around and realized that I was at the end of the hallway, and he gave me a look."

"A look?"

"Yes, a look," Ethan confirmed. "Like he was pissed off that I had seen him—like he was going to do something."

Ethan stopped. He could feel his face growing hot. What kind of pansy complained about a look?

"Okay," Detective Lee said patiently. "So, you go to the funeral, stand in an unlit hallway, and see this man, Carlos Silva, run his hand down Leah Runar's back. She whispers to him and then he gives you a look? Is that right?"

"Yes," said Ethan, "and I am telling you it was a...a... disturbing look."

"Did he do anything when he looked at you? Did he come towards you?"

"Well, no," said Ethan, his words getting slower. "It was just—I don't know—unsettling, I guess."

Detective Lee nodded and continued to write on her pad. When she raised her eyes, Ethan could read the passive boredom in her expression.

"Well, that's all very interesting," she said. "Is there anything else?"

"No," Ethan said softly. His neck now felt hot. Sweat was rolling down his back.

"Well, thank you for coming in, Ethan," the detective said as she stood and offered her hand.

Ethan extended his hand and silently cursed himself for his own damp palm. He turned to leave, hoping for a quick way out of the room.

"Exit is to the left," Detective Lee called behind him as he reached the doorway. With his stomach in knots, Ethan walked hastily towards the front of the station. He felt like a total jerk.

In his car, he put on his aviator sunglasses and pulled out of the parking space. Grinding his teeth, he punched the gas to enter the highway that snaked back to the mill. His car jerked forward as he took a curve. He didn't even care if he was speeding. In his rear-view mirror, the station disappeared.

Furious thoughts filled his mind. What a wasted lunch hour just to relay a stupid observation! Why had he even tried to talk to the authorities? What happened to John was terrible, but what good was his pointless information?

Whatever he saw wasn't that important. People did all kinds of weird things at funerals. Wasn't life busy enough these days without adding to the small-town drama? Maybe Detective Lee would just forget their idiotic conversation.

He pulled into the Delta Paper parking lot and grabbed his hard hat from the passenger seat. There was plenty of work to do in his own department for the rest of the day without losing any more time on a wild goose chase.

Ethan headed towards the plant entrance at a quick pace. At least he was done with that ridiculous errand. As he approached, Finishing looked like a beehive of activity. Crossing the production floor, he put his safety googles in place and surveyed his dayshift in the control room. Ethan took long strides towards his office. When he settled into his desk chair, he looked out at the plant and made one final decision. Today was absolutely the last time he would go to the police.

CHAPTER TWENTY-NINE

"Well?" Simpson asked, looking up from his computer monitor with his thick fingers poised over the keyboard.

"Ethan Weir came back in to tell me about what he witnessed at the Runar funeral," Lee said with a sigh as she stood next to her partner's desk.

"Oh? Did he see something that we missed?"

She rolled her eyes and opened the notepad in her hands.

"He thinks that he saw a man named Carlos Silva run his hand down the back of John Runar's widow. Said it was, and I quote, 'an intimate touch' followed by a whisper from the woman to the man and, get this, 'a disturbing look'–also a quote."

Simpson leaned back in his swivel chair, his expression deep in thought. "So, what's your take on what he said?" he finally asked.

"I think Mr. Weir believes he saw something out of the ordinary, but it's hardly much to go on."

"You know that Weir guy struck me as a pretty sharp guy on our first interview at Delta. Sort of a straight shooter with brains."

Lee pulled out her desk chair with a shrug and said nothing. Simpson turned towards her; his face was serious.

"Unfortunately, the problem is that we still don't have much to go on with this case. John Runar was murdered, that much we know, but our leads are starting to shrink. Travis Hutson has no firm alibi for the night of the accident, but a workplace argument isn't much of a motive. Besides, his cell phone pinged off a tower close to his house all evening long and he passed the voluntary polygraph that we gave him."

Lee sat forward and nodded her head.

"Then there's Starla Pittman's husband," continued Simpson. "Even though he doesn't have recorded whereabouts for the whole evening, he seemed genuinely shocked to learn about his wife's affair."

"I agree that something is missing with Glen Pittman but there was a love triangle, remember? I still think that the relationship with Starla is at the center of Runar's murder."

"I know, but in this case, I feel like we're missing something—another fact, something that would make all the pieces fit together."

"So, what do you want to do?" asked Lee. "Do you want to talk to Leah Runar? Should I bring her in?"

The older detective shook his head in deep thought.

"Not yet. We need to be smart about this. What'd you say the man's name was—the one Mr. Weir thought he saw?"

"Carlos Silva," she answered, reading her notes.

"Carlos Silva," Simpson said slowly. "Doesn't he run the soccer program in town?"

"Yeah, Weir said that Silva runs the team that his kid is supposed to join."

Simpson was tapping away at his keyboard, starting to smile. "Doesn't Carlos Silva also own one of the liquor stores in town? The one in Campton Center?"

"Hang on," Lee answered. She started searching on her phone.

"Yeah, that's right. He owns Sweetwater Wines and Liquors, and he runs the soccer program in Campton."

Simpson narrowed his eyes and studied the ceiling. "That's just what I wanted to hear."

"Do you want to go talk to him?"

"I've got something better in mind," he said. "Remember the new cameras that the city put into the shopping areas of the Campton Center and the Walmart? Well, I bet that one of those lenses is aimed just about right to see the Sweetwater Liquor Store."

Lee looked intently at her partner, trying to follow his train of thought.

"Let's go look at some film footage from the night of John Runar's murder," Simpson urged. "It might be a waste of time, but we've got nothing else that makes sense. You never know what a camera can reveal."

CHAPTER THIRTY

Ethan eased his car over the ruts in the road and felt the entire interior of his SUV start to sway. He looked over at Hayley Shaffer as she grabbed the support bar above the passenger window.

"Sorry, it's a bit bumpy," Ethan said as he glanced in the rearview mirror at Daniel Matthews in the back seat. The young intern rocked back and forth as the car wheels sunk in yet another sandy depression. "They don't put in the best roads out in the timberlands."

"So how much land does Delta Paper own?" Daniel asked as he braced against the front seat.

"About thirty thousand acres, give or take," replied Ethan.

"Wow, that's a lot," said Hayley. "It's much more acreage than my family's peanut farm in North Carolina, and we own one of the larger tracts in Bertie County."

"Well, it is a large holding of land, but remember that Delta Paper runs 24/7 and requires a constant source of trees. Believe it or not, the company still has to buy pine from loggers as well as to contract production out to landowners. All that in addition to the forest that you see."

Ethan slowed his Explorer down and turned onto a small side road that narrowed and twisted into the trees. He searched for compact ridges of clay among the sand. The last thing he wanted to do was to get stuck and have to call for some sort of help. His tires found a raised shoulder on the side of the road as he brought his car to a stop.

"Let's get out here," Ethan explained. "There are things you should see."

Early morning heat engulfed the trio as they emerged from their seats. Ethan checked his watch. He knew from experience that the interns needed to get a feel for the size and scope of the managed timberlands, but they needed to be efficient with their time. The air was already sweltering.

"Follow me for just a minute," Ethan said to the students as they both instinctively wiped their brows. "We won't stay here too long," he promised.

As Hayley and Daniel followed him into the row of pine trees, Ethan looked back, careful not to walk too far. The trees that surrounded them had been planted in perfect lines, and he knew how easy it was to get turned around and lose his car in the woods.

"This is a type of twenty-year Slash pine," Ethan announced as he reached for the slender branch that seemed to fluidly bend in his hand. "It's similar to a Loblolly pine that grows well in this region and is ideal for our production at the mill." The young people examined the intermediate length of the tree needles and felt the trunk that resembled scales on a fish.

"One of the concerns for Delta is the pine beetle. While the insect is native to this region, it can devastate a managed forest," Ethan continued. He moved deeper into the row of spreading limbs with Hayley and Daniel close behind him. "Now, what you should note—," his words froze in mid-sentence as the students practically bumped into him.

"Okay, guys. We need to stop," Ethan said trying to remain calm. "I need you both to back up slowly."

"What is it?" Daniel asked.

Ethan took a step backward. A huge coiled snake rested against the base of the next tree. The black and gray mottled body lay in thick rings as the head moved with a flickering tongue towards the visitors.

"It's a snake, and a large one. Looks like a rattlesnake," he told them.

Ethan took another step back and looked over his shoulder. The space behind him was empty. In the distance, he heard the car doors slam shut.

When Ethan walked casually out of the forest, he looked towards his vehicle and smiled. The students obviously preferred the sauna-like temperatures of his car's interior to the possibilities of meeting the natural inhabitants of the southern woodlands.

"Sorry about that," he said easing into the driver's seat. "Snakes are a part of the ecosystem, and we certainly have our fair share in Alabama."

Hayley and Daniel sat still, their eyes wide with fear, breathing heavily. Ethan felt momentary guilt for bringing the students out on a timberland tour in only their steel-toed mill boots. He had never intended to do more than stay close to the road.

"Tell you what," Ethan continued, "how about we finish our look at the timber production, but we do so after we put on some snake guard shields that come up to our knees?"

"Okay," Hayley mumbled.

In the rearview mirror, Ethan could see that Daniel was pale, his skin the color of a waxy honeydew melon. For a moment, he wondered if the young man was going to faint.

"There is a forestry building about a mile from here," Ethan began as he backed out onto the larger dirt road. "We can go there, put on the proper leg wear, and then finish up what we need to see."

From the back seat, Ethan watched the young man open and close his eyes. When his head rolled to one side, the sweat on his upper lip made Ethan wondered if he was going to vomit.

Please not in my mill car, Ethan prayed. *It already smells bad from the plant, and barf will only make my ride to and from work a form of hell.*

"Daniel, you okay?" Ethan asked looking in his rearview mirror. "How about I roll down the window."

"Yeah," he responded, as he stuck his head out into the hot air.

"I'll tell you what," Ethan said brightly, "after we finish, we'll go through town on our way back to the mill. We can get some sodas, maybe some food, my treat."

Hayley nodded, and Daniel said nothing. Ethan turned up the air conditioning and increased his speed, careful to avoid the largest holes in the unpaved road. Getting the interns out of his car was the first order of business. A low brick building, about the size of a gas station, came into view on the horizon.

"Okay, we're here!" Ethan announced as he navigated towards the front of the one-story outpost. He pulled to a quick stop and three car doors simultaneously opened.

Ethan watched Daniel stagger out of the back seat as Hayley took his arm. Both students had sweat stains on their shirts.

"Let's get inside, out of this heat," Ethan said, leading the students to the front door. "There are usually bottles of water for the loggers in the fridge."

The temperature had climbed so that the late morning air felt like a clothes dryer. In the tiny slice of shade created from the overhanging roof, Ethan pulled out his phone. He searched for the access numbers to the security keypad that was mounted on the door frame.

"Got it!" he said trying to sound cheerful.

Ethan moved his fingers quickly to punch in the four-digit passcode. He glanced again at the students. They were under the roof line, leaning up against the barely sheltered bricks and looking more like wilted flowers with every passing minute. He turned the door handle. Nothing happened. Once again, Ethan carefully pushed in the numerical sequence and jiggled the knob. The door remained tightly closed.

"Well, it looks like we'll have to solve this problem a different way," he said.

Stepping out into the glaring sunshine, Ethan dialed his cell phone. Of all the people who knew the fine details of Delta Paper, one person stood out in his mind. He smiled back at the bedraggled students as the number started to ring. After a full minute, the call rolled to voicemail. Ethan rubbed his hand through the back of his now damp hair.

"Hey, Starla, this is Ethan Weir. I am out in the northwest part of the timberlands at building number two and I was wondering if—"

"Ethan?" a familiar voice boomed onto the line.

"Roger? Is that you? I was trying to call Starla. I am out here in the timberlands with some student interns and we need to get into one of the buildings. My passcode isn't working, and I knew that she would know the right one."

"Hang on," Roger McVann replied. "I picked up Starla's line because she went to make some copies down the hall."

"I'm sorry to bother you," began Ethan. "We can just leave this area if you don't have the access code." He looked over at the young people who were whispering and wiping their faces with their sleeves.

"Don't be silly," Roger assured him. "I have that code right here. Building number two, did you say?"

"Yes," confirmed Ethan.

"I think there was even a meeting for the loggers and the security team in that building this morning. Okay, try this sequence."

Ethan carefully pushed the numbers and heard the door give a dull buzz. He turned the handle and felt a cool rush of residual air conditioning coming from inside.

"Thanks, Roger."

Holding the door, Ethan led the students into the darkened building as he put his phone in his pocket.

"Thanks, Ethan," Hayley said, crossing the threshold.

"It's all about teamwork," Ethan told them both as they moved inside, and he reached for the light switch. "Remember, you have to always realize that someone at the mill knows the missing information that you might need."

The interns nodded as he opened the refrigerator against the far wall to hand them each a cold water. Easing into chairs, the young people started to sip from their plastic bottles while Ethan continued, "And sometimes you just need to dig for the answers, even when you feel like you should already know. Not everything is obvious, so you can't be afraid to ask questions."

The students nodded again, and Ethan realized they still looked frazzled.

"Finish your water. We have leg protection in one of the back closets, and we'll make a quick forest survey from around this building. After that, I promise that I'll buy you lunch in town."

Hayley and Daniel both smiled and mumbled their thanks.

"And tomorrow is Founder's Day," added Ethan. "So, we have a company-wide picnic."

He paused and looked at Hayley, remembering Jerry Hillar's antics at the mill and thinking about the snake they had just seen. Maybe the actual reptile they ditched today would be preferable to the unwanted advances of a paunchy middle manager tomorrow.

Ethan smiled and tried to make his words sound upbeat. "It will be a fun day," he said, aware of his boldface lie.

The interns merely nodded as he continued.

"The barbeque will give you both opportunities to meet all the characters that make up the manufacturing environment—the good, the bad, and the ugly."

CHAPTER THIRTY-ONE

Nick Simpson rubbed his fingers through the coarse bristles of hair along the back of his neck. He stole a glance at his partner who sat with her head resting on her fist while struggling to keep a look of dull boredom from her face.

"How many hours have we watched so far?" asked Lee.

"Three, so far," he responded. "I can fast forward it just a bit, but we have to just keep slowing down to see everything in the parking lot."

"And Runar was killed at what time, approximately?"

"Sometime between eleven and one, give or take."

Both detectives shifted in their seats and stared at the slightly grainy images. Cars and people moved through the parking lot of the Campton Center with regularity in the fading evening light.

"Fast forward and let's jump to a bit later," said Lee as she watched the patrons of the shopping area milling through every frame. "What kind of car does Carlos Silva drive?"

"He has a Chevy truck registered in his name. It's one of those extended cabs, and I think he has soccer emblems on the back window, if I remember correctly from seeing it around town," answered the older officer.

"You mean like that one?" On the monitor, a long vehicle came into view.

"Maybe," said her partner. "Let me go to still frames so we can look at the model and license plate."

"That's it—look, it has to be. It's a truck that has those soccer ball stickers on the window. What's that in the bed of the truck?" The images froze on the screen as the Nick Simpson peered closer to the monitor.

"I think it's a net bag with what looks like soccer balls in it," he replied.

"Well, that's definitely him. He's pulling in front of the liquor store. What time is it on the film?"

"Just after 8:30—the sun is almost gone, but that's him."

The two detectives let the film roll for a few minutes, each watching intently as Carlos Silva stepped out of his truck and headed into his business.

"Kind of late to be heading into the store, isn't it?" asked Lee.

"Maybe he came to look at the receipts for the day or close up the shop," said Simpson as he studied the continuous film stream.

"Fast forward again and let's see what time he leaves."

The staccato movements of cars and shoppers darted across the screen in an uncoordinated dance as the parking lot emptied. Only the large truck remained under a pool of light from a lamp. Suddenly, Simpson took a sharp breath and sat up in his seat.

"Well, would you look at that?"

A minivan came into the camera's view and parked beside Carlos Silva's truck.

"What time is it on the film?" asked Lee.

"The clock shows 10:30."

They watched intently as someone emerged from the driver side door. The familiar figure proceeded to enter the liquor store.

"Well, I'll be damned," said Nick softly as he stopped the film and looked at his partner. "We need to run the plates, but I do believe that this," he said, putting his burly finger onto the screen, "is none other than Leah Runar. The two detectives looked at each other and nodded.

"Well, Mr. Weir was right about a little something going on between those two," admitted Lee.

Simpson narrowed his eyes as he started piecing together this new information about the case.

"Yeah, but let's not get ahead of ourselves," he agreed. "I must admit, this looks like the lead we've been looking for, but let's watch the rest of the film. Maybe there's some sort of explanation."

"Like Leah Runar just happened to need a fifth of vodka late at night, the very night her husband is murdered?"

Simpson turned back to the monitor and let the video roll. The parking lot was empty except for the two cars.

"Speed this up," urged Lee impatiently. "I want to see what time they leave."

The older detective set the footage to fast forward.

"Stop," she said quickly, as the picture changed.

The film slowed to regular speed as the profile of two people emerging from the liquor store came into view. In the glow of the lamppost, the two figures moved towards the minivan.

"What are they doing?" she asked, studying the screen.

"Well, we don't have any audio, but I think it looks like they're having some sort of argument."

In the silent footage, the camera caught the two figures flinging their arms out as they appeared to be yelling, their bodies contorted in emotion.

"It doesn't look very lovey-dovey to me," noted Lee. "Let's just hope they're only arguing about which position her kid would play in the next soccer game."

In the dim light, Leah Runar appeared to yank open her car door.

"Oh, it's not about soccer," Simpson said as the images continued. The clip showed Carlos Silva yanking Leah and spinning her around to face him. "This is definitely something else."

With that, the flickering recording showed the two of them melting into an embrace as the minivan door shut. The couple leaned against the car with obvious yearning in their stance. As her head fell backwards, his lips dropped onto her neck while his hands moved under her top.

"Okay," said Simpson with a smile of satisfaction. "Now we have enough to bring them both in for questioning, but let's take a day and get warrants."

CHAPTER THIRTY-TWO

"I can't find his other shoe," Abbey said to her husband as he stood by the back door with Charlie on his shoulders.

"Where's your other shoe?" Ethan asked, tugging his son's leg.

"I dunno," responded Charlie as he kicked his one bare foot against Ethan's chest.

"We have to find his other tennis shoe. He's outgrown his old pair, and he can't run through the Delta Park for Founder's Day in just his flip flops," said Abbey.

With a sigh, Ethan lifted Charlie off his shoulders and placed him on the kitchen floor. He bent over to look his son in the eye.

"Okay, I'll buy you a pack of Skittles if you can find your shoe in the next five minutes."

Charlie darted out of the kitchen in lightning speed, his feet echoed from the hallway.

"Skittles? Ethan!" Abbey chided. "He's four. The books all say that he is supposed to keep up with his things out of a growing sense of maturity."

Ethan looked at his wife and shrugged his shoulders.

"He needs to learn to manage his belongings," she explained.

"Got it!" Charlie announced as he ran to his father's leg, clutching a new light-up shoe in his hand.

"That's what I'm talking about!" Ethan exclaimed as he placed his son on the dryer and fumbled with the small sock and Velcro straps.

"Oh, come on," Ethan said to his wife as he placed Charlie on the floor and opened the side door to the carport. "One bag of Skittles won't kill him. Besides, it got the job done."

Abbey rolled her eyes as she grabbed her purse and followed her son into the muggy morning air that was already thick with the sound of cicadas.

"And there'll be plenty of junk food at the picnic anyway, so a bit more won't hurt," Ethan said as he strapped his son into his car seat.

As the minivan eased out of the driveway, Spanish moss hung limply in the trees, hinting at the sultry day to come.

"I want my Skittles!" Charlie called from the back seat.

"On the way home," Ethan told him, looking in the rearview mirror. "And you have to be good at the picnic, or you won't get them."

Abbey glanced at her husband and shook her head.

"Oh, come on, it's a two-for-one deal," Ethan explained as his hand covered hers. "One bag of candy and we got the shoe and good behavior for the day."

"You're hopeless." She put on her sunglasses and looked over her shoulder at her son. "But also smart," she admitted.

Ethan maneuvered the car through the almost empty streets of Campton. Open businesses, with silent store fronts, seemed to beg for customers.

"I guess everyone's at the picnic today," Ethan said looking at the unusually quiet town square.

As the municipal park came into view, carnival rides rose above the flat terrain. Booths and a midway filled the entire recreational grounds that had become choked with people. Smoke from large grills billowed skyward from the covered pavilion.

Ethan pulled in by the large Delta signage and scanned the already full parking lot. Finding a spot would be a nightmare. Parking attendants directed a line of traffic by pointing to a row of grassy spaces on the greensward. Ethan waited his turn and dutifully pulled his minivan into the designated slot.

As the family unloaded, Ethan tried to suppress his growing sense of resignation about the day. The annual Founder's Day picnic was a tradition for most Delta Paper employees. While managers were expected to attend, most of the crowd consisted of hourly employees who came out to enjoy the day in spite of their constantly changing southern swing rotation at the plant. The celebration was an opportunity for Abbey and Charlie to see a large number of company families and enjoy a free festival, but the entire event ended up feeling like a workday merely masquerading as a party. Ethan reached for the folding chairs in the trunk as Charlie tugged at his leg.

"I got to go potty," he said.

Ethan looked at his wife before hoisting the seats from the trunk.

"Let me take him," she said with a sigh. "I'm going to need to go any minute myself."

"At least let me walk you over to the park facilities," Ethan offered.

"Don't do that," she said. "I would rather you go ahead and get a spot in some sort of shade. And you can start talking to all the Delta people that you need to see so that you can take Charlie on some of the rides when I get back."

She took her son's hand. "Come on, Sweetie, let's make this quick."

Abbey and Charlie strolled off together as Ethan gathered the portable chairs in his arms. He trudged across the Bermuda grass towards the picnic shelter. In the mid-morning heat, his cotton shirt clung to his back.

A large, white tent loomed next to the picnic area, and Ethan joined the throngs of attendees moving towards the shelter. He nodded to fellow employees and their families before ducking into the canvas enclosure.

Giant fans lined the back of the shaded tarp. Ethan made a beeline for the parched turf near the rear flaps and dropped his chairs onto the ground to survey his position. On the one hand, the propeller-like blades behind him sounded like an aircraft carrier was ready to take flight. But on the other hand, the area was cool and shaded with enough breeze to counteract the humidity.

Ethan turned around and inspected the entire area from his current vantage point. Rows of folding metal chairs rested in front of a raised podium at the far end of the tent. His carefully chosen location would be the perfect place to watch the Delta hierarchy make their annual remarks to the employees. He nodded in satisfaction.

People were starting to trickle in by the stage. Ethan scanned the crowd for Hayley and Daniel. They were due to join him and listen to the company remarks before having lunch with his family. Searching the faces in front of him, he suddenly stopped.

At the far end of the tent, Leah Runar made her way through the swelling assembly of people. Within seconds, Carlos Silva moved to her side. Ethan frowned as he studied them. Was it his imagination, or were they standing just a bit too close to each other? He watched as their hands appeared to touch.

Without warning, a group of laughing teenagers chased each other through the side of the tent and almost bumped into Ethan. He reached out and caught one of the girls before she fell onto his chairs.

"Sorry," she said breathlessly.

He helped her stand and tried to look past the giggling group that had slowed down and drifted in front of him. Craning his neck, he stepped to the side, but Leah had disappeared into a streaming throng of people.

"Hey, Ethan."

Starla Pittman stood beside him with a camera in her hand.

"Oh, hey, Starla," Ethan answered as he moved aside to scan the crowd again.

"Looking for someone?" she asked.

"No, I just, well no," he said, giving up his search and turning to her.

The fading bruise on her arm caught his attention. Purple hand marks peeked out from under her short sleeve.

"What are you up to?" he asked, trying to sound bright and cheery.

"Just taking pictures for Founder's Day."

She followed his eyes to her arm and dropped the camera to her side. They stood in awkward silence. Ethan smiled. He wanted to say something, but he wasn't sure what.

"Do you have anyone to eat with?" he began. "Abbey and I would love for you to join us. Of course, we have Charlie, and my interns are planning to picnic with us, so it won't be glamorous."

"Thanks," she said, "but it's kind of a workday, you know. I need to get pictures of the events today. The photos need to go on the company's Facebook page."

Ethan nodded and watched Starla shift her weight from one foot to the other while she looked uncomfortably around the growing flood of families. He could sense her hesitancy. Without effort, he could almost read her thoughts. She reminded him of someone, probably himself when he was young and getting knocked around by his old man.

People were not always kind to Starla, Ethan realized. They often forgot that people like her were really incredibly lonely. He decided to change the subject.

"So, are you taking pictures of everything today?"

"Yeah, I'm trying to get the entire event. I'm focusing on all the speakers and any new employees."

"New employees, eh? Would you be willing to get a shot of each of my interns? I'd love to have a copy of those pictures to put on my department bulletin board."

"Be glad to," she said. "I'm making hard copies of everything so that folks can take the pictures if they want to. I'll finish the electronic updates on Monday, and I plan to have actual photos on Tuesday, probably in the break room in the front office."

"Great. I really appreciate it."

Bill Hackman sauntered across the makeshift stage and grabbed the microphone. He pulled the black tip down towards his chipped buck teeth, smiling at the seated audience.

"Testing, testing," he said into the mouthpiece.

"Well, I gotta go," Starla said. "The speakers are getting ready to start and I'm supposed to get pictures of them as well as all the other folks in here."

"My interns are meeting me at these chairs in just a bit," Ethan said. "Can you come back after the speakers?"

"No problem," she assured him.

Starla raised her camera and started slowly clicking as she moved towards the lectern. Ethan watched her go forward and wished, once again, that he could do something to really help her.

"Daddy!" Charlie squealed as he spotted his father from the edge of the tent. His face was smeared with blue from the cotton candy that he clutched. Hayley and Daniel chatted with Abbey as they followed the darting preschooler.

"Hey, little man," said Ethan as he scooped up his son. "You're a mess. Cotton candy? Already?"

"Sorry, Ethan," confessed Hayley. "He said he wanted some, and he's just so cute that I couldn't resist."

Ethan kissed the side of his son's sticky face, licking his lips afterwards. "It's okay. Just don't let all the cuteness fool you," he said as he cradled his son and took a wet wipe from Abbey to begin the clean-up process. "Remember, it's always the lovable ones that will get you every time."

CHAPTER THIRTY-THREE

Leah Runar followed the detectives into the Campton County Sherriff's Department. She looked around the single-story headquarters with an expression of passive disgust. Dressed in jeans and thick flip flops, she brushed her maple-colored hair from her round face. In the early morning light, Leah Runar resembled the proverbial soccer mom to the few patrolmen who looked up from their paperwork long enough to notice.

"Follow me," Simpson said over his shoulder as the trio made their way to one of the interview rooms.

"Have a seat," the older detective offered as his partner shut the door.

Leah settled into the plain chair as her eyes swept across the nearly barren room. Noticing the red blinking light of the camera mounted to the corner of the ceiling, she crossed her arms and leaned against the back of the seat. Her eyes bore into the detectives in front of her.

Nick Simpson opened his notebook and began, "Leah, I'm sure that you're wondering why we invited you down to the station."

"Invited? Is that what you call it?" she asked defiantly. "I wasn't aware that I had a choice. You show up at my door with a search warrant and insinuated that we needed to discuss things that my children should not hear. You practically twisted my arm to come to the station. So, if that is an invitation, then I guess you did give me one."

"We need to ask you some questions, and we thought that it would be best not to have your children present."

"My children have already lost their father," she said flatly. "So, a few questions are par for the course with what they're dealing with right now."

Simpson leaned across the table and said, "We need to ask you about Carlos Silva."

With a slight twitch of her mouth, Leah locked eyes on the pair in front of her. She could feel her anger rising.

"What about him?"

"What is the nature of your relationship with Mr. Silva?"

"He is my son's soccer coach."

"Is that all? Do you have any kind of personal relationship with him?"

Leah remained silent for a moment; her eyes narrowed as she studied the officers. She knew her next words would be scrutinized.

"I hardly think that my relationship with a community leader is something that should concern you," she finally answered.

Detective Lee sat watching from her chair; her words were slow. "Leah, your husband was murdered and right now we are in the middle of a full investigation. We're looking at every possible angle."

"Every angle? So, you think I had something to do with John's murder?" she asked incredulously.

The two detectives remained motionless, blank expressions on their faces.

"Did you?" asked Simpson.

"No!" Leah exclaimed in surprise. "Of course, I didn't!"

"Where were you the night of your husband's accident?" he asked.

"At home with my children."

"And Mr. Silva? Did he have anything to do with the death of your husband?" asked Detective Lee.

"Of course not!" Leah said hotly as she sat up in her chair. Her fury was rising. This needed to stop. "You know, this really beats all. My husband is murdered on his way home from the mill and you have the audacity to ask me if I had anything to do with it? You've got to be kidding!"

"Your husband was actually murdered out on the Mill Highway, going west, and you don't live out in that direction. Do you know where your husband was going on the night he was killed?" asked Simpson.

She glared at the officers, letting several seconds elapse.

"I guess John was probably taking the long way home," she said coolly.

"The long way home, eh? You can't get to your house from the Mill Highway going away from town," responded the older officer. "Was he perhaps going somewhere else?"

Leah sat back in her chair with sheer outrage on her face.

"John had a habit of being social," she said sarcastically. "So, like I said, he was taking the long way home."

"Did you know your husband was having an affair with a Delta employee?" asked Lee.

Darting her eyes to the camera, she exhaled and then looked back at the two stoic detectives.

"Do you know what it was like to live with John Runar?" she asked.

"Why don't you tell us?"

"Are you married? Either of you?" she asked. "Well, let me tell you what life with John was like."

"Please, go on," said Simpson.

"When we were first married, it was the military, all military. John did multiple deployments. What I wanted in life really didn't matter. In fact, I even had both my children stateside, on post, while he was leading his unit through the mountains of Kyrgyzstan."

Leah paused, and there was silence in the room. She looked at both officers and wondered if they would understand.

"After he left Special Forces, I thought that we could finally make it, you know, as a family. But then the post-traumatic stress symptoms started. At first, it was just the not sleeping at night–hour after hour, cleaning his guns in the middle of the night. But then it was the anger, the yelling, even a few fists through the drywall."

"And you didn't get counseling?" asked Simpson calmly.

"Of course, we did," scoffed Leah. "He tried everything– medication, talk therapy, a service dog. Hell, he even did yoga."

"Was he suffering from PTSD while he was working at Delta?" asked Lee.

"That's the thing," admitted Leah. "The only thing that really saved John from himself was his job at Delta. In many ways, he viewed the paper industry like being back in the military. He loved it. When he started and moved us to Campton, I really thought that this time it would be different. I thought that he could make it–that we would finally work everything out this time."

"So, what happened?" Simpson inquired.

Leah sighed as a rueful smile spread across her face. The rest of the story was no better. "Delta was just a substitution for what he had lost in the army. In fact, Delta became his army, his mission, if you will. And it only got worse when he was assigned to work on his special project."

"How so?" asked Lee.

"A new cellulose grade," Leah said, mockingly flashing her fingers in air quotes. "John said that it could change the packaging capabilities for the distribution of food and medicine, maybe even lessen wars. It was everything that he ever wanted, and it gave him purpose. He just forgot to notice me or the kids along for the ride," she said in a fading voice.

"So, you met Carlos Silva. Is that what happened?" asked Lee.

"Don't you dare judge me!" Leah spat.

"We're not judging you," said Simpson.

"You don't know what it was like, what I sacrificed for John, for all of it! Not only did John always have Delta as first in his life, but then he had the audacity to have an affair," she said, practically shouting. "John had three M's in life—the military, the mill and his mistress. So, I hardly made the cut."

She paused, breathing heavily. Her head was starting to pound. Everything that had been so hard was being painfully dissected.

"Do you think I didn't know about his little play toy? I'm lots of things, but not stupid," she finally added.

"We never said you were stupid," said Lee evenly.

"Carlos is the first decent thing to happen to me in a long time," she said, "so, don't make this into something that you don't even understand."

"But Leah, you have to see how this looks," explained Simpson. "Your husband is killed driving away from the plant, but not towards your house. You knew about his affair, in fact, you had also met someone else."

"His accident had nothing to do with me!" she shouted.

"Where were you the night that your husband was killed?" asked Lee evenly.

"At home with my kids! You've already asked me this!"

The detectives glanced at each other. They leaned across the table as Simpson took the lead. "We have evidence that you were not, in fact, at home that night."

Leah opened her mouth in surprise, but then took a sharp inhale. "I went out, for milk, to the grocery store," she mumbled.

"We have you on film with Carlos, in front of his store. You were with him."

Dropping her gaze, Leah looked at her hands.

"Where did you go when you left with Carlos? And where did he go when you both drove away from the liquor store?"

She raised her eyes and said, "I want my attorney."

CHAPTER THIRTY-FOUR

Ethan leaned towards the computer monitor as Calvin's fingers flew over the keyboard. The soft summer rain that dripped steadily from the entrance of the Finishing area punctuated the continuous rhythm of his rapidly tapping fingers.

Despite the gloomy sky, a hum of midmorning activity filled the department. Workers moved bales and rolls of pulp onto beeping forklifts and shouted at each other. Ethan looked up and turned his attention to the day team and the current production. As if on cue, a spreadsheet comprised of numbers filled the screen. He turned back to look at the data.

"So, this is as far as I can get," Calvin said as he pointed to the monitor.

Ethan leaned even closer, studying the figures in front of him.

"I can replicate John's results for the new cellulose grade— and they're great numbers—but that's as far as I can go," Calvin explained.

"So, what's the exact problem?" asked Ethan.

"There are files that I can see on the hard drive, but I can't seem to access them."

"Let me guess," deduced Ethan. "They are password protected."

"Exactly."

Rubbing his chin in thought, Ethan's eyes scanned Calvin's work area, searching for some sort of clue or divine intervention among the items on the special assignment desk. He had been afraid of this problem.

"And you looked everywhere? He didn't write anything down?" Ethan questioned.

"Nothing," answered Calvin sitting back in his chair. His aqua polo shirt creased stiffly from heavy laundry starch as he folded his arms across his chest.

Ethan narrowed his eyes in thought. "What have you tried, in the way of passwords," he asked slowly as possibilities started to crowd his mind.

"All the usual things—the names of his family, his schools, his hometown. I even tried his Army nicknames, that I heard at his funeral," responded Calvin. "All of it came up denied."

Ethan remembered watching John work at his desk. Another thought raced across his mind. "And you never found a thumb drive?"

"Nope. The police even came and searched, but they never found anything. Apparently, John kept his work area perfectly clean, thanks to his military training."

"You may have to call I.T. to help you," offered Ethan.

"But that's the problem. John was the I.T. expert at the mill. I can call some of the tech support in the main office, but I don't know if they can hack into his files."

Ethan bit his lower lip as he glanced sideways at Calvin. He felt resigned to reveal the truth.

"I do have something to tell you," he confided.

Calvin's chair swiveled, and his eyebrows arched in question. "What?"

"I might know something that could be a clue to the passwords," began Ethan. He moved closer to Calvin to continue. "John was having an affair," he said quietly. "Did you know that?"

Calvin's eyes opened wide with surprise. "No," he said.

Ethan rubbed the back of his neck, looking intently into Calvin's chocolate eyes.

"John was having a relationship with someone here at the plant. It was fairly hush-hush. And now that he's gone, it doesn't matter for him, but it's not something that I really wanted to broadcast for her sake."

For a moment, he remembered rounding the corner in the front building, seeing John with his hands on both sides of Starla with her back pinned to the wall. Their lips had been so close, but even more that the posture, it was the look of total desire on their faces.

"I didn't know," Calvin said. "Did other people know?"

Ethan thought about the ongoing rumors of the mill. No one had mentioned the affair outright, but he knew that John had used the internal phone system to call up to Starla's desk. Ethan often saw him on his extension, head down and whispering. For the second time, he remembered John's name flashing across the caller ID screen of the phone system when he was in Roger McVann's office having his monthly department review meetings. Since Roger and Starla shared an office, Ethan wondered again if the relationship might have been noticed in the front building.

"Well, I don't know how many people really knew. It wasn't something that I ever discussed. But I'm wondering," Ethan said as he pointed to the screen, "if possibly the password could be linked to that relationship."

"I could try it," Calvin said.

"You are probably going to have to try a bunch of versions or phrases, but you might start with the name of one person."

"Tell me."

"Try the name of the one woman who John really needed. Start with the name Starla Pittman."

CHAPTER THIRTY-FIVE

Nick Simpson pushed the Styrofoam container to the edge of his workspace, trying to ignore the odor of catfish and collard greens that seemed to engulf his desk. Rain clouds darkened the police station windows as he studied the detailed papers in his hands.

"So, where are we?" he wearily asked his partner.

Lee moved in front of the whiteboard with a capped marker gripped in her hand. Names and pictures covered the writing surface.

"Well, we have three suspects, and even two unlikely ones, and none of them have a complete alibi," she responded.

"Okay, let's start one more time with Travis Hutson," said Simpson as he leaned back his chair and rubbed his thick neck. Fatigue was settling in his shoulders. This case was not getting any better.

"Well, he clearly fought with John Runar at work. He even admits it, and he has no one to corroborate where he was the night of the murder."

"But there's nothing else there, right? I mean, a workplace argument is hardly motive for murder."

Lee turned around to face her partner, a serious expression on her face. "Tell that to all the people that get shot at work because of some disgruntled employee. People are crazy these days. You don't think anyone would murder over a disagreement at the industrial facility, but you never know. Besides, he had a restraining order issued against him by his ex-wife."

"Well, let's not dismiss him all together, but I still think that other suspects need to be considered as more likely than Travis. What about Glen Pittman?"

Lee circled his name as she spoke. "He certainly has holes in his schedule the night of the murder, but he clearly didn't seem to know about his wife's affair."

"But he has the strength to break someone's neck, and we know that he's an abuser. However, I'm with you. If he did it, then he should definitely take up acting," agreed Simpson. "He just didn't strike me as someone who knew much about John Runar."

"He's ultimately kind of dumb, isn't he?" asked Lee as she faced her partner. "I must admit, he just can't be that good of an actor. I also can't see tiny little Starla as a part of the murder."

"It's a bothersome love triangle, but all right, what about Carlos Silva? No alibi after leaving the liquor store with Leah Runar, except that, according to him, they both went back to his place for a roll in the hay."

"Kind of convenient, isn't it? Both of them can cover for the other one. And don't forget, Runar's cell phone is missing and his laptop has never been found."

Simpson stood up and then perched on the edge of his desk, studying the information written in large blue lettering. He was silent as he looked at the names. What was he missing?

"Well, Leah Runar is tough in her own way," he said, standing up and stretching his back. "And living with her husband was no picnic, so that's something to consider. But sleeping with another man does not make her a murderer."

Lee studied the board and shook her head.

"How did a mill town like Campton become such a hot spot for adultery?" she asked. "My kids complain that the whole community practically rolls up the sidewalks in this county after dark."

"It's always the quiet little whistle-stops that will fool you," answered Simpson. "All the real drama always happens in small places, mostly because there's nothing else to do."

Lee nodded in agreement as Simpson began to pace, his eyes squinting in thought. How could the leads in this investigation be withering? He looked at the board and wondered if this murder would become a cold case.

"You know what we need, right? Really the only thing that is important at this point," he finally asked.

"What's that?"

"Hard, unequivocal, solid evidence that links someone to the murder. We just need something," Simpson said as pointed to the names. "Just one thing that will tie one of these people to the crime scene."

CHAPTER THIRTY-SIX

Ethan took one last look over his shoulder before heading out of the Finishing Department and into the light rain. A sense of guilt crowded his mind as he left Calvin and made his way through the misty drizzle. Talking about John's misdeeds was hardly the problem but revealing the secret affair of an abused woman like Starla left him feeling uneasy.

A humid summer depression had settled over Campton following the Founder's Day Picnic. The damp weather made the Delta employees look like images from some mysterious other world as they walked around the plant, their presence shrouded in low hanging clouds. In the thick haze and steam from the mill boilers, Ethan wiped off the front of his safety goggles as he trudged towards the front office.

Pulling open the glass door, he removed his hard hat and stomped his wet shoes on the large industrial mats at the entrance. Instinctively, he smelled his limp cotton shirt sleeve. The stench made him wrinkle his nose. The only thing worse than being wet at the mill was smelling like he was wet from the mill. The aroma, thanks to the sodium sulfide compounds that clung to his clothes, could only be described as resembling human excrement.

"We turn trees into paper to wipe up crap, but we end up smelling more like crap than anything else," he muttered to himself.

He looked around the office building at his fellow engineers. Everyone who moved between the production areas and the main business center looked slightly soggy and disheveled. Ethan shook his head and shrugged. The only saving grace at Delta Paper was that everyone ended up feeling communally sodden and smelling equally awful.

Tucking his hard hat under his arm, Ethan made his way towards the break room. Long ago, he had learned the value of low-tech bulletin boards. A central communication area, especially in a mill that was running three continuous shifts a day, was vital.

His weekly updates were already a day late in posting, but with a little luck, he could get the photos of his interns tacked up to the board with his other announcements before the end of the day. Email blasts were great, but Ethan knew that Hayley and Daniel would love seeing their pictures on display. Including them in the department news was an important aspect of team building.

Ethan approached the doorway. The humming of the fluorescent lights reverberated through the empty lounge. All the tables were abandoned, littered only with unused napkins.

"Well," he said aloud. "I guess that I'll just have to find the pictures myself."

The well-lit entrance of the plant manager's suite stood open at the end of the hallway.

"I'm in here," Starla called out to Ethan as he walked to the front of her empty workstation. Ethan turned and saw that she was sitting in an adjacent boardroom, pictures spread across the large polished conference table. A young woman was talking with her.

"Let me guess," she said with a smile at Ethan. "You came looking for some pictures to put up in Finishing."

"Guilty as charged," he confessed. "I'm trying to gather all my current information for the week, and I was hoping to get those photos you took."

The young woman rose. "Thanks, Starla," she called over her shoulder as she made her way out of the room. Ethan couldn't help but notice her dyed blue hair and her nose ring as she passed him. He gave Starla a questioning glance as she hurried down the hallway.

"She's a new temp," Starla explained from her seat. "The old hens in the accounting department are giving her a hard time. I was just giving her a pep talk."

He moved to the doorway of the meeting room. A rich mahogany table filled the midsized space. The gleaming surface surrounded by thick leather chairs created an atmosphere of formal beauty.

"I took several shots—some casual ones of everyone—so come take a look," she beckoned.

Ethan hesitated. Just walking into the impressive boardroom always made him feel slightly out of place, and he paused now in his damp clothes. The sleek meeting area was the domain of senior company officials from Memphis when they visited the plant. The decor reminded Ethan of something powerful, like the helm of a kingdom. He secretly longed to attend those meetings as an officer of the company.

Walking carefully to the beautifully inlaid table, he saw rectangular snapshots of speakers and employees scattered across the top.

"Wow, these are great," Ethan said with admiration.

"I took over a hundred pictures," Starla confided. "That digital camera that we keep for mill usage is incredibly good and fast."

Scanning the images in front of him, a likeness of Daniel Matthews, his fresh face and tousled hair, grabbed Ethan's eye. He reached his hand towards the picture but stopped.

A print of the crowd from the Founder's Day Picnic rested on the table in front of him. Taken in the tent, the picture showed a gathering people, their backs to the camera. Leah Runar and Carlos Silva were captured in the photograph, their fingers entwined.

"Hey," said Ethan slowly. "Let me ask you about—"

Starla's cellphone let out a blaring ring as it vibrated on the table. "Hang on," she said.

Ethan stared at the picture of Leah and Carlos. He hadn't been wrong at all. Even though he felt silly about talking to the police, he had been right with his suspicions. There was definitely something going on between those two.

"But that can't be!" Starla stood up defiantly as she spoke on the line. "I know it's wrong!"

Ethan moved next to Starla; she was starting to cry.

"Okay!" she wailed. "I will! Yes, I know," she exclaimed into the phone as she hung up and let it drop from her hand.

"Starla, what is it?"

"The police got an anonymous tip," she said with a sob. "They searched Glen's locker out in one of the buildings in the timberlands and they found something—some sort of chain something or other—chainmail, I think they said. It punctures tires. They think it's the stuff that flattened John's tires the night of the accident."

"What? They found what?" Ethan asked, trying to process what she was saying.

Starla trembled, tears streaming down her face.

"Oh Ethan, they just arrested Glen for John's murder!"

Starla gave a slight sway. Instinctively, Ethan tried to steady her as she reached out to grab the edge of the table.

"Are you okay?" he asked. "Why don't you sit down. I think you need to rest a minute."

He eased her into a chair as she stared blankly around the room. Ethan studied her shocked face. Whatever had happened between her husband and the police had left her shaken and pale.

Images of Glen Pittman started to fill Ethan's mind. While they only met a few times, Starla's spouse always appeared arrogant, almost rude. Getting arrested would probably make him want to hit someone.

"Oh Ethan," she said in a quivering voice. "I don't even know what to do."

"It's okay, Starla. Everything's going to be fine. I'm sure that there's been some sort of misunderstanding," he soothed.

"I should go to him," she whispered.

Pushing back from the table, she stood up and started towards her desk. Halfway there, her knees began to buckle.

"Hold on," Ethan said as he caught her crumpling figure from behind. "You're not going anywhere until you can at least walk."

"I'm fine," she said. "I just didn't eat anything this morning, and then I got busy at work."

"Well, we're going to rectify that problem immediately. There's some food in the break room. Let me help you there so we can raise your blood sugar."

Starla reached out and gripped Ethan's arm as his other hand went around her waist. They began to move down the hallway together.

"Ethan, you're a good man," she began as she leaned against him, "but you don't have to do this. I know that you're busy in your department. Help me get to the break room, and I'll be fine."

"Starla," Ethan said, trying to lighten the mood as they entered the lounge. "I'm paid big bucks to solve all sorts of problems at Delta, and at the moment, you're the most important person for me to help." Easing her into a seat at one of the tables, he opened the small refrigerator and started rummaging among the shelves.

"Here we go—I knew that this was in here," he said, producing a can of Pepsi. "I told the plant nurse that one of my hourly guys in Finishing is a diabetic, and she agreed to keep a couple of cans of soda up here." He bent over and checked the chilled racks one more time. "Although, it looks like the other ones have been taken, at least we have this one."

He popped the tab and handed her the cold drink. She took a tiny sip and sighed as she rubbed her eyes.

"Oh no," Ethan urged, "that's not going to cut it. I want to see a real sip."

Starla took a large gulp and smiled.

"Ethan, you're really a nice guy," she said gratefully. "Your wife is lucky to have you."

"Well, you haven't seen anything yet," he assured her as he went to the cabinets that lined the walls of the small room. "There should be something here, something that I put here for the same employee, and I purposefully hid it." Ethan's long arms reached behind cans of coffee. "Here it is!"

The crinkly cellophane wrapping of a Moon Pie rested in his outstretched hand. He gently placed it in front of her.

"Yeah, I know," he said, "it's a Pepsi and a Moon Pie, but what can I say, we live in Southern Alabama."

Pulling open the clear wrapper, Starla pinched off a piece of the sweet chocolate cake and put it in her mouth. She smiled again.

"I'm feeling better already," she assured him.

"Good," nodded Ethan as he sat down beside her. "And I really think that the police probably got hasty with your husband. I'm sure there's a logical explanation."

Starla took another mouthful of the soda and looked intently at Ethan.

"He didn't do it," she said. "I know he didn't."

Ethan nodded sympathetically, unsure of what else to say. The room grew quiet. He glanced at the bruise that had become a yellow outline on her arm. Trying to avert his eyes, Ethan found himself wondering if Starla really knew what her husband was capable of doing.

"Glen didn't kill John. I'm sure of it," she said adamantly. Ethan remained silent. She leaned forward and spoke in a low voice. "He didn't do it. I have proof."

CHAPTER THIRTY-SEVEN

Ethan stared at the resolve in Starla's face. He tried to take in her words.

"Starla, if you have some sort of proof, that's great. You can go to the police and tell them," he said. He thought about Glen getting out of jail. Maybe if his wife could help him, then he would be grateful and possibly less angry.

Chewing her lower lip, Starla leaned across the table. "But I can't do that," she said quietly.

"Why not?" Ethan asked with surprise.

She straightened up in her chair; her eyes darted around the empty room. Tears slid down her cheeks. "Go shut the door," she pleaded, in a hushed tone.

Ethan pushed his chair out from the table and closed the heavy break room door. When he returned to his seat, the expression on Starla's face reminded him of a frightened animal.

"I can't go to the police," she said again in a whisper.

"Why not?"

"I can't do that because, well because….," her voice trailed off as she dropped her head into her hands.

"What is it?" Ethan questioned gently.

"Oh Ethan, it's a mess."

"What's a mess? You mean John's death?"

Starla looked up at Ethan. He thought that she searched his face as if she was calculating the risk of her words, as if her own safety needed some sort of guarantee.

"You know that John and I were…"

"I know that you were involved with each other," Ethan said softly as he finished her sentence. "Starla, I never judged you for that," he assured her.

"I know."

"I didn't, really."

"I know. I know that you didn't judge me. Like I said, you really are a nice guy. I've always known that about you."

Ethan leaned closer to the table. "Starla, I'm not going to lie to you. I don't think that your husband has always been nice to you, and it really bothers me. Maybe it reminds me too much of my own childhood. My old man knocked us around plenty when I was young."

"Really?" she asked. "You hardly seem like the type."

"Oh, most definitely," he said with a nod. "In fact, one of the few places that I always felt safe was school, especially in the library. The result, I'm afraid, is that I became a bit of a nerd."

"Oh, you're not a nerd!" she said with a small laugh.

"Oh, but I am," he said. "But all that nerdiness helped me earn an engineering scholarship to college, and then my tuition was later covered by the pulp and paper program of my university."

"Well, you certainly made the most of your opportunities," she acknowledged.

"Not always. I had my share of youthful indiscretions. But what can I say, everything in my life has led me to all this glamour," he said with a laugh and a wave of his hand around the break room.

Starla laughed and Ethan smiled. For a moment, he noticed that she appeared to relax.

"So, now that you know some of the pieces of my sordid past, why don't you talk to me? Tell me what is going on. Why can't you go to the police?"

Starla exhaled. "I don't want to get you involved in anything. It might not be safe."

Ethan furrowed his brow, trying to understand. "Why don't you let me be the judge of that," he said. "Let me try to help. You know what they say, two heads may be better than one." She was silent for a full minute while Ethan sat and waited.

"Starla, whatever you tell me, I promise to keep it in confidence. I don't run my mouth."

Tears slid down Starla's cheeks. Ethan waited as she dried her eyes. "Starla, I can't force you to talk, but I give you my word that anything you share will stay only with me."

"All right," she said with a sigh. "I'll tell you. John and I each had disposable phones that we used to talk to each other."

Ethan listened and nodded. Somehow, he knew that this was only the beginning of the story.

"The police found his extra phone, which they pretty quickly linked to me. They came to my place and took my phone right off the bat. But after John's accident, I started getting messages, awful messages. One note was left on my car and then I got a call at home on my regular cellphone. They were both warnings."

"What do you mean, warnings?"

"They were weird threats—things like I should forget what I know and to keep quiet."

"Did you go to the police?" asked Ethan, trying to put the pieces together in his mind.

"How could I?" Starla asked. "The messages warned me that if I didn't keep quiet about—well I didn't even know what I should be quiet about—that I would be sorry."

"These messages were threats?"

"Yes," she said, pleading in her voice.

"Do you have any of the messages? Did you save the note on your car?"

"No," she said. "I didn't want anyone—especially Glen—to find it, so I got rid of it. I flushed it down the toilet, and I deleted the unknown number from my phone."

Ethan sat and thought about everything that he'd heard. The details Starla shared were odd.

"I know that Glen didn't murder anybody. He didn't even know about John. The police actually told him about my affair when they came to talk to him after the accident. So, you see, he couldn't have killed John."

She took a breath and smiled ruefully. "And besides, sending messages is not Glen's style. He preferred a more direct approach, as you already know."

"But couldn't you go and tell the police about the note and phone call? Surely, they could protect you somehow," he said thoughtfully.

Starla shot Ethan a look of derision. "You think the police are going to care about me? They can't even catch whoever did this to John, and he was a veteran and a manager."

"But—"

"Ethan, you just don't get it, do you? Nobody's going to care about a bunch of weird messages to someone like me. And they very clearly said that I should be quiet if I know anything."

"But do you know anything, anything that the messages are alluding to?" he asked.

"No!" she said emphatically. "All I know is that John was murdered and now my husband has been arrested because they found some sort of evidence out in a building that they think is his."

Ethan sat in silence trying to figure out how the pieces of the story went together. There had to be a way that the facts could make sense.

"Ethan, think about it," she continued. "Someone knew about me and John. They sent messages for me to keep quiet and now my husband has been arrested. Whoever is behind this is capable of anything."

She pushed her chair back and stood up to leave. "I have to go. I need to get to the police station to check on Glen."

"Do you need some help? Do you want me to go with you?"

Starla gave a faint smile and shook her head. "The last thing Glen needs is for me to walk into the Campton Police Station with another man. Besides, you have a job to get back to doing at the mill. You know, all this glamour, as you said."

"But Starla, I really think you need some help—"

She put her hand on Ethan's forearm and gave a gentle squeeze. "I know," she said. "You're a nice man. But, please, let me handle this. I probably shouldn't have told you anything. Just forget it all."

"You need a good lawyer," he urged. "You and Glen really need to retain someone to help you."

Starla stopped, growing serious. "Ethan, Glen and I are just common people. We can't afford to hire some fancy big shot. Besides, what decent attorney would want to represent someone who has a police record for domestic assault and an alibi with hours that can't be verified due to his job?"

"But—"

"You're a nice guy," she continued, "but you simply don't understand. This really isn't your problem."

Without another word, she opened the door and disappeared down the hallway. Ethan watched her leave, feeling both mystified and concerned.

"Well, this whole thing just beats all," he muttered to himself as he rose. Was she right? Was the person who murdered John playing with even more lives?

He walked to the doorway and thought about the kaleidoscope of characters, both good and bad, that worked at the plant. Whoever said a pulp facility was just made up of chemical processes and production had never worked a day in the paper industry, certainly not at Delta.

Ethan headed out of the break room. For a moment, he paused and watched the bustling cubicles that lined the hallway of the main building. The business of turning pine trees into usable cellulose was more primal, more dramatic, and more dangerous than most people knew, but it was always the secrets behind the scenes that were truly hazardous. The reality was starling enough to leave him both astonished and unnerved.

Deep in thought, Ethan walked back to the boardroom. His gut told him that Starla was telling the truth. Her husband, however lousy, probably didn't know about her affair. If Glen had ever suspected anything, he most likely would have confronted his wife, probably with his fists. And if he really didn't know about the affair, which made sense, then he had no reason to go after John.

He stopped outside of the plant manager's suite and shook his head. The whole bit about the messages sent to Starla was just plain weird. What kind of sick joke was someone playing?

From where he stood, Starla's desk looked forlorn and empty. If Ethan hadn't known that she left the building, he would have merely assumed that her absence was only momentary.

The door behind her desk was closed. Roger McVann was probably in his office unaware of all the drama that had unfolded. Ethan wondered if he should knock and tell him that Starla was gone. Roger would probably want to know, but something made him hesitate. The bizarre story that Starla shared with him was a secret and told in the strictest of confidence.

Ethan turned towards the adjacent boardroom. All he wanted to do was to get the photos that he needed and return to work. He glanced at his phone. The morning was quickly getting away from him.

The snapshots were still scattered in loose rows on the table reminding him of a sort of freeze frame sequence of the picnic. He reached for the pictures of Hayley and Daniel before seeing more photos of the employees from his department. All of a sudden, he froze. Something was wrong.

He stared at the hundreds of photographs and tried to think. What was it that seemed off, that felt different?

Ethan studied the images in front of him. His fingers reached out and then stopped. That was when the obvious change hit him. The picture, the one of Leah and Carlos holding hands, was gone.

CHAPTER THIRTY-EIGHT

"**D**amn it!" Ethan said as he threw a pen onto his desk. "Not again, not one more time!"

He rose angrily from his chair and surveyed the area in front of his desk through the glass partition. Loud alarms and shouting from his day crew rang out across the Finishing floor.

He narrowed his eyes in irritation knowing exactly what was happening. For the fourth time that morning, power had fluctuated in his department creating breaks on the paper machine and damage to the cutting and baling process. Perfectly good rolls of pulp were being ruined.

"What am I in? The reject business?" Ethan muttered to himself as he tightened his hearing protection into his ears and marched onto the Finishing floor in search of the shift manager.

"Travis, what's going on?" Ethan shouted.

"It's that damn Powerhouse!" Travis yelled back, in exasperation. "They can't keep steady electricity in here, and the rolls keep breaking!"

Ethan put his hands on his hips. Thanks to the late June temperatures, the production area felt like a hellish oven. The entire morning had revolved around nothing but a series of power outages and problems

"We can't sell these rolls as prime!" Travis bellowed over the blaring buzzer. "Shit, Ethan! I have rail cars and trucks waiting to be loaded today! What am I going to do?"

Hourly workers were scurrying around the machinery trying to salvage rolls of cellulose as Travis began to gesture in rage. Ethan looked at the chaos and felt his own temper rising, knowing the real culprit resided deep in the center of the mill.

Typically, production problems were handled methodically. Under Ethan's leadership, the standard practice involved data collection followed by problem solving. As a nod to his level approach, the workers in his department had even nicknamed their boss "Weir the Tear Genius" for his cool head under pressure.

But now as he stood in the center of his own snarled domain, Ethan could feel himself getting furious. Why was it that Finishing was always the last part of the plant to get any consideration? What was his department, the butt end of the horse?

"I'm going to handle this!" Ethan called to Travis who was barking orders to the forklift drivers.

Whipping his head back around to his boss, Travis held up a hand to stop the rolling machinery as he stared at Ethan.

"You're going to the Powerhouse? Shit, Ethan. You know that Wymon's an asshole."

"Yeah, I know," shouted Ethan. "But I also know that I'm tired of the crap we get from his department."

"But Wymon is the worst," Travis began loudly. "Everybody hates him, and I should know. He and I grew up together as swamp rats in Citronelle."

"Well, I don't really have a choice, now do I?"

Before Travis could continue his protests, Ethan took long, determined strides out of Finishing. Confronting the main person responsible for losing production was one way to solve the problem.

In the hazy morning sun, the latticework of overhead pipes and buildings that lined the center of the mill appeared to dwarf the employees who darted along the main industrial driveway. Ethan often walked into the heart of the manufacturing areas of the plant and felt a type of awe that came from realizing that every process at Delta worked together on a grand scale to create a true engineering marvel. But today, as he made his way past the brick-lined building that housed the production chemicals, irritation rose within him. Even the pulp digesters that soared into the air as magnificently round stacks of concrete made Ethan snarl.

On some level, talking to Wymon Hicks was probably a colossal mistake. If he had been sleeping better at night, resolving power outages in Finishing would always begin with a conference call involving several leaders of the production team. Major problems were usually handled best in a collaborative manner. But Ethan felt anything but cooperative at the moment.

He was exhausted and had been for days. His shoulders ached, and he was starting to nurse a headache that no amount of coffee or ibuprofen would relieve. Ever since Starla confided her strange story to him last week, Ethan had been unable to get a good night's rest. The odd details of her threatening messages and the constant small-town gossip about her husband's arrest filled his head whenever he tried to sleep.

"What is it?" Abbey finally asked Ethan as he got up in the middle of the night to pace the floors for the third time in a row.

"I just have a lot on my mind," he told her, trying to sound nonchalant. "You know that the annual shut down period at the mill is coming up and there's always a lot to do."

If he had to guess, Abbey probably wasn't buying his flimsy excuse, but she stopped asking him questions at some point in the pitch darkness of their bedroom. She merely rolled over and announced what she always did these days.

"I've got to pee."

Ethan watched her round shape move to the bathroom and worried. The last thing he wanted to do was to tell her about Starla and what she confided to him. It was so bizarre, and he was sure that the idea of an uncaught killer playing games with people would frighten her.

Now as the Powerhouse stood before him, Ethan realized that his nerves were frayed from fatigue. Having a "discussion" with Wymon was probably going to be a huge mistake.

For a full minute, Ethan entertained a fleeting fantasy. If Wymon acted the way he usually did, maybe there would be a way to lean over and smack the familiar, condescending smirk off his face. Ethan smiled at the thought of watching his round head roll to the side. Taking his frustration out on someone who really deserved it was the only truly satisfying outcome of the morning that he could imagine.

Ethan stopped long enough to quell his imagination and gather his thoughts. The Powerhouse sat before him with lines generating electricity and steam that flowed out from its center. Ethan knew that the pace of manufacturing was ultimately governed by the single department before his eyes. Like the huge center of a spider web, this part of the plant ultimately dictated all work functions.

He wiped his brow from the sticky humidity, opened the glass door, and started to climb the stairs that led to the second- story control room. With his jaw set, he became aware of a central thought. Whether it was the actual creature or the Powerhouse, Ethan absolutely hated spiders and webs.

He was shaking his head in disgust when the odor hit him. The condensation from the dripping chemicals of the area created a stench that almost made him gag. No matter the time of day, the Powerhouse always managed to smell like rotten eggs.

On the stairs, Ethan tried to hold his breath, but the steps were too steep. Like his previous visits, attempts to restrict his oxygen were futile. He was already drenched in sweat and unable to avoid sucking in the foul air.

In the control room, the shiny bald head of Wymon Hicks rose from the center chair. With a telephone up to his ear, he sat in front of a panel of various screens. He appeared consumed with his multitasking.

"I know it's not working!" he half shouted into the receiver. "The boiler is generating more than one reading. Let me analyze the data and I'll get back to you," he spat as he slammed the phone onto its cradle.

"Wymon," Ethan called as he moved into the room. "We need to talk."

With a slight turn of his balloon-like head, Wymon squinted his eyes towards the voice.

"Ee-than," he said as he eyed his visitor. "What brings you to my part of the world?"

Ethan felt his neck tighten as his right hand involuntarily made a fist. Wymon always said his name that same way, elongating syllables with his southern accent like he was stretching out some sort of taffy. The exaggeration always sounded stupid.

"Wymon, we can't keep power in Finishing. I've lost electricity four times this morning, and we have orders that have to get loaded today," Ethan said hotly.

"Well, Ee-than," Wymon began as he leaned back in his cracked leather chair. "This may come as a surprise to you, but you're not the only recipient of power at the mill. In fact, Finishing isn't even in the main production line. Believe it or not, the other areas of the plant actually have precedent over you," he said with a taunting smile.

"I'm generating rejects faster than I can count, and my trucks and rail cars are going to leave without enough prime pulp to fill orders," Ethan said between clenched teeth.

"That's too bad, but as you may have noticed, we're having a few problems of our own this morning. In fact, when you came in here, I was in the middle of analyzing data, as I've been doing for several hours," he responded smugly as he turned back to the control panel. "Now, Ee-than, if you will excuse me, I have to get back to the numbers."

"Wymon," Ethan said angrily. "You need to do more than just have analysis paralysis! You need to fix this!"

Wymon spun around to face his visitor. "And you need to accept the fact that you are just a manager in the Finishing Department! Maybe if your career ever gets off the ground, you will realize that your little corner of the mill isn't the whole world!"

With that, Ethan took a lunging step at the man in front of him. Wymon shot out of his chair. The top of his circular shiny head reached the lower part of Ethan's chin. Wymon grabbed a worn clip board from his control desk and waved it in front of him.

At the sight of the short man trying to defend himself, Ethan started to laugh. "So, what are you going to do, Wymon, analyze me to death with your calculations?"

"I mean it Ee-than," he said as raised the plastic clip board like a martial arts tool. "I can use this on you. I can stick this where the sun don't shine!"

The telephone on the control panel gave a shrill ring and one of the screens started to beep. Ethan looked over the glistening head in front of him towards the monitor.

"Your fan club is calling, Wymon, so I should go and let you get back to it."

Wymon whipped his head around to survey the controls that resembled the blinking lights of a Christmas display. Immediately, he sank down into his chair and reached for the phone.

"Don't come back!" Wymon barked as Ethan headed to the stairs to leave.

"I won't," called out Ethan over his shoulder.

"You're just a middle manager, Ee-than, who can't make it out of Finishing!" Wymon yelled behind him. "Everyone knows you're never really going to make it in this industry or with Delta!"

CHAPTER THIRTY-NINE

Ethan stomped away from the Powerhouse and ground his teeth in frustration. As his steel-toed boots pounded the asphalt, the taunts from Wymon rang in his ears.

On any other day, Ethan would have dismissed pronouncements about his future as the mere rantings of a confirmed idiot. After all, everyone at Delta knew that Wymon Hicks was an insecure loner. But as he trudged along the pavement, Ethan knew what really bothered him. Maybe, on some level, Wymon was right about his lackluster career.

He made a quick check of the time on his phone and thought about the morning. Going to the Powerhouse had been a complete error on his part. He should have chosen a better approach for solving a manufacturing problem. His own actions had merely escalated a production glitch into a nasty confrontation. Or maybe, on some level, he was simply itching for a good fight.

Ethan gazed at the tall brick buildings that lined the center road of the plant and admired the natural stability of the industrial processes. There was something comforting about working with technical systems.

Ever since John's murder, Ethan's sense of confusion was growing. Life at Delta Paper was completely unsettled these days. As if having some sort of killer on the loose wasn't bad enough, the strange drama that Starla shared made the events of the past month all the more troubling. These days, nothing seemed to be quite right.

Sidestepping a truck that was beeping in reverse, Ethan wiped the sweat off his brow as the Woodyard came into view. Maybe it was time to be honest with himself. Maybe his career was stalling. Or maybe the eerie happenings of the last few weeks had just left him uneasy. Whatever the reasons, having a fight with a clearly obnoxious buffoon was probably what he had subconsciously craved.

Ethan turned into the low building that housed the mill auditorium and wondered if he would be late for the scheduled employee meeting. Checking his phone again made him breathe a sigh of relief. He was right on time and his screen remained free of messages. Hopefully, Travis had the department at least up and running, ready for the afternoon release of product.

In the large conference room, the scuffle of work boots mixed with the murmur from dozens of voices. Managers from every area of the business huddled together along the rows of seats designated for the audience. The scraping of chairs across the terrazzo floor signaled the beginning of the assembly. Ethan canvased the area for an open spot.

"Ethan," Jerry Hillar called out and waved his arm from across the room. He motioned to the empty place next to him.

"Saved you a seat," he mouthed pointing to the thinly padded folding chair.

For once, Ethan felt relieved to see a friendly face. If ever there was a day that he needed camaraderie, this was the one.

"You okay?" Jerry asked.

"Yeah, I'm just having a totally horrendous morning and I'm starting to get a killer headache," Ethan responded as he sank into the seat.

"Power been out for you this morning?"

"You don't know the half of it," said Ethan. "I even went to the Powerhouse to try to talk to Wymon."

Jerry twisted in his chair, looking shocked. "You went to see Wymon? He's the biggest pain in the ass ever. How'd that go for you?"

"About like you think," Ethan acknowledged. "Wymon did offer to give me a colonoscopy though, free of charge, with his clip board."

Jerry threw back his head and howled with laughter. "If he wasn't such a pathetic little jerk sitting up there in his Powerhouse, I'd have to give him a swirly."

"A swirly?" asked Ethan, rubbing his temple.

"Yeah," said Jerry dropping his voice. "I would love to take that ugly mug of his and introduce it to one of the mill toilets," he said with a wink.

"Excuse me, but if you could all take your seats," Bill Hackman stood at the front podium and spoke into the microphone as he motioned for quiet.

A sea of hard hats settled into chairs as conversations came to a halt. Cell phones appeared from pockets for one final check before being placed on silent mode. Bill Hackman glanced around the auditorium and cleared his throat.

"I want to thank everyone for coming this morning. I know we are facing some production challenges today, but senior management felt it was still important to gather everyone together in order to honor some very special employees."

Ethan let out a sigh and rolled his eyes to the ceiling. Was this the "critical meeting" that had been announced in an email before seven in the morning?

"And here to lead today's meeting is our own chief at Delta, Roger McVann!"

Applause filled the hall as Bill stepped away from the microphone and the plant manager took confident paces towards the front of the room.

Jerry leaned over to Ethan's ear. "If Hackman's pointy nose was any higher up McVann's butt, it'd be brown."

"Good morning," Roger said cordially. "Today we felt it was important to honor some of the hard-working employees here at Delta. While many of you push tirelessly to ensure that our products are the best in the marketplace, we should always celebrate those among us who are at milestones in their careers."

Jerry leaned over to Ethan again. "I wonder who the pet is today," he whispered sarcastically.

"This morning, we want to begin by recognizing one particular individual. He is achieving his ten-year anniversary with our company, and I think that I speak for all of us when I say that he is the epitome of a team player."

Ethan sat in his chair with a stoic look on his face. He thought back to his own tenth anniversary with Delta last year. Starla merely placed a catalog of products in his Finishing mailbox so that he could pick his own gift. Each memento in the booklet had been generic, with the Delta logo affixed to it.

"I handle all the gifts for employees," she told Ethan when he called her on the phone to inquire about selections. "Just pick one. But only choose from the section of small items, since you've only been with the company for ten years."

After surveying the half dozen items that were available to him, Ethan finally chose a paperweight. It arrived unceremoniously in a brown box on his desk one morning. On any given day, the shiny anchor rested next to his computer atop department reports and out-going correspondence. The oval disk had a green "D" visible through the thick glass that matched the lettering on the company signage.

Now, Ethan wondered if the paperweight was somehow synony-mous with his career. One "D" item for a D—rated manager.

"So please help me honor a new ten-year employee with our com-pany," Roger announced. "Mr. Calvin Jones."

"Didn't you have an anniversary last year?" Jerry asked quietly. Ethan shrugged, trying to hold a neutral expression. Clapping erupted as Roger extended his hand, and Calvin sprang from his seat to head to the podium.

"Calvin, we have a gift for you today," Roger said as he held up a small metallic object. "It's a pocketknife with your name and date engraved on the side. We hope you will use this around the mill and remember your achievement with Delta."

Calvin took the tool and smiled. His perfectly pressed striped dress shirt, off-set by his crisp khaki pants and round glasses, made him look like the perfect engineer. Ethan felt his mouth go dry.

"Wow!" Calvin said enthusiastically as he took the award. "I'll definitely put this to good use as I take lots of samples for the new cellulose grade. This will really help me around the mill. Thank you all very much."

Ethan remained in his seat without moving. He stared straight ahead as Roger began sharing stories from his college sports career at the University of Florida before he continued the presentations.

In a single file line, middle-aged managers with expanding waist-lines and scuffed hard hats moved towards the podium to be recog-nized. Ethan surveyed the dozens of Delta employees in his midst. Was this his future? Was he merely destined to become some faceless department manager consigned to oblivion?

As employees with decades of service moved back to their seats, recognition gifts in hand, Ethan felt numb. Were his own contributions to the business so mundane that his career milestones could be forgotten?

"That's all our awards today. Like I always said on the baseball field as player number #32, 'Play like a champion!' Thank you all for attending and please feel free to congratulate our newly awarded members of the Delta family as you head back to your departments," Roger said into the microphone.

The lights in the auditorium brightened as the clapping subsided and people began to rise to their feet. Jerry looked at Ethan and shook his head.

"You should have been recognized, too," he said. "I bet if you talk to Starla—"

"It's fine," Ethan said, cutting off the flow of Jerry's suggestions.

"You want to get lunch? My treat," Jerry offered.

Ethan turned to his colleague and stared in disbelief, trying to process what he was hearing. Jerry Hillar was known throughout Campton as someone who only spent money on himself. Folks often joked that Jerry put his own wife on a shoestring budget so that he would always have cash to go fishing in Mobile Bay. If he was offering to buy Ethan lunch, then the gesture went beyond just simple kindness. It was an act of pity.

"Another time," Ethan said, trying not to have his words sound too stiff. He headed for the exit door.

At that moment, he saw them. The two detectives, Mia Lee and Nick Simpson were standing at the entrance of the auditorium. They caught Ethan's eye and moved towards him.

CHAPTER FORTY

For a split second, Ethan froze. What were the detectives doing at Delta again? He felt the color rise to his cheeks as he remembered the last time he spoke to the police. Hadn't he said some really stupid things about touching that made him sound like some sort of sissy?

Starla—Ethan watched the detectives making their way through the crowd and wondered suddenly if she told them about the creepy messages. When he sat in the break room with her, Starla was clear about not telling the police about her threats. Had she changed her mind? Did the detectives want to know about Ethan's conversation with her? And hadn't they arrested Glen for John's murder? What were the cops doing back at Delta if they already had their man?

Ethan stood in the middle of the auditorium and tried to think about how much he should say to the detectives. Telling the truth was always the safest policy, but he made a promise to keep Starla's secret. He could feel his heart starting to pound in his chest.

Managers swirled past him in every direction making their way to the open exit doors. Ethan remained immobile, unsure of what to do.

A figure emerged from the front of the auditorium and called to the officers. Bill Hackman walked forward to greet the detectives. Ethan watched them shake hands. Slowly he moved towards the side of the large room. Whipping out his phone, he pretended to check his messages while his peripheral vision kept tabs on the trio.

"Are you sure about lunch?" Jerry was at his elbow, a concerned look on his face.

"Nah, I can't," said Ethan, trying to come up with an excuse. "There's a bunch of crap going on in Finishing."

"Want me to walk there with you?"

Ethan felt his stomach tighten. Why was he always such a lousy liar? Excuses raced through his mind as he tried to look nonchalantly at Jerry.

"No, it's okay. I really have to make a quick call before I head back. You go on and go."

Ethan put his phone to his ear, pulled his lips into a thin line, and started to nod. "Uh huh, all right, yes... I got it," he said into the silent phone in his hand.

He turned his back to stare at the brown wall in front of him. With his head still bobbing, Ethan prayed that Jerry would take the hint. He counted to ten while studying the color of the auditorium paint. The interior stain was probably the exact same color of the vomit that he felt churning in his throat. When he glanced over his shoulder, there was no one beside him.

Ethan scanned the room. The meeting space was almost empty. He felt both guilty for what he had done to Jerry and relieved to be rid of him.

With his phone still resting on his cheek, Ethan resumed watching Bill and the detectives. The three of them were just out of ear shot. He stepped farther to the side wall to watch them closely.

Bill Hackman now reached into a folio that he carried and handed something that looked like a photograph to Detective Lee. Squinting his eyes, Ethan caught a glimpse of what the officer took in her hand.

The photo wavered and reflected in the bright overhead lighting. The familiar image made Ethan widen his eyes. He had seen that picture before, just the other day. It was the missing shot from the conference room, the one of Leah and Carlos holding hands.

Ethan scrutinized the detectives as they leaned forward while Bill appeared to be explaining something important. Their heads bent together with their eyes locked on each other as if some secret was being revealed. Straightening up, both officers looked at each other with a hard stare. One by one, they shook Bill's hand in what appeared to be a gesture of gratitude.

As the threesome strolled through a doorway on the opposite wall, Ethan thought about everything that he had seen. Was Hackman behind the disappearance of the photo from the conference room the other day? And if he took it, could he also be responsible for what happened to John? And what about Starla? Did the police know Glen was innocent and were now looking at other suspects?

Deep in thought, Ethan jumped at the sound of loud ringing. He looked at his hand. With his attention on the detectives, he had forgotten that he was still clutching his phone. He brought it up to his ear.

"Ethan, come quick!" Travis shouted on the line. "We've got an emergency in Finishing!"

216

CHAPTER FORTY-ONE

Ethan sprinted through the entrance of the Finishing department and saw a crowd huddled together in front of the pulp rollers. His eyes swept the scene. A body was on the ground, surrounded by the blue jeans and work boots of the day shift.

Travis, in the middle of the group, was screaming something that was lost over the sound of the machinery. Once again, Ethan could feel his stomach churn as he pushed through the swarm of muscular torsos. Blood covered the floor.

"What happened?" Ethan shouted to Travis.

"Hell, I don't know," yelled Travis, trying to be heard above the churning of the paper roller. "He stuck his hand in the machine!"

Ethan dropped to his knees. The employee, a young new hire, was clutching a mangled right hand and writhing in pain. Gently Ethan touched his arm. From the elbow down to the wrist, the skin was all but gone. A crimson mess of protruding bone made up his hand.

"Call the nurse and the safety manager!" Ethan barked.

"They're on their way!" Travis confirmed as he dropped to the floor to begin first aid.

Blood started to pool under the injured man's back.

"Apply pressure!" Ethan directed Travis.

Thick hands held the mangled arm as a widening circle of red began to spread onto the mill floor.

"He needs a tourniquet!" shouted Ethan as he watched the veins in the man's arm spurting rhythmically with every heartbeat. "Give me something to use!"

One of the workers took off his T-shirt and handed it to Travis. Ethan snatched the fabric.

"I need a knife—something to cut this with!"

Calvin stood at the feet of the young man. He was holding his new pocketknife with a look of utter shock on his face.

"Give me that!" Ethan commanded as he grabbed the knife and made quick slices of the fabric. With the shirt in long pieces, he quickly tightened it on the upper arm of the moaning employee.

"Hold his arm up!" Ethan said to Travis as the mill nurse elbowed her way into the gathering throng. Ambulance sirens were blaring in the distance.

Examining the wound quickly, she checked the man's eyes and put her hand on his chest.

"Who did the tourniquet?" she called out to the men.

"I did," Ethan answered.

"Good job," she said. "You may have saved his arm and his life."

The workers parted as the mill safety manager ran up to the scene. His puffing red face was dripping with sweat. His large frame crouched down next to Travis.

"Well?" he asked the nurse.

"He's going to make it, but we need to get him to the hospital," she replied.

"I'm gonna need a full safety report!" he bellowed, rising to his feet, as his eyes sought out Ethan.

The crowd widened as the paramedics rushed into the department. Ethan and Travis began to answer questions while the first responders motioned for the stretcher.

With the ambulance loaded, Ethan and Travis temporarily suspended all departmental operations. Both men moved to the center of the floor and gathered the remaining crew to begin a safety incident investigation. After two hours of intense review, the floor was wiped clean of blood.

Ethan looked around at the somber workforce. He noticed that the employee who offered his shirt now had on a dirty wife beater undershirt that was presumably borrowed.

"Way to give Delta the shirt off your back," Ethan joked as he clasped the man on the shoulder. "Thanks for the quick response."

Ethan looked around the department. Calvin was sitting off in the corner. He was alone with the pocketknife in his hands and seemed to be deep in thought.

"You okay?" Ethan asked as he made his way to the edge of the production floor.

"Yeah," Calvin said as he studied his knife.

"You sure?"

"Yeah, I'm okay. You were great today, Ethan," he said with admiration as his gaze was still fixed on the tool in his hands. Looking up at his boss, his eyes widened. "Oh wow, you're really covered in blood." Ethan looked down at his own shirt. It was a stained mess.

"I'm afraid that goes with the territory," Ethan replied with a smile, trying to forget that Calvin had been the darling of the earlier plant meeting. "Just remember, always keep your knife with you in the mill. You never know when you're going to need a tool like that."

Calvin nodded and put the knife in his shirt pocket.

"How's the computer work going with John's files?" Ethan asked, ready to think about something beyond manufacturing safety.

"I've been able to access a few more files," Calvin told him. "Your suggestions about the passwords were really good. I just can't get into one final area."

"Keep trying," urged Ethan. "Use the female name we discussed earlier," he said instinctively lowering his voice, "and maybe something about his truck. He really loved that vehicle he drove. He called it a joyride, or something like that."

Calvin grabbed a pad of paper and made notes. "Thanks, man," he said.

Ethan walked back to his desk. He sank down in his worn seat. Where had the day gone? His neck felt like a drum as he rubbed the tired muscles with one hand. He opened his bottom drawer and grabbed the extra golf shirt that he kept for emergencies. With a distracted swipe of his arm, customer reports and his Delta paperweight started to slide to the floor. Instinctively, he stuck out his foot as the heavy disc smacked him on the shin.

"Shit," he howled as stars danced before his eyes. The glass hit the floor. Ethan bent over to rub his sore leg and grab the paperweight from under his chair.

A new crack ran down the middle of the glass and a chip was missing from one side.

"Well, that figures," he muttered. "Another casualty of the day."

He was still massaging his tibia when his phone started to ring. Through the glass partition, Travis was stomping towards him with a scowl on his face. Without warning, his head started pounding again.

All this glamour, Ethan thought as he reached for the blaring line. *Who could ask for anything more?*

CHAPTER FORTY-TWO

Ethan pulled into his subdivision just as the thermometer in his car dropped below ninety degrees. The late afternoon sun cast long shadows from the live oak trees onto the empty lawns of his quiet street. Not a single person appeared outside. He looked at the deserted neighborhood, knowing that the furnace-like weather made even die-hard southerners seek indoor refuge.

Only the loud hum of his air conditioner vibrated against the dashboard. Ethan usually played his favorite hard rock station on his stereo, but not today. Now, he drove home in grateful silence while saying a prayer of thanksgiving for the dull whirl of tepid breeze that wafted against his sweat-stained skin.

Abbey had her back to the side door as Ethan entered the house. She was rummaging through the refrigerator, pulling out plastic cartons that she stacked onto the counter.

"Hey, Sweetie," she said without looking in his direction. "It's just too hot for anything but a cold supper tonight. Hope you like pasta salad and some cold chicken."

"It'll be fine," Ethan answered as he untied his work boots by the washing machine. He dropped his bloody shirt on the floor. The tone of his voice made her turn around abruptly. At the sight of his appearance and the crimson polo at his feet, her eyes grew wide.

"My God, Ethan! What happened to your shirt? Are you all right?"

"I'm fine," Ethan assured her tiredly as he slipped out of his heavy shoes. "It's blood on my shirt, but not mine. We had a safety incident in the department today. I had the joy of being one of the first on the scene until the mill nurse and the ambulance arrived."

"What happened?" she asked.

"We had a new hire stick his hand all the way up past the elbow in between two metal rollers."

"Is he going to be okay?"

"I think so. They took him away by ambulance. Of course, it threw the whole day into a madhouse," he said as he kissed her on the check.

"What was he doing?"

"Don't ask me. Travis told me the guy is known as a pothead around town. For all I know, he could have been high."

"Why don't you go take a shower? Just drop your clothes in the bathroom, and I'll come and get them," Abbey said as she started to follow him down the hall. "We'll eat dinner after you clean up, and you can tell me all about your wild accident."

Ethan stood under the shower nozzle and let the water fall over his shoulders. He wanted nothing more than to wash away the awful memories of the day. If only his muscles would unknot. Placing both hands on the green tiled walls, he lowered his head under the spray, cursing his height. Getting completely wet was almost impossible.

The entire master bathroom of his ranch house was barely bigger than a walk-in closet. Ethan turned sideways. His shower bordered on being the size of a vertical coffin. Living in what was considered the "manager's neighborhood" meant that most of the houses had been built decades earlier. Updating the bathroom was on his list of home improvements. As he stood under the meager drizzle from the overhead fixture, he vowed to get started on his renovations.

Dressed in shorts and a loose cotton shirt, Ethan appeared as Abbey was fixing a plate for Charlie. She took one look at her husband and spoke to her son.

"Do you want to eat watching television tonight?" she asked.

"Yes, plesth," Charlie lisped.

"Okay, go in and turn on the TV. I'm going to let you eat on a tray like a fancy cafeteria. I'll bring you your dinner, so just get settled on the sofa and turn on your Daniel Tiger show." Charlie's chubby legs pounded into the living room as Abbey returned her gaze to her husband.

"I hate for him to have too much screen time, but I would hate for him to hear about a mill accident more," she explained. "What can I say? It's the lesser of two evils."

Ethan opened the refrigerator and pulled out a beer while Abbey carried a plate to her son.

"Now, what happened today?" she asked when she returned to the kitchen.

"Well, I don't even know where to start. First of all, we had production problems out the wazoo this morning. The Powerhouse couldn't keep electricity to Finishing, and we made way too many rejects. Then we had a plant meeting, and I got to watch everyone get service awards, even though I never seem to get remembered. And then, to top it all off, we had a safety incident." He took a long swig from his beer and looked at his wife. He felt twinges of guilt for telling her about his less-than-successful day. She probably longed to be married to an industry star. "And all of this happened before lunch, so the rest of the day was just kind of a bust."

"Oh, Ethan," she said as she put her arms around him, "I'm so sorry that you had such a rotten day." She rested her head on his chest. "You really are a great manager."

"Well, I'll take your word for it any day of the week," he said as he rubbed her back.

She pulled away from him with a knowing gleam in her eye.

"After hearing about all that, I really hate to tell you what happened to me today."

"What?"

"I had a phone call," she told him. "It was from my mother."

Ethan felt himself groan. He let his head drop back so that he stared at the ceiling and wondered, for a moment, what he had done to deserve his hellish existence. His mother-in-law was one of his least favorite people.

Janet Vandersmith always conjured up images of merciless disapproval in Ethan's mind. At just five feet tall, her perfectly matching sheath dresses and pumps accentuated her stiff blond bob that never moved. She reminded her son-in-law of a cool, calculating shark ready to bite off his manhood, if only the right opportunity presented itself.

She prided herself on finding just the right moments.

"Ethan," she said during her last visit, managing to sound annoyed just by saying his name. "Did I tell you that one of my friends from my country club bridge group has a son-in-law who is also a chemical engineer?"

"Is that so?" Ethan replied, steeling himself for what he could envision was coming.

"Yes," Janet Vandersmith answered as she pierced him with her cool, blue eyes. "He has a job, a top position really, making macaroni and cheese—the kind that comes in a box. He has been extremely

successful. He even managed to buy his wife a new home in the sub-
urbs of Atlanta."

"Well, good for him," Ethan responded, trying to sound ami-
cable. He smiled at his mother-in-law, too polite to mention that one
more person making boxed processed food was hardly a monumental
achievement.

"I just thought that you would like to know what your peers are
doing. You know, the ones that are making money and living in nice
places," she said with a sniff.

At that point, her litany of disfavor got the better of him. Ethan
had enough of her digs, and he changed his tone.

"I'll keep that in mind, Janet," he acknowledged, with a hint of
sarcasm, "as Delta continues to make the box and the packaging that
your friend's son-in-law probably uses for his dehydrated cuisine."

Ethan dropped his head back down to look at his wife. She had an
expectant look on her face. "What did your mother want?" he asked
wearily.

"She wanted to know if we want to come to the beach this week.
She and Dad went down to Destin and rented a house with another
couple, but their friends had to leave because the wife's elderly mother
fell and broke her hip," Abbey explained. "They have a whole house
to themselves. It's all paid for, and they've invited us to come for the
rest of the week."

Ethan sighed and pulled away her arms. He reached for his beer
and took a long sip. A host of rude comments formed in his mind,
but he kept silent. He might be an obscure, underappreciated vanilla
manager, but nobody could call him a stupid husband.

"Do you want to go?" he asked her.

"Well, it's a free vacation," Abbey said. "I don't have a doctor's
appointment this week, and Charlie doesn't have summer preschool

camp. We could head out tomorrow, and since it's Monday, you could get a break from work. You'd only have to take a few days off from the mill."

Ethan studied his wife. He could see that the wheels were already turning in her head. From experience, he knew that his input at this point was relatively inconsequential. Talking to Abbey when she had made up her mind was like a tennis match that was already on the last serve. Point. Set. Done.

"I just don't know," Ethan said slowly. "I haven't requested any vacation plans on the schedule, and it's hard to leave right after a safety problem."

Abbey bit her lip. He could tell that she was starting to pout. In spite of himself, Ethan smiled. She was always so cute whenever she started to plot her strategy in a discussion.

"Why don't you and Charlie go? I'll just stay and work," he offered.

"But I don't want to leave you," she protested.

Ethan thought about what it would take to get a few days off from work. A change of the vacation schedule was probably doable, but then he remembered the inevitable problem. If the three of them went, he would be stuck in a beach house with his mother-in-law. Her endless barrage of comments would make swimming with the real sharks in the ocean look appealing.

"No, you should go," he offered. "You need some time with your folks, and it would be fun for Charlie."

"But I hate to leave you here," Abbey insisted. "You're working so hard at the mill, and I don't want you to be alone. Besides, even though the police made an arrest in John Runar's case, the whole town is still whispering that they didn't get the real killer. People are saying that he'll strike again."

Ethan looked at his wife. He was so tired that he had forgotten about the detectives coming to the mill until she mentioned the case.

Glen Pittman was not the killer. Starla had all but confided that her husband never knew about her affair until after John's death. Besides, the cops wouldn't come back to the mill and talk to management—looking at the picture of Leah and Carlos–if they had a perfect case. With everything he knew, Ethan would stake money on the fact that the wagging tongues of Campton were probably right.

Maybe getting Abbey and Charlie out of town would be safer.

"No," Ethan said with determination. "I want you both to go. Really, I insist," he said with a forced smile. "And I'll tell you what, I'll leave early Saturday and drive over to Destin. I bet I can be there before lunch."

"But–," Abbey began.

"No buts," said Ethan. "I'll even get up early tomorrow and pack the car for you to go before I head to the mill."

"Oh, Ethan," she said as her lips brushed his cheek. "What would I do without you?"

Ethan took another sip of his beer and thought about his mundane life that managed to dribble and plop along despite all the drama of their small town.

"Well, let's hope that you never find out, darlin'."

CHAPTER FORTY-THREE

The papers landed next to Ethan's computer with an angry smack. He heard the derisive snort before he could hang up his phone and raise his eyes from his desk.

"We are behind!" Travis exclaimed, pointing to the paperwork. "Those damned salespeople are selling grades that we can't get through the mill. We're never going to make these customer orders!"

Ethan returned the phone to its cradle and turned to his shift manager.

"Oh, and I made you some coffee," Travis added as he set a mug down on the corner of his boss's workspace.

Ethan furrowed his brow and reached for the reports. He rarely mistrusted his foreman's verbal pronouncements but verifying how far behind schedule their output lagged was always wise. The data on the sheets looked bleak.

"How are we running right now?" Ethan asked, flipping through the pages.

"At this moment, I'm steady. But I can't make up for the Powerhouse problems and the down time from the safety incident yesterday."

"Head back to the floor," instructed Ethan. "Keep everything running. Let me make some phone calls, and I'll see what I can do. Oh, and thanks for the coffee."

Travis sighed and clomped out to the floor. Ethan leaned back and wearily rubbed his closed eyes. The exhaustion of the previous day still lingered in his pounding head. If the production problems weren't enough to drain him, then his own lack of recognition at the plant meeting yesterday managed to further erode any flickering hope he held for career advancement. When he added to that the safety report that now sat partially complete on his desk, he felt spent.

For a brief moment, Ethan wondered about going to Destin with Abbey and Charlie. A vacation would have recharged his battery. Ethan could see himself playing with Charlie in the waves and enjoying a sunset dinner with his wife.

But he opened his eyes and stared out at the Finishing Department. The responsibility to get rolls and bales of pulp out the door ulti- mately rested on his shoulders. Despite the fact that yesterday had been brutal in more ways than one, the duty of leading his team fell squarely to him. Besides, he really couldn't stand more than an hour with his mother-in-law.

Ethan reached for the cup on his desk. Papers littered his work surface, but he needed to soldier through the day. He took a sip and winced. The coffee was more bitter than usual.

A headache started to throb in his temples in spite of the caffeine that he sipped. Ethan put the mug down in disgust. Maybe his lack of rest was to blame for his sensitive taste.

Trying to sleep last night proved all but impossible. Every time he started to doze, he was back at the mill. First, he saw blood on the Finishing floor, followed by Wymon's screaming face. But seeing the police in his dreams made him constantly jerk and twitch in the darkness. They were always gazing at him, then moving towards him to ask questions. As he stared at the detectives in his nightmare, a dark figure suddenly emerged in the distance. Ethan woke up multiple times, covered in sweat and gasping for air. At five in the morning, he couldn't take the torment anymore. Silently getting out of bed, he started to load the car for Abbey.

"How long have you been up?" she asked as her bedroom slippers softly plopped into the kitchen.

"Just a little while," he lied. "I packed the minivan like I promised, and I even made breakfast for you and Charlie."

In the golden morning sunlight, she looked at her husband with concern. "Ethan, why are you not sleeping? What are you not telling me?"

"I've told you—I've just got a lot on my mind. Yesterday was wild at work with an injury in the department. Look, I even made you a breakfast sandwich for the road."

"If I didn't know better, I would think that you are trying to get rid of me," she said with a rueful smile as she filled the tea kettle with water.

Ethan continued to pack a small cooler with snacks for the road. He tried to hold a blank expression on his face, like an engine idling in neutral.

"Of course, I'm not trying to get rid of you. I just want you to go have some fun. You and Charlie deserve to get out of Campton. The beach will be great, and I bet the water will be warm."

"And your coming Saturday, right?"

"As soon as I get up, I'm packing my car with a suitcase and an energy drink and heading your way."

Abbey merely nodded as she disappeared down the hallway to get dressed. Ethan watched her go before slipping quickly out to the carport to finish stuffing beach toys into the hastily packed trunk.

By eight o'clock, he was waving both of them off as they backed out of the driveway. When the minivan rounded the corner, the smile fell from his face.

Walking back into his house, Ethan couldn't hide his worry anymore. The John Runar case was far from settled, and a killer was still at large. His family was better off outside of Campton.

Now at his desk, Ethan shook his head and tried to focus. Struggling to put aside his concerns about the murder investigation, he grabbed the incomplete monthly report in front of him. Between writing about procedural adherence and crafting a report on the safety incident, he was already behind with his daily work. Noise from the production floor filled his office. Grabbing his coffee, he chugged the entire mug, grateful for the jolt.

After three hours of nonstop activity, he needed a break. He stood and stretched. Choosing to ignore the remaining unopened emails in his inbox, he strolled towards the control room. Walking along, Ethan watched the dayshift working. The fast-paced activity of the department triggered the first telltale signs. As if on cue, his right arm started to tingle, and an aura appeared in one eye.

"Oh no," he muttered, "not today. I just don't need a migraine on top of everything else."

Travis approached as Ethan began to wipe his now sweaty forehead. "You okay?" he asked.

"I have a headache," Ethan confided.

Suddenly, his stomach lurched. Ethan turned abruptly and started sprinting to the mill bathroom. He barely made it into a stall before the retching began.

As the cold water ran over his hands, Ethan bent over the ancient sink to splash his face. He forced himself to take deep breaths. Patting his clammy skin, he tried to look on the bright side. Maybe the fact that he was able to vomit would help him make it through the day. But standing there, he noticed his hands. The skin all the way up his arms was flushed and he was feeling worse by the minute.

"Are you all right?"

Ethan jumped as he looked into the blurry mirror to see Travis standing behind him.

"I didn't see you there," Ethan said, rattled by both his illness and the hushed nature of his foreman's footsteps.

"Well, you've got the water running full blast, but I didn't mean to startle you."

Ethan stared at the reflection in the glass. Travis stood completely still; his dark expression was enhanced by his penetrating stare.

"You don't look so good," Travis said.

"I don't feel so good," admitted Ethan, unable to take his eyes off the man behind him. For some reason, he studied his unmoving shift manager and found himself suddenly wondering if Travis knew more about John's death than anyone realized.

"Why don't you go home," Travis suggested.

"I've got a lot of work to do."

"Well, you can't do it sick," he leveled at his boss.

Ethan said nothing as he turned off the water. Drying his hands, his legs started to ache. For a moment, he tasted the remnants of coffee in the back of his throat. He started to question if maybe his illness was more than a migraine. Maybe, he needed to reevaluate staying at the mill for the afternoon.

"Do you want me to help you to your car?" Travis asked, his eyes locked on Ethan.

"No," Ethan replied, wanting only to get out of the bathroom.

As he walked back to Finishing, Travis followed silently. Ethan felt odd. Sweat was starting to roll down his back, and his hands felt weak. Staying at work would be foolishness. He grabbed his laptop and keys.

"I need to go to lunch," he told the crew assembled. "If I don't come back today, I'll call you."

"Let me know if you need me to bring anything to you," Travis offered.

"I'm going home, but I should be back."

As he hurried to the exit, Travis called out behind him. "Get some rest, and don't worry, Ethan. If you need anything, I know where you live."

CHAPTER FORTY-FOUR

Calvin looked up from his monitor as Ethan rushed out of the Finishing Department. He frowned at the computer in front of him.

Leaning back in his chair, he could feel his frustration growing. Folding his arms across his chest, he drummed his fingers along the starched fabric of his shirt. What was he going to do? His project was completely stalled.

If his own cowardly behavior hadn't been so embarrassing yesterday during the safety incident, then he would have found the courage to interrupt Ethan earlier in the morning. He stared again at the open spreadsheet before him and vainly tried to figure out what was wrong. Appearing whiny and in need of help from his peers made him feel like a loser. He knew the daily production was running tight, and Ethan had his hands full. Managing an entire department was far more fast-paced and critical than special project work.

Calvin looked at his cluttered desk. So far, his day consisted of checking his own email and moving papers around to different piles. Everything made sense on the project except for the data that had been omitted. Parts of John Runar's work and communication remained incomplete, left like a puzzle with missing pieces. He pushed his roller chair away from his computer and stretched his back. The muscles in his neck were tight, and he needed a break. Besides, he didn't know what else to do.

Without meaning to, he looked out into the department and thought about everything from the last twenty-four hours. The employee accident had been so awful that Calvin was awake for most of the night. He was astonished at how quickly the entire event unfolded. All the blood on the floor only reaffirmed his belief that medical school would have been a mistake, despite what his parents said to try and persuade him.

He grimaced at the stack of paperwork on his desk. Opening all the files that John left on his computer led to endless speculation. The project was more revealing than he could have ever guessed, but something was still missing.

Calvin stood up and stretched his legs. His work was definitely at a standstill. He thought about eating an early lunch. Maybe getting away from the numbers was the ticket to clearing his head. Papers and notes covered his work area, and he vainly searched for his phone and keys. His gaze moved to the shelf above his printer and he smiled in relief. Calvin reached up to get his phone at the same moment that Travis shouted on the production floor. Loud alarms started to blare from the control room.

Memories of yesterday's gory disaster made Calvin whip his head in the direction of the noise. His fingers splayed out, and he knocked a ceramic coffee mug that functioned as pen caddy off the shelf. The green cup fell to the floor and shattered.

Calvin bent over to pick up the array of pencils and pens. In the shards of broken porcelain, a thumb drive was taped under what appeared to be a rubber disk that once lined the bottom of the mug.

Carefully, he picked up the external component. What was this doing in the cup? Did John leave it here? He stared at the small device, wondering what the thumb drive contained.

The police meticulously inspected the entire department after the accident. Had they missed this during their search of John's workstation? Calvin held up the memory stick while thoughts ran through his mind. If he never looked at the bottom of his pencil holder until this moment, then the authorities probably missed it too.

Calvin moved back to his desk. He remembered Ethan asking about a thumb drive for John's files. Ideas started to swirl in his head.

Sitting back down, he logged onto his computer. Whatever was on the external memory might be important. He had a hunch, but there was always the possibility that he might be wrong. His fingers moved over the keyboard as he narrowed his eyes. He could feel his heart starting to pound. With a little luck, he might finally uncover John's secrets.

CHAPTER FORTY-FIVE

Ethan moaned as he bent over to untie his steel-toed boots. His head was killing him, and he could hardly see out of one eye.

Out of habit, he sniffed his shirt sleeve and wrinkled his nose. His clothes totally smelled like the mill. With weary fingers, he unbuttoned his shirt and walked out of his entire outfit, leaving the heap in front of the washing machine.

The house was saturated in sunlight and silence. Only the hum of the air conditioner broke the stillness. As Ethan wandered to the bedroom to find something to wear, he realized how much he missed his wife and son.

Too tired and sick to fumble with a clean shirt, he grabbed an old reddish bathrobe. He pulled on the garment, grateful for the simple comfort. A weak smile crossed his lips as he remembered unwrapping the mahogany-colored fabric.

"You'll look like Hugh Hefner," Abbey teased as she placed the gift in his hands. Ethan rolled his eyes and then pranced around the house in his new attire until they both shook with laughter.

He ran his hands over the soft front of the robe and wished that he could hold his wife. Maybe he was wrong not to tell her everything that Starla shared with him. Perhaps failing to reveal to her that the detectives had returned to the mill yesterday was also a mistake. When he strolled into the living room, he wondered for the first time if trying to protect his family was the right choice.

The old gray sofa looked incredibly inviting. Ethan stretched his long frame onto the worn cushions and took a deep sigh. He knew that Abbey really wanted new furniture, but his arguments convinced her to wait until after the baby was born. Settling down onto the lumpy pillows, he felt both guilty for not splurging on his wife and grateful for the familiarity of his old couch.

He put one arm over his face and shut his eyes. Breathing deeply, his concerns and thoughts started to melt away as he drifted into sleep.

All at once, he was wide awake. A sound, repetitive and loud, filled the room. His eyes tried to adjust while his brain scrambled to process the noise. Ethan could feel his heart pounding in his chest.

Shadows made long lines along the living room wall. How long had he been asleep? He only meant to take a one-hour lunch. What was happening in Finishing?

Ethan looked around, disoriented. His head still hurt, and he tried to think. He swallowed, but his mouth was dry. With difficulty, he sat up and swung his legs to the floor. Noises were coming from somewhere. The thudding was beginning again in earnest. Ethan rose unsteadily to his feet. A voice called to him.

"Ethan, let me in. Ethan, Ethan!"

Someone was outside, and they were pounding on the front door. From his spot in the living room, Ethan could see the wood bumping with each blow. He took a few steps towards the foyer but then hesitated. A thought raced through his head. His family was gone. He was completely alone.

"Ethan, I know you're in there. Open up."

At that moment, he grew uneasy. He couldn't place the voice of the person on the other side of the door. His eyes darted wildly back to the living room looking for his phone. Where did he leave it? He tried to decide what to do, but before he could move, the doorknob started to turn.

Ethan crept forward, balling his fists and listening. He could hear mumbled words coming from his front porch. Thoughts of a home invasion started to race through his mind.

Instinctively, he searched for a defensive weapon to use. A small coat tree holding rain gear stood next to the front door. If he was going to peek outside, at least he wanted to be armed. He reached onto the wooden base to get the only golf umbrella in the stand.

With his hand on the deadbolt, Ethan suddenly realized how stupid he probably looked. What was he going to do, beat the intruder to death with a plastic handle?

"Who is it?" he shouted, trying to project his voice.

"It's me—it's Calvin," he heard through the thick wood.

Flipping the lock, Ethan opened the door a small crack and peered outside, still holding his weapon out of sight. Calvin Jones stood on Ethan's brick doorstep. With a huge stack of papers under one arm, he held a plastic bag in the other hand. A look of concern and worry covered his face.

"Ethan, I'm sorry to bother you, but I really need to talk to you," he began.

Ethan stood completely still, staring at the man in his doorway. For a moment, he was unable to think.

"Can I come in?" Calvin asked.

Ethan blinked and opened his door. "Yeah, sure," he said, remembering to be polite. Calvin crossed the threshold and looked embarrassed.

"I, uh, like your bathrobe," he said, trying to hide a smile.

Ethan looked down at his garment that hit just above his hairy knees. Plaid boxer shorts peeked out from the open front of the robe. He quickly bunched the fabric together as he tossed the umbrella behind the door.

"Oh, uh, yeah. Sorry. I wasn't expecting company," he muttered. "Come on in. You've got quite a load. Can I help you with all of that?"

"No, I've got it. But Ethan, I need to show you some things. Is there a place we can sit? I really need to put this down so that you can look at what I've found."

"Why don't you go to the dining room?" Ethan offered. "We can spread out in there."

"Am I interrupting your family time?" Calvin asked, looking in the living room as if he expected to find other people.

"Oh, they're out of town."

Calvin merely nodded and followed Ethan past the old sofa to the large wooden table at the far end of the room. Ethan turned on the overhead fixture and grabbed a stack of papers to help.

He tried to hide his curiosity with a pleasant smile. What could possibly be so important that Calvin had to come across town to his home? Mounds of computer printouts were starting to cover the dining surface.

"I need to make a quick call to the mill," Ethan confided as he pulled out a chair for his guest. "Why don't you make yourself comfortable and just give me a minute."

He disappeared into the kitchen and retrieved his phone from the shirt he left by the back door. Hastily redressing into his work clothes, he called his department. When he returned to the dining room, Calvin had the papers arranged in stacks.

"Okay, I touched base with Finishing. I told them that I would work from home the rest of today, so I'm all yours," Ethan confirmed.

Calvin rose from his seat and offered Ethan the plastic bag that he was holding.

"First, I want to give you this. I'm sorry for coming to your house and everything," he said. "So, I brought you a present."

Ethan stuck his hand into the bag and pulled out a bottle of vodka. His face went slack with surprise.

"Let me explain," started Calvin. "My mama told me to never come over to anyone's house empty handed, so I brought you some Grey Goose."

"I can see that," said Ethan still a bit stunned.

"Second, I know you were sick today, so I thought, maybe you might need this. You know, the hair of the dog and all."

"Well, I wasn't drunk," Ethan said with a laugh. "I had a migraine, actually."

"Yeah, I know," said Calvin with a nod as he motioned to the paperwork on the table. "But when I get through showing you what I found, you're going to need a drink. Probably several of them, maybe even more tomorrow. In fact, we both are." Ethan looked questioningly at the documents resting on his table.

Calvin put his hand onto Ethan's shoulder. "We're going to need some of that vodka because you're not going to believe what I've found."

CHAPTER FORTY-SIX

Ethan took the bottle and placed it on the edge of the dining room table. Racking his brain, he couldn't imagine what Calvin meant. How could looking at a bunch of papers possibly be so concerning? He sat down at the table to listen.

"Okay," Calvin began, "let's start with this stack." He shoved the closest vertical pile towards Ethan. "Start looking through those reports and tell me what you think."

Ethan flipped through the pages. The forms were familiar industry documents.

"Well, these are the lab reports that you generate. The ones on the new cellulose grade," Ethan said.

"Right," agreed Calvin, "and if you go down to the bottom of the pile, these labs go all the way back to when John Runar was running the testing. But what do you notice about all of them?"

Ethan looked closer at the sheets before him. Consistently, the new grade of pulp tested high in viscosity while also low in overall impurities. Their chemical analysis revealed that the samples met every parameter that would be required for the new packaging application.

"All the numbers look good—great actually," surmised Ethan as he carefully studied the data. "Looking at these reports, there's no doubt that the new grade would really make an impact in the marketplace." He looked up at Calvin, who was watching him expectantly, and continued, "New material made from this base product would change the landscape of distribution for all sorts of things–food, medicine, anything really."

"Exactly," conferred Calvin. "Now notice the name that John gave the new cellulose grade."

"St*r-10," said Ethan. He shook his head and laughed softly. "I know whose name he had on his mind when he was naming his work."

"Yeah, he clearly named it after Starla. Everything made sense after you told me about the two of them," added Calvin. "Now look at these," he said as he slid another group of papers over the tabletop.

Ethan studied the next stack of documents. They were emails that had been printed. He started to read one after the other.

"This is an email thread," Ethan said.

"Yep," said Calvin, "that's what I started to find when I got into the first set of files that were password protected. Thanks to your hints, I tried a bunch of different variations of Starla's name. When I added his nickname for his truck, I could finally open the remaining files."

"I see that address is John, but who is the other?"

"Keep reading. You see that it's someone here at Delta in Campton. When I clicked on the email address, it was hidden. I couldn't tell who was communicating with John. They also purposefully never use any names in the emails, either of them."

Ethan settled back in his chair. The exchange was lengthy, with John doing the majority of the writing, disclosing every aspect of the creation of St*r-10.

"I did a bit of scratching around on my computer, so to speak, and I finally found the sender's address. It is Mitt32UFB1."

Ethan looked up puzzled. "That's an odd email handle coming to John. Did you check the server at Delta to find out who it was?"

"I tried," said Calvin, "but all these online correspondences were sent from a private device right to John's personal email account. They were never sent using the server at the plant."

"So how did they end up on John's mill computer?"

"That what's strange. It looks like the emails were put into a file on his work computer two days before he died."

Ethan felt his brain start to click.

Calvin pointed to the papers and dropped his voice. "They never found John's personal cell phone at the accident site, remember? Supposedly, nobody ever knew what happened to it. So, I would think that these emails probably came to his phone, and then he put them on his work computer."

Ethan stared at the pages in front of him. For some reason, he thought about Starla. Didn't she get some weird warnings about keeping quiet about something? He stared at the pages and tried to figure out what the emails could mean.

Calvin continued, unaware that Ethan was half listening. "I have read through every email. The mystery person writes about Delta and everything going on at the plant. The way the emails are written, the sender is someone in upper management, someone at this mill. They mention Product Development at headquarters in Memphis, but the sender is clearly here in Campton," Calvin explained.

"Okay," said Ethan. "Since John was on special assignment, he probably had to keep upper management informed about his progress on the project."

He set the paper aside and looked up again. Calvin had a worried expression on his face. Ethan leaned back in his seat. Maybe nothing was really all that unusual, and Calvin just didn't understand the protocol for communication.

"I don't see anything out of the ordinary. John probably had to take direction from the hierarchy at the mill. He may even have been told to forward these emails on to Product Development in Memphis."

"But that's the thing," Calvin said, "if you read through everything, the person who writes to John is telling him to be purposefully vague to everyone in Delta outside of the Campton facility. They are telling him to give Product Development at headquarters only the barest facts."

Ethan looked at Calvin with uncertainty. He picked up the stack and starting reading, one page after the next. After an hour, he stopped.

"I must admit," said Ethan, "this doesn't make a great deal of sense. All I can surmise is that whoever is instructing John in these emails wants some sort of glory for our plant when the product is released."

"Yeah, that's what I thought, too," replied Calvin. "The mill has struggled to make a profit with some of our commodity grades and I assumed that St*r-10 would be the big new product that nailed the future for Delta in Campton."

Ethan nodded. Trying to obtain a healthy bottom line for the plant was nothing new. The cyclical pulp market wreaked havoc on the profits of the mill when the output of traditional products ran high and the demand was low. Too much inventory was a killer for the company bottom line, and Delta had been left with full warehouses lately.

Looking at the emails, Ethan thought about the implications of having a successful product made only in Campton. Employees would benefit tremendously from having a new marketplace invention. Ethan always found himself worrying about the future of the industry whenever Campton struggled to meet their sales goals. The lean times often gave him sleepless nights about his own performance and career. During those periods, he often woke up at dawn to recalculate his retirement accounts.

"But then I read these," Calvin said as more papers slid across the table. "I found something today. After you left, I knocked that Delta coffee mug off my shelf, you know, the one that had pens in it. Well, the cup broke, but I found a flash drive taped to a rubber pad on the bottom of the mug."

Ethan started looking at the thick mountain of papers. Something in Calvin's tone made him uneasy. He picked up the pages, one by one, and began reading. Confusion clouded his face.

"These aren't from John."

"Nope," Calvin said shaking his head, "they're from that hidden sender. Check out the email addresses. Whoever wrote to John is now writing to someone else."

Ethan read the correspondence. The mystery person at Delta, Mitt32UFB1, was outlining the details of the creation of St*r-10 to another party. He studied both addresses.

"How did John manage to get emails between two other parties?" Ethan asked.

"Beats me," answered Calvin, "but he had an assignment in Information Technologies in the front office before he came on special assignment in Finishing. If I had to guess, I would assume that he hacked into the email account of the Delta person. I don't know if any of the emails were saved to the Cloud, but John definitely saved it all on his flash drive that he hid in his office."

Ethan read in silence, his eyebrows knitting together in thought. Something felt wrong.

"It's like he stopped trusting whoever was directing him here at Delta, and he suspected that the information would be valuable—maybe too valuable—to someone else," added Calvin.

Ethan narrowed his eyes as he studied the pages, noticing a familiar name.

"This looks like the other party is Stellar-Caldmore Paper. I recognize their email address. We've sold product to them for years," said Ethan.

Calvin nodded, a worried look on his face. "I know. Almost all the specifications of our brand-new grade are right there, given to one of our biggest customers."

"This isn't our customer," Ethan said as he dropped the pages. "Not anymore. They're our competition now."

CHAPTER FORTY-SEVEN

For a moment, both men sat in stunned silence. They stared at the table covered in papers.

"Ethan," said Calvin softly, "this is why I needed to come to your house. I knew you would want to see all this. What does it mean?"

Thoughts were racing through Ethan's brain and he could feel the blood start to pound in his temples.

"Well," he replied, "while there is nothing wrong with our plant in Campton trying to keep products from direction at headquarters, it's not great company policy. But this problem is bigger than that. All of these communications reveal an email trail that leads to a traitor somewhere in upper management."

"That's what I thought," confided Calvin. "So, I guess you should see this now."

From the bottom stack, he pulled out a neatly paper–clipped pile of computer sheets. He handed them to Ethan.

"These were the final emails that John put in the folder. They are between the mystery person at our mill and Stellar-Caldmore. He put them in there right before he died. Take a look."

Ethan read through the pages, feeling his stomach start to twist. The situation was only getting worse.

"Oh shit," Ethan muttered. "The Delta person wants a payout in exchange for the final bit of information that will be provided to Stellar-Caldmore." He raised his eyes toward his dining room ceiling and let his head drop back. "Of course, they do. Why else would someone from our plant have given away competitive market information?"

"What do we do?" Calvin asked.

For the first time, Ethan thought about what it would take to fix the situation. What was the best thing to do? Another company now had insight into their unpatented process for a new market grade of cellulose. Someone within Delta was going to sell all the information required for production. Ethan ran his hand through his hair. On top of all this, John was dead, and the police had a suspect—or did they? Was this betrayal behind the murder?

"I don't really know," Ethan said slowly. "This is a company problem, but we don't know the identity of the Delta sellout. Whoever this is, if they get wind that we have this information, he or she will bury it." He paused and looked over at Calvin. "That is if they don't take matters into their own hands."

Ethan stared at the papers in front of him. Was this enough to make someone murder? Should they go to the police? But what would he tell the detectives other than someone was selling protected information? He inwardly shuttered remembering his discussion with the detectives when the subject centered on touching. His last interview with the police had made him sound like some sort of jerk.

Calvin sat with his head buried in his hands. When he turned to Ethan, his eyes were wide. "I think we should go to Roger. He's the plant manager. If we show him this data, he can most likely get to the source."

Ethan ran through a mental list of the upper managers at the plant. Suddenly, he remembered Bill Hackman meeting the detectives in the auditorium and handing them a picture of Leah and Carlos. Had he been trying to cast doubt on the current investigation, or was he trying to create additional suspects?

"Who do you report to on this project, at our facility, I mean?" Ethan asked.

"I circulate my weekly status reports to the project management team in the front office and copy the headquarters group in Memphis."

"Does anyone from the mill discuss your results with you?"

Calvin shook his head, deep in thought. "The only person that stops by and looks at my results is Bill Hackman."

Ethan felt his stomach tighten. Bill Hackman. That name kept popping up in his mind. Everyone at Delta knew about his unbridled ambition. Bill was the one person that consistently had so much information at his disposal, thanks to his position.

"So, what should we do?" asked Calvin.

"Let me think about it," Ethan answered. "This is really complicated, and we need to be smart about this."

"Well, while you're thinking, I'm pouring the Grey Goose."

CHAPTER FORTY-EIGHT

Ethan stood in his kitchen and stared at the open cabinet full of glasses. He knew that he should just reach out and take one, but his mind felt numb. All he could think about was the paperwork in his dining room. Instinctively, his hand grabbed two small tumblers.

"Do you want ice?" he called to Calvin.

"Sure."

Ethan brought both glasses into the dining room. He stopped and rubbed his tight neck.

"I can hardly think. My head is starting to kill me," Ethan explained. "Hang on, I really need to get some food for us. Wow, it's dark outside. Have you had dinner?"

Calvin shook his head. "No, but I don't want to put you to any trouble."

Disappearing back to the kitchen, Ethan surveyed his choices in the pantry. Why was the only snack option always Goldfish crackers or fruit snacks in their house these days? He took a discarded box of Wheat Thins from the shelf. A block of cheese from the refrigerator landed on a plate with a knife.

"Sorry my snacks aren't much, but I can't think about heating anything up in the microwave right now."

"Hey, this is great," said Calvin gratefully as he reached for the food. "I did the honors of pouring for us. Do you always have your drinks straight?" He motioned to Ethan's glass.

For a moment, Ethan stared at the clear liquor in his tumbler. Drinking had not been his intention. He only brought two glasses to the table out of habit. Now he didn't know how to respond.

"Well, uh," he stammered, "I'm not usually much of a drinker."

The last thing that Ethan wanted to talk about with Calvin, or anyone else for that matter, was his decision concerning alcohol. Only Abbey knew about the car wreck and DUI when he was nineteen. The whole disaster had been a wake-up call, especially when the result of his big mistake was a two-week stay in the intensive care unit. His final punishment came when he lost his engineering scholarship due to his time away from campus. Only a Pulp and Paper Fellowship, awarded the next semester, allowed him to finish school.

"I usually just have an occasional beer," Ethan explained.

"I'm sorry," apologized Calvin. "I didn't mean to bring the wrong thing."

"No," Ethan said, trying to smile, "it's fine."

How could Calvin know that Abbey only ever kept a single beer in the refrigerator at any given time? The limit was something that both of them had decided was best for their marriage.

Ethan stared at the half-filled glass that sat in front of him. He thought about the problems at Delta and his own career. Liquor had been the one thing that led him inadvertently to the paper industry, and now it was the one thing sitting right before him again in a professional dilemma. He swore off drinking hard spirits years ago. The last thing he ever wanted to do was have a problem like his old man.

He picked up the glass to move it to the edge of the table. In his hand, the vodka swirled against the lip of the tumbler. The clear liquid merely looked like water. He felt himself start to waver.

The situation at Delta was a mess. His own future in the paper industry was mediocre at best. Maybe Abbey would get sick of their small-town life. His fingers tightened around the glass. All the choices that he ever made merely resembled a series of points on a set of intersecting lines. Every crisis seemed to ultimately begin or end in booze for him, like oddly placed bookends along his life's trajectory.

Raising his glass, Ethan swallowed his drink in one swift movement. Calvin widened his eyes in surprise, as Ethan dropped the empty cup onto the table and poured another round.

"So, what should we do?" Calvin asked.

Ethan stared at the full glass in his hand. The liquor was warm in the back of his throat. He had forgotten how good vodka felt. He ran his tongue around his mouth. A warm buzz was starting at the base of his skull. Holding a brimming drink made him want another round and then another. Somewhere deep inside of him a switch was being flipped. For the first time in days, he felt powerful. He took another sip, forcing himself not to gulp.

"Well," Ethan said slowly, "I think that we have to do something. Since it's a problem at our mill, I think the right person to tell is Roger McVann."

"That's what I thought. Roger is the plant manager. He assigns all special project oversight to different senior leaders. He has to know who was directing John's work on the new grade and who was emailing him."

Ethan nodded as he finished his second drink and reached for the bottle.

"Ethan, why don't you have something to eat?" Calvin offered, handing him some cheese.

"Good idea."

He began to stuff food in his mouth while Calvin pulled piles of documents to the center of the table. Effortlessly, Ethan reached over to freshen both glasses.

"Let's figure out what are the most important things to show Roger when you meet with him," Ethan said.

Calvin simply nodded as he gathered pieces of evidence. Ethan could read the concerned expression on his guest's face, and he felt a sense of shame. Calvin was clearly worried about the situation with Delta, and now he could obviously hear the slur in Ethan's words.

Ethan dropped his eyes to the tumbler that he still cradled in his hands. Embarrassment made his cheeks flush. He knew that he should stop drinking. They both needed to stay focused. He straightened up in his chair and only took a small sip.

After an hour of work, the most crucial documents rested in neat stacks on the table. Ethan leaned back in his chair. The vodka bottle, which was now almost empty, sat nearby.

"I think we did it," he said thickly.

"Yeah, I've got it all together," agreed Calvin.

Ethan wiped his red-rimmed eyes. He was so tired. Tears wet his fingers.

"Are you okay?" asked Calvin.

"I'm sorry, man. I just miss my wife and son," he mumbled. "And this is such a mess. How did everything get so uncertain?"

"Ethan, why don't you lay down on the couch, and I'll just clean up all my papers?" offered Calvin.

"But I need to help you get all this stuff to your car."

Ethan stood up and swayed. With careening steps, he tried to move around the dining table. Calvin caught his arm to guide him towards the living room.

"Maybe I'll just sit down for a few minutes while you get your stuff into your car. You're gonna talk to Roger tomorrow, right? You need to do it first thing, and then you need to call me."

Ethan slumped sideways onto the sofa and leaned his head back. He shut his eyes.

"Yeah, I'll do it first thing," soothed Calvin. "You just rest. I'll take care of everything."

Soft breath rose from Ethan's open mouth. His splayed arms and legs that stretched across the furniture made him look as if he was running a race in his dreams.

"Get your sleep," Calvin said quietly to Ethan as he moved back to the table to gather his paperwork. "We're all going to need some rest because tomorrow everything is going to hit the fan."

CHAPTER FORTY-NINE

The noise started in earnest. Persistent ringing made Ethan open one eye, then the other. He turned his head and tried to find the offending sound while his hands involuntarily reached into the air for the source of the commotion.

Red glowing sunlight, the color of Tropicana roses, filled the living room. The coffee table by his outstretched leg was awash with bright streaks of morning color. Ethan tried to adjust his eyes. What time was it? Birds were singing outside in the live oak tree next to the window. He scrambled to piece together memories. His head still ached.

He looked down and moaned. The shirt he was wearing gaped open across his chest and his pants were twisted. Had he really slept in his mill clothing? Ethan wiped a hand across his clammy face. He was plastered in sweat. Only his bare feet felt comfortable.

Sitting up, he turned and looked over the back of the sofa to the dining room table. The empty surface prompted memories from the previous night. Calvin had been there with vodka, but now he was gone. For a moment, Ethan wondered if the evening had been some sort of dream.

The ringing stopped, plunging the house into a kind of empty stillness. Without warning, the ringtone started again. Ethan rose to his feet, trying to remember where he left his phone.

Walking into the kitchen, he spotted two empty glasses resting on top of a plate by the sink. The sight of the dirty dishes made him uneasy. Events of the previous night started running through his mind. He shook his head at the memories. Sharp flashes of drinking vodka and uncovering corporate drama were piecing together in his mind. The evening was coming into focus, only now the visit from Calvin seemed less like a dream and more like a nightmare.

A call on his cell phone made the top of the washing machine vibrate. Abbey's name flashed across the screen.

"Hey there," Abbey said cheerfully on the line. "I'm sorry that I didn't call you last night, but I fell asleep after I went out to dinner with Mom and Dad and read to Charlie."

"That's okay," Ethan said hoarsely. "I fell asleep last night too."

"Did I wake you? You still sound sleepy. I thought you would just about be ready to go to the plant."

"I worked late," he said. "so, I'm just about ready to get in the shower."

Ethan rubbed the back of his neck while he listened to his wife's chatter. So far, he had avoided an outright lie, but the few words he uttered hardly conveyed what really happened with Calvin.

"Well, I won't keep you. Go ahead and get cleaned up so you can go to work. But just think, by the weekend, you'll be at the beach with me!"

"I can't wait."

Ethan looked out of the sunny kitchen window and thought about Abbey. Telling her he couldn't wait to see her was the first completely honest sentence that he had spoken. He felt a lump in his throat.

"Mom and Dad have a beautiful place here. You're going to love it."

"I know that I will. I'm going to love it because I love you."

"Well, I love you too," she said, sounding surprised.

Ethan shut his eyes. Having Delta in such a mess made him long for his family. What he wouldn't give to hold his wife and son.

"I mean that, Abbey. I really love you and Charlie. Don't ever forget that, okay?"

"Ethan, are you, all right?" she asked with concern in her voice.

"I'm fine," he assured her. "I just miss you."

"Well, I miss you too. But hurry up and come to Destin so we can have a Babymoon!"

Ethan smiled at the sound of her voice. "I'll be there at the end of the week. I can't wait, but I have to go now and get ready for work."

He was still holding his phone as he moved down the hallway. His breathing started to quicken as he thought about the day to come. The discovery from last night nagged at him. Calvin promised to call him as soon as he spoke to Roger. Hopefully, the two of them would be able have a meeting first thing this morning before the day got too crazy at the mill.

Standing in the hot shower, the remnants of a dull headache throbbed at his temples. Ethan bent his head and shoulders under the spray. For a moment, he longed to stay in his bathroom, or at least in his house for the day. There was something safe about the wonderfully lived-in space that Abbey and Charlie shared with him. Their modest brick house, sitting quietly along the street in their small Alabama town, felt familiar and solid, like a haven from any storm they would ever face.

As the water ran down his long limbs, Ethan thought about the next few hours. Looming like a giant game of Russian roulette, everything could turn out well—or not. Bill Hackman was most likely betraying Delta Paper, and he, or one of his underlings, would be exposed within hours. A sense of dread started to gnaw in his gut.

As he dried off and dressed, Ethan mentally ran through his past assignments with Delta Paper. The last few years had taught him more than a few lessons about human nature.

There was always the way that things should turn out at the plant—and then there was the way that situations often did. In a perfect world, Calvin and Ethan would be rewarded for their ability to spot a problem and alert top management. But, in real life, not everyone wanted to see the issues, especially if the truth was inconvenient and damaging.

In the kitchen, the coffee dripped as he checked his phone again. Calvin still hadn't called him. Hopefully, he was already in a meeting with Roger.

Ethan popped two ibuprofens into his mouth and swallowed. He was a bit late for work, but hadn't he learned his lesson more than once? Having a migraine one day meant that eating well and drinking his caffeine would be more important than ever the next morning. The worst thing for his department would be for the boss to need a second sick day in a row.

Opening the refrigerator, he surveyed the leftovers that lined the shelves. He grabbed a sausage biscuit to chase away his lingering mental haze.

With his steaming mug in hand, Ethan grabbed his laptop and made his way into the living room and turned on the television. Watching sports was a guilty pleasure that he never got these days. His set was always streaming children's shows in the morning for Charlie. He smiled at the fact that baseball highlights were running on the morning news show.

Settling into the sofa, Ethan sipped his coffee. The slow java buzz was delightful. He could afford fifteen minutes to relax. His shoulders started to unwind as he swallowed.

Out of habit, his gaze drifted down to his laptop on the coffee table. He sighed in resignation. The only way to rationalize his time with Sports Center was to check his work emails while he was still at home.

He picked up his computer and logged into his account. As if on cue, the assignment from Hayley and Daniel popped into his inbox. He opened the message and read the words that filled his screen:

Hello Ethan,

Please find the attached summaries that Daniel and I have completed. We each did as you asked and identified problems and solutions for everything we found in each department in the mill.

This assignment was valuable because it taught us that problems can't be seen as just small, isolated situations, but rather as parts of the greater whole. When we found things that were wrong in production, we learned to step back and look at the entire process to see the bigger picture. Often, what looked small was really the result of something larger.

Ethan stopped reading and stared at the words before him. Facts, like little parts of an equation, started to collide in his brain. Why had he not stepped back and seen it all together? For a second, he couldn't breathe. He looked at his television that was blaring with action.

"Out!" the umpire called on the video clip.

"Oh shit," Ethan said. "What have I done?"

CHAPTER FIFTY

Calvin rounded the curve and glanced at his phone. He pushed his glasses into place to look carefully at the clock on his screen. With his Italian driving shoe pressing the accelerator, he tightened his grip on the steering wheel. The last thing he wanted was tardiness after practically begging for a few minutes of Roger's time.

His hands were damp as he sped down the highway. He knew that having a plant manager actually agree to such an early morning meeting was atypical. Usually, young managers didn't get much of an audience with the mill hierarchy.

Calvin thought about his phone conversation with Roger thirty minutes ago. He knew his call sounded urgent, maybe even a little panicked. He was sure his voice had sounded strained, but whininess was par for the course. He had to push.

"Well, I'm headed out to a meeting with the Land and Timber group this morning. Can it wait until later?" Roger asked when Calvin when he called.

"Not really. I need to see you now. It's confidential."

"Well, I'll tell you what. I need to lay my eyes on the condition of a storage facility that we lease before my meeting this morning. Do you want to join me? I know that it's just seven o'clock, but I need to

261

be there in about twenty minutes. I don't know if you know where it is, but we have an extra warehouse out on the edge of the woodlands, on Piney Tar Road."

"That would be great," Calvin said with relief. "In fact, the items at that warehouse are probably just what I need to show you."

As his car headed out of town, Calvin reviewed everything that he needed to share. He hoped that the facts would speak for themselves. Nervous energy made his legs twitch.

He tried to imagine what Roger would say when he heard the news about the status of the project. Probably the realization that a traitor within Delta was selling privileged information would be enough to make him furious. Swift terminations were probably on the horizon, maybe even criminal charges.

Calvin took deep breaths and tried to relax. The only bright spot in telling Roger was the anticipated relief in ridding himself of all the sordid information. He could just envision a weight off his shoulders by the afternoon.

His GPS warned him to reduce his speed and he turned off the main road while he rubbed his tight neck. The past week had been grueling. Dealing with an industrial accident was bad enough, but learning about company betrayal kept him from sleeping for a second straight night.

Through his bug splattered windshield, a warehouse rose in lonely isolation on the flat horizon. Like a giant rectangular box, the building stood forlornly in the middle of the backwoods terrain.

Dry dust billowed in clouds around his car as Calvin pulled to a stop in front of the first large roll-top door. He got out of the driver's seat as hot wind made his stiffly pressed shirt swell around him. Reaching back onto the passenger seat, he pulled a stack of papers across the seat.

"Can I help you?"

Calvin jumped and turned around.

"Roger, you startled me! I didn't see you there," Calvin said as he pushed his glasses into place and looked around. "Where's your car?"

"I pulled around back. The electricity is off to this building and I was trying to look at the power box on the far wall. We've had a number of problems with lights out here," Roger said.

"You can start looking at these papers, but can you open the bay door? Part of what I need you to see is in the warehouse. I think seeing the inventory will help you understand what's on the sheets in your hand." They moved towards the mounted keypad and Roger punched in a numerical code. The door didn't move.

"We're going to have to manually open it," Roger said. "When the power is out, the doors have to be opened by hand."

Calvin pulled the door up and led the way into the cavernous opening. Rolls and bales of pulp that smelled of sulfur compounds and wood chips soared vertically towards the metal roof. Calvin walked over to one of the tagged rolls, studying the information listed, and looked back over his shoulder.

"Okay, on the documents in your hand, you will see that the grade of cellulose referenced in the email stream is St*r-10. That was the name that John gave the new process that he developed. It's the same grade as this tag here," he said, pointing to the bright blue wrapper that encased the pulp.

Calvin pulled out his pocketknife and cut a small sample of cellulose off the end of the roll, walking back to Roger.

"You can feel that it's a bit different from other grades. The surfactant used in the new design gives the product a slightly slick but uniform texture."

Roger took the pulp in his hand, examining the layered fibers.

"You know, I never had the opportunity to actually see John's new grade in the final form, ready for the customer, but this is really impressive," he said with admiration.

Calvin set his knife onto a short bale of pulp in the center of the warehouse and continued. "The first five emails here show that John was emailing someone at Delta. Neither John nor the other person identify themselves, but they are talking about the creation of St*r-10. I don't know exactly who was directing his work at the mill, so I don't know who that person was."

"John reported to Product Development in Memphis," Roger said. "He only made periodic reports on his progress to the mill leadership team, but his project fell under Bill Hackman's management."

Calvin looked serious. "Whoever corresponded with John in these emails helped him decide to keep most of the process details a secret, even from Product Development at headquarters."

Roger pulled the pages close to study them. "He did? That's not right."

"That's why I wanted to meet you so I could show this to you."

"But how did you get these emails?"

"They were left on John's computer at work, in separate files. Honestly, I was stumped until Ethan helped me with the passwords. These emails were uploaded right before John's car accident. The Delta person that writes to him used a private server and an unusual email name." He paused and leaned closer. "Ethan and I even talked about it. I showed him all this last night, and we both wondered if possibly Bill Hackman might be involved."

Roger said nothing as he studied the pages and shook his head in disgust.

"Ethan and I weren't sure, but the emails read like they came from someone who handles special assignments, and we knew that Bill's current role included project oversight."

Scratching his head, Roger flipped through the pages. "Good God. I can't believe it."

"But there's something else," Calvin said.

"You mean this isn't everything?"

Calvin shook his head. "The rest of the emails are in my car. The paper trail is going to be really disturbing, I'm afraid."

"Show me," commanded Roger.

Both men started walking back out of the opened bay as sultry breezes filled the warehouse.

"You're going to be shocked at the amount of paperwork I have," said Calvin. "But before you see all of that, you need to focus on the most important pages. Flip over and look at the back two sheets in your hand," he said as he opened the passenger door of his car.

Roger's eyes widened at the stacks of papers on Calvin's front seat, but he quickly started studying the bottom sheets in his hands.

"This is the most important part," Calvin confided as he pointed to the documents. "The mystery Delta person is emailing another party at another company in those last two pages. They are discussing St*r-10 and setting up payment details for providing process secrets."

"My God, I can't believe it. How did John ever get all this?" asked Roger in amazement.

"I couldn't tell you, but he figured all this out before his death. He put everything on his computer, protected by passwords. It was like he stopped trusting somebody at Delta," Calvin said as he bent over to pick up the discarded sample that Roger had dropped onto the ground.

Deep in thought, Calvin held the fluffy fibers in his fingers and studied them. With a resigned expression, Roger's right hand went into his pocket as he spoke.

"John did stop trusting someone at Delta. Me."

For a moment, Calvin didn't say anything. He just looked up blankly, like a deer in the forest, all soft eyes and unsuspecting. Then Roger raised his gun and fired.

CHAPTER FIFTY-ONE

The blast was surprisingly loud. Roger could feel his ears start to ring. After a lifetime of hunting during deer season, Roger thought that he knew exactly what his handgun sounded like at close range. He listened in amazement. The barrel of his Colt Mustang had an echo that rippled across the empty countryside like a pebble thrown in a pond. The reverberating noise made the shot feel like a slow-motion movie.

Force from the bullet kicked Roger's hand upward as he stood and gripped the trigger. He noticed that the smell of gunpowder was sharply stunning. The burst of scent was reminiscent of being too close to the Fourth of July fireworks, the way he was as the Master of Ceremonies for the Campton festivities last year.

Calvin crumpled inward, then stumbled back and fell. A bright red stain started to spread across his starched plaid shirt. With one hand, Calvin clutched his chest as his back bounced onto the open passenger door. His foot kicked out of his left shoe, and fire ants started to run up his pants leg. Small, gagging noises, like a gargle, rose into the air as he slid to the ground.

For a moment, Roger stared at the blood that was smeared across the interior handle of the car. Long crimson teardrops fell into the dirt.

He lowered his gun, trying to judge how the ammunition probably dispersed upon impact. The imagined trajectory made him satisfied.

Silently, Calvin's expression went from twisted to slackened. The sky was still and hot as Roger stepped back and returned his gun to his waistband. He grimaced as he studied the scene.

Why did everyone have to stick their noses where they didn't belong? Technology created such a difficult trail to erase but people were always the ultimate wildcard. Who would have ever thought that John, so intent on his grand new project and his sleazy little affair, would have the foresight to hack into a private email account and save his findings on his computer? The commercialization of a new product should have been left to those that really knew how to capitalize on a revolutionary idea. But maybe everyone tries to cover their bases, Roger thought. Maybe that fact was the true irony.

Walking towards the open car, he pulled latex gloves from his back pocket. He could feel his heart pounding. Fury was rising in his brain. This was such a mess. He only brought the gun because Calvin sounded so desperate when he called. His tone had been just frenzied enough to cause deep concern.

Roger surveyed the body, fighting the urge to start shouting. Calvin was never supposed to dig so deeply. All he needed to do was to give Sta*r-10 the final push to get the product ready for the marketplace. If he had just been content to mind his own business, then none of this would have happened.

Rapid thoughts crowded his mind. He needed to be smart. The situation was getting out of control. Going forward would require some creativity. Clearly, it was time for his back-up plan.

From the front seat of Calvin's car, Roger grabbed all the paperwork and started to move. The documents proved heavier than they looked. Both of his arms strained to carry them to the back of the building. Fortunately, the stacks loaded easily into the empty boxes in his truck. He tossed the gun on top of the papers and shut the door. Quickly, he drove his car back to the front of the warehouse. From under his driver's seat, he pulled out the white fabric.

The muslin slipped easily over Calvin's face and shoulders. Roger stepped back and surveyed the image. A dead black man in Alabama with a hood over his head would keep the police guessing for a while.

In the front pocket of Calvin's pants, Roger found the car keys. With one quick movement, he hoisted the body into the open door, watching the torso crumple like an accordion on the passenger seat and floorboard. He picked up the lone shoe and threw it in the back seat. Satisfied that nothing had been left behind, he drove the car behind the warehouse and stopped in front of a muddy retention pond.

The car idled in park. After a final review, he got out and reached back in through the window. Roger put the gear shaft into drive and stepped out of the way.

Like a magnet pulling metal, the engine simply gained momentum as it rolled forward into the dirty water. Roger watched the car tip sharply and sink up to the roof.

The morning sun was beginning to bake the scorched Alabama ground as he walked back to the open bay. He took one last look at the sliced cords on the side of the building. Severing power to the warehouse was a stroke of genius. His decision to cut the electricity before Calvin arrived ensured that the cameras on the roof were disabled before the meeting even began. Roger congratulated himself on the foresight to arrive from a back road. His car would never appear on any of the recorded images. He looked down at his feet and smiled. His footprints were disappearing in the scorching wind that blew across the sandy maroon soil.

At the front of the building, Roger made a mental checklist of details. Inevitably, the crime would be discovered. Calvin was clearly murdered, and his body was sufficiently victimized with his car submerged in a murky reservoir. Everything would look exactly like a hate crime. Only a single pool of blood remained on the ground in front of the warehouse.

With a tree branch, Roger kicked loose earth over the red stain. He stood back. The sun would dry the dirt. Rain was in the forecast.

A glance into the open bay door confirmed that the everything inside the building was untouched. He walked to the keypad to wipe it clean and shut the warehouse door.

Final details ran through his mind. By the time anyone discovered the body, decomposition would be well underway. He wondered for a moment if the animals in the Delta timberlands would possibly help the process—if they would venture into the water for the corpse.

It was only when he gave the warehouse one final glimpse that the problem appeared. Calvin's engraved knife rested on a bale of pulp in the middle of the room. Roger swore under his breath.

With one quick movement, he took the knife and shoved it in his pocket. Carefully, his eyes searched the space. Everything in the warehouse was perfectly intact. The metal door slid shut with a bang.

As his sedan roared to life, Roger realized that he had only one problem left. What was the best way to deal with Ethan Weir?

CHAPTER FIFTY-TWO

Starla looked up from her computer monitor as Ethan rounded the corner of her office. She stopped; her fingers poised over her keyboard. Widening her eyes, she froze in place. Her expression was one of shock and Ethan realized that she had never seen him look so angry.

"Where's Roger?" he demanded.

"He's——," she started.

Ethan stormed to the side of her desk, knocked once, and shoved open the heavy door.

"Where's Calvin?" Ethan asked through clenched teeth.

Roger sat behind his large polished desk. Papers lined his workspace. He looked up at his visitor with a smile.

"Hello, Ethan. Good morning," Roger began.

"Where's Calvin? I know he was supposed to have a meeting with you this morning. He's not answering his cell phone. Where is he?"

"Why don't you come in and close the door," invited Roger.

Ethan didn't move. He glared at the man in front of him. This wasn't a game. Roger was going to tell him where Calvin was.

"Where is he?" he repeated slowly.

Roger moved his papers aside and folded his hands in front of him. "If you have something to discuss with me, why don't you shut the door so we can confer?"

Without taking his eyes off the man in front of him, Ethan pushed the door towards the frame. The heavy wood slammed shut with a bang.

Ethan stared at Roger. He slowly shook his head knowing that the pieces of the puzzle finally fit together. Like unlocking a complex equation, every clue lined up in his mind. He suddenly felt amazingly calm.

"He came to see you, didn't he?" Ethan asked.

Roger said nothing, but Ethan saw a twitch in his eye. The subtle movement confirmed his biggest fear.

"The whereabout of your employee, one that is currently assigned to work in your department, is not something that I can say with certainty," replied Roger.

So, this was how it was going to be? Ethan took several deep breaths, aware that his heart was pounding. He needed to stay focused. Only Calvin's safety was ultimately important.

"I'm asking you again—where is he?"

Roger shifted, leaning back slightly in his large leather chair. His expression was almost one of amusement, of knowing the truth yet finding it annoying.

"And I'm telling you again that the work schedule of a millennial minority engineer is hardly something that I can know. I've been at my desk since eight. Did he not come into the mill this morning?" Roger asked calmly.

"No, he did not. He's not answering his cell phone and his car is not in the parking lot. No one has seen him this morning at Delta."

Roger shrugged dismissively, his gaze starting to move to the window. Ethan could feel his fury rising.

"I know about everything, about John, about the emails directing his work, about the proprietary information that you intend to sell. What happened—did John finally realize what you were doing? Was that it? And what was your payout? I'm betting that Stellar-Caldmore has made it more than worth your effort to betray Delta."

"I don't have any idea about what you think you know," Roger said coldly, staring back at his visitor.

"It took me a while to put everything together," continued Ethan. "The clues were all there, but I didn't step back to see it all. You knew about Starla and John. I remember being in this office when you saw that he called her on the mill phone system. You were hardly surprised because you had figured out that they were having an affair. So, that little fact played to your advantage when you planted the chainmail out in the timberland building, knowing that it would implicate her husband in John's death. Doing that was easy enough because, of course, you have the code to every remote keypad. You actually helped me access one of the buildings with my interns, because you know all that information. You even frightened Starla with a note on her car just in case John told her anything before you killed him."

Roger stared at the man in front of him and said nothing.

"But then you also realized that another suspect would be handy, so you took the picture of Leah Runar and Carlos Silva holding hands out of the board room and made sure that your right-hand man gave it to the police."

Ethan shook his head. With two steps, he moved towards the framed photos and trophies mounted against the wall.

"But it was really the email handle," Ethan said pointing to the wall. "Mitt32UFB1. That was the final clue that pulled it together for me. You played baseball in college, didn't you? Number 32 for the University of Florida? You're always weaving your sports metaphors into your talks to the employees in the mill." Ethan shook his head. "It all fit together. I just needed to step back to see it."

"If you know so much," Roger returned calmly. "Do tell me, where is your evidence?"

Ethan paused. All the evidence was with Calvin. He had taken everything with him late last night. His stomach tightened.

"I saw it with Calvin last night. He showed the paper trail to me."

"Oh, so what you are telling me is that you are here in my office, slinging wild accusations all over the place, but you don't have any hard proof?" Roger asked. He stopped speaking as his mouth upturned. "Well, isn't that interesting?"

"I'm going to the police right now unless you tell me where Calvin is," Ethan demanded. The words were out of his mouth, sounding harsh, but the deepest recesses of his mind started to grind painfully. He could feel the shift starting in the room.

"No, you won't go to the police," assured Roger as he swiveled in his chair. "First of all, you have no real proof to your crazy theories. Second of all, you will merely look like a disgruntled, angry ex-employee."

The words hung in the air for a moment. Ethan felt a sound of disbelief leave his throat.

"You're firing me?"

"Sad, but true," said Roger in a matter-of-fact tone. "I've needed to reduce head count, and you've had a recordable safety incident in your department this week. Your little fiasco in Finishing will force us to deal even more closely with the corporate industrial safety department in Memphis and that is contrary to our mill goals."

"You can't be serious?"

"Oh, I'm serious," he said. "But you can rest assured that you were well liked by fellow employees. In fact, paperwork is in the process of being sent to me this week that would have given you a promotion and an opportunity to transfer to Headquarters," he said, leaning forward on his desk. "The folks in Memphis always thought you did good work. They had spotted you a while back and were eager to have you join the corporate group." He paused letting the knife twist. "But that won't happen now."

"I'm going to the police," said Ethan flatly.

"Oh, you won't do that," answered Roger, smiling again. "Because there is also a third reason for you to stay silent. If you go to the authorities, I will personally blacklist you in the paper industry. Yes, that's right. I will put so much information out to other companies about you that you'll struggle to find so much as an entry–level position. And yes, I can do that," he stated. "I have that much power."

Before Ethan could say a word, Roger picked up his mill phone and punched a red button.

"Security, I need you in the plant manager's office ASAP."

"You'll never get away with this," Ethan told him. "I'm going to find Calvin. He also knows that truth."

The office door flew open and two burly security guards burst into the room. They looked at Roger and then Ethan. Concern gave way to confusion on their faces.

"Please escort Mr. Weir to the front gate and see that he leaves the mill property immediately."

One of the guards put a hand on Ethan's shoulder.

"Come on," he said quietly.

"Where is he? Tell the truth!" Ethan said between clenched teeth.

"Good day, Ethan," dismissed Roger. "And good luck. Remember what I said. You need to make the right decision for your future and the future of your sweet little family."

CHAPTER FIFTY-THREE

Starla's mouth dropped open as Ethan walked out of Roger's office flanked by two guards. Was this really happening? Even though she had clearly watched security march past her desk, the sight of a manager being forced off mill property was almost incomprehensible. She stopped what she was pretending to do and simply stared.

Ethan caught her eye as he passed her chair. His expression told her that something was terribly wrong. There was pleading in his face. She held his gaze. A look of worry and then resignation passed between them.

Starla watched the three men walk into the hallway. Words tried to form in her mouth, but they were out the door before she could speak.

Unable to process what she was seeing, her inner voice wanted to scream out that something was deeply wrong. Never in her wildest dreams did she ever see something like this coming. There had to be a mistake. Ethan Weir embodied Delta Paper, maybe more than anyone else at the mill. He was one of the good guys in a sea of lesser men. Besides, she had been listening through the door.

Obviously, there had been an argument in Roger's office, but the heavy wood allowed her to hear only snippets of the confrontation.

Something was going on with Calvin Jones, that much she had been able to ascertain, but the rest was lost in muffled sound. The fact that she worked for a paper company always made her curse whenever she was straining to eavesdrop. Thick doors had a way of blunting the best information.

"Starla, I need you to hand walk these papers to Human Resources," Roger said as he stood next to her.

She took the sheets, looked at them in surprise, and then glanced back at Roger. For the first time, she noticed that he had a sheen of perspiration on his face although the air conditioning in the office was almost frigid.

"Roger, Ethan is…," she began.

"Starla, Ethan Weir will no longer be working here at Delta," he explained hotly. "You know, I run this facility as I ultimately see fit. Everyone is either on board or not. There are employees who never know when to keep their mouths shut. They talk too much, and then they are sorry."

Starla felt Roger's eyes on her face. The words rang in her ears. That phrase—talk too much and then are sorry—where had she heard those words? Why were they so familiar and frightening? A chill ran down her spine.

"I've written some additional comments on the standard forms, and they need to be dealt with immediately."

"Of course," she managed to say.

Long ago, Starla learned to agree to everything that was asked of her and then to figure out what was really going on in the paper business. The forms in her hand would definitely need her scrutiny before she did anything else.

"Are you ready to go?"

Bill Hackman stood in the doorway; he nodded to Roger.

"Just about, I just need to get my briefcase."

As Roger disappeared back into his office, Bill winked at Starla and touched his tongue to his upper lip ever so slightly. He grinned at her. Starla looked at Bill and tried to hide her disgust. She wished that she could stand up and slap the stupid look of lust off his face.

Ever since John's death, Starla noticed the increasing overtures that seemed to come her way from the men at work. More than a few managers apparently wondered if she needed a new relationship, some sort of sugar daddy. All the repeated advances only left her wanting to plant her knee in whatever offending crotch was standing in front of her.

Starla looked at Bill and said nothing. Evidently, such indignity was the price she was going to pay for a while. There was an inevitable cost to having an office affair in an industry where nothing is ever truly private.

"I'm driving Roger to the airport in Mobile," Bill told Starla as he sauntered closer. He said the words almost like he was bragging. "Time for him to head up to Memphis to tell them what a fantastic operation we have here. The folks in corporate need to know what great people work here." He dropped his voice to continue. "Roger is going to tell them which one of us needs a promotion to the next level."

He was obviously talking about himself, she realized. His inflated ego forced her to hold a blank expression. Starla turned away in her chair. His presence, so close, was revolting.

She also needed a better view of Roger. Glancing at her boss, Starla noted that his briefcase was open on his desk. She could tell from his body language that he was reviewing everything he would need for his trip.

As she watched out of the corner of her eye, Roger put his hands on his hips in thought. Suddenly, one hand dropped into his front pocket.

Pulling out something shiny, he opened a small desk drawer—one that was always private—and dropped the object inside. His fob for his car followed the item. With a swift twist, he locked the drawer and put the keys in his bag.

"I'll be back next week," Roger said, hoisting his hanging bag over his shoulder. Bill reached out to grab his briefcase. "I'll be in touch via my cell and email."

"See you then," Starla said with a forced smile.

She watched them disappear down the hall. Getting rid of both of them flooded her with relief. For the first time, she looked carefully at the papers that Roger had given to her. Ethan was clearly being fired. She read the comments in disbelief. Roger described Ethan as everything from reckless to uncaring. At one point, the document even outlined how the Finishing Department had allegedly sabotaged production. Nothing on the dismissal forms was true, and she knew it.

Starla gathered the pages in a pile and neatly tapped them on end. The moment to make an executive decision had arrived. She nodded her head and smiled as the papers moved towards their destination.

Quality work systems were incredibly important, Starla always said. In fact, she always felt a sense of shame when paperwork got misplaced or even destroyed. Roger would undoubtedly be annoyed at the clerical error, but such was life. She turned on the shredder and fed the machine everything in her hand.

CHAPTER FIFTY-FOUR

Starla felt an incredible sense of peace as the last page buzzed through the shredder. Like finally figuring out how to master an opponent, getting rid of the termination paperwork for Ethan Weir felt incredibly empowering. She sighed. Doing the right thing created such an amazing sense of calm.

She made a mental note to call Ethan later in the day. He was one of the nicest men she knew, and he deserved some help. Starla had some ideas about how to appeal his termination, maybe even thwart the process. Hopefully, he would take her up on the offer. Ethan needed to remember that decisions were never really final until Human Resources had their paperwork, and they certainly wouldn't be getting any of the necessary forms or notifications in Roger's absence.

In the past, Starla knew that she wouldn't have dared to interfere with decisions from management. But that was then, and this was now. The way she saw life nowadays, the top people were often the ones most in need of correction. Their choices, bolstered by power, were often the most dangerous. This was one of the many things that she had learned in the last month since John's death.

Starla searched her desktop for just the right tool, thinking about how much her life had changed. Glen was finally given an initial court hearing, and she sold most of her jewelry just to hire a Campton lawyer for him. Glen was surprisingly grateful for her sacrifice. The olive branch made her move out of the trailer so much easier for both of them.

These days, her new apartment sat on the edge of a rural highway. She had only two pieces of furniture. In fact, everything she owned, including her dog, could fit in the back of her Camry. But being on her own proved to be surprisingly wonderful and liberating. No one could lay a claim to what she had, but then again, she didn't have much.

Starla often found herself remembering John. Their time together had been a blessing even if their relationship meant that the small-town tongues often wagged. No, she knew that she wasn't his wife, but she had learned how to love herself, in part because of him.

In the beginning, Starla thought that the affair merely taught her about the finer things in life. Now, she knew that type of exposure was only part of the transformation. Her greatest realization was that she, little old Starla, was strong and smart. Her life could be anything. But John would also be proud to know that she had finally left Glen.

Opening her desk drawer, she spotted the very thing she needed. A diamond nail file—once a small gift from John that she kept at work as a remembrance—rested in the front tray. There was something about a good sharp point that was always the perfect choice.

She pushed back her chair and got to her feet. Starla crept into Roger's office and gently shut the door. With the knob still in her hand, she made sure that the deadbolt was set. Without making any noise, she moved towards the desk with the lightness of a stalking cat.

Her eyes narrowed at the nail file in her hand. The tip was almost too wide for the task. Getting the lock open would require precision. In total silence, she carefully slid the pointed end into the small latch. She knew that her success would depend on her ability to feel the inside of the mechanism. Fortunately, this was hardly the first time that Starla had ever picked a lock. The drawer slid open in less than a minute.

Two objects rolled together in the empty wooden compartment. A long metal piece caught her eye. In confusion, Starla bent down for a closer look. She started to reach out and take the item, but her hand stopped. Her heart was starting to pound. Fingerprints could always be incriminating, and she was already guilty of breaking into Roger's desk.

Starla furrowed her brow in confusion. Obviously, the long tool was a penknife, but the question was why Roger would be putting something like that in his private drawer? She read the inscription without touching the smooth, shiny silver. The lettering on the handle had Calvin's name engraved on the side. Starla felt her stomach tighten. She had ordered the special gift just a few weeks earlier. What was Roger doing with it? Staring at the knife, she remembered how furious Ethan was this morning. When she listened at the door, she heard him ask Roger repeatedly about Calvin's whereabouts. Something started to feel strange.

Her attention shifted to the fob. For a moment, she wondered about Roger's car. He certainly didn't need to start his vehicle if he was traveling by plane, but he usually left personal keys in a hidden box in the back of his credenza along the wall. Starla stared at both items. Little pieces of information were lining up like dominoes in her brain.

The phrase that Roger said when he stood next to her desk sprang to her mind. Those oddly familiar words had been on the note on her car. Suspicions started to ping in her brain. Starla grabbed the car fob and shut the drawer.

Going to the parking lot and opening Roger's car was hardly a problem. She could always claim that she thought he needed a file that he left in his trunk. Nobody would suspect that she was snooping. She turned from the desk and headed for the door. The time had come to do her own digging.

CHAPTER FIFTY-FIVE

"May I take that, sir?"

Roger stared at the small plastic cup that he was holding. Absentmindedly, he nodded and handed over the remnants of his cocktail to the flight attendant, realizing that he had barely touched his second scotch.

His gaze drifted to the small oval window next to his seat. Rain pelted the glass. He watched the water drops scurry across the outside of the plane. For most of the trip, he had been too lost in thought to notice the wet sky. For the first time, he saw that the ground was getting closer, making the cars and roads larger by the minute.

The trees that dotted the terrain below the wing caught his attention. They looked like miniature landscape props. Out of habit, Roger studied the sweeping forests. Lone brown saplings, victims of the summer heat, were evident from his elevation.

"Dead roots," he muttered. "Poison to the forest."

His thoughts returned to Delta Paper as he looked at the lifeless trees. John and Calvin clearly failed to know their place. Both of them refused to take direction and work only on what was required. Neither one of them could see how much was at stake. Their constant probing meant that Roger ultimately had no choice. He had to deal with them like foresters would deal with dead a tree. They had to be removed. They were poison roots.

For the first time, he looked around at the fellow passengers on the small plane. The smell of sunscreen and sweaty bodies permeated the stale cabin air. Vacationers with carefree expressions were returning to Memphis from the Gulf coast. Roger noted their presence with detached disdain.

Returning his focus to the gray window, Roger thought about checking his phone. Would he have a string of messages that required his attention? The trip failed to yield the work time that he had anticipated when he boarded.

"I'm sorry, sir, but the summer storm has the captain asking that all passengers refrain from electronic devices at this time," the flight attendant told him at takeoff.

Roger chafed at the restriction, but after the second scolding, he gave up and put his phone in his briefcase. As a peace offering, the flight attendant handed him an extra drink from the serving cart.

Flying first class without his digital tools ended up being just what he needed. The ride gave him some needed time to finally think and plot for the future.

Roger rested his thick hair on the reclined seat and tried to relax. In the large leather chair, he decided to use the time to mentally strategize about his deal with Stellar-Caldmore. His long legs stretched out in front of him. He closed his eyes and leaned back, determined to use the last few minutes of the ride for planning. He felt spent.

The situation at Delta had all but spun out of control. Fortunately, getting the final bit of information to Stellar-Caldmore was still doable. The company contact was planning to meet him at his hotel tonight. They had agreed to join him in the lobby of the Peabody for a drink, followed by a private dinner. The final process details were in his briefcase, ready to disclose if the deal went well. With a little luck, Roger would have the money by midnight. There just didn't need to be anymore missteps. Spur of the moment revelations were proving tragic for everyone.

He winced at the thought of his car left in the Delta parking lot. His trunk was full of documents that would require shredding. If only he had not run out of time, he would have destroyed all the paperwork. But he did the right thing by showing up at his office by eight. Keeping a regular schedule was as important as an alibi. The police, with their slow, methodical investigation, were already proving easy to throw off course.

Calvin should have never pressed so hard to look at the parts of the project that were outside of his manufacturing scope. But then who would have thought that John could have accessed so much information only to leave the trail behind on his computer? If only Roger could have simply taken John's devices in the bathroom that night, maybe their ultimate fates could have been different. Roger thought about both men and shrugged. Calvin and John had been perpetrators really, more like culprits than victims.

Ethan was the final wildcard. There was always the chance that he would go to the police, but the look of fear in his eyes had been telling. He would probably think long and hard about his options. If he did go to the authorities, it would only be after much contemplation. With a few phone calls, he could all but blacklist Ethan from employment.

A smile started to form on Roger's lips. He would have the money from Stellar-Caldmore in an offshore account within the day. As a safeguard, he made a mental note to call a few paper companies once he was on the ground. The smear campaign against Ethan needed to begin immediately.

Roger's neck bounced against his head rest as the wheels of the plane found the tarmac. He felt himself pulled forward, a pawn of inertia, as the small jet applied its roaring brakes.

At the gate, Roger unfolded from his padded seat. After taking his bags from the overhead compartment, he moved to the door. Being first out of a plane was a lovely perk for his frequent flying status.

A faint smell of barbeque from an unseen restaurant on a different concourse drifted through the airport gates. Roger readjusted his bags on his shoulder and wondered if his private driver could make a stop for ribs on the way downtown.

He noticed an ad for a real estate office along the airport wall. Roger looked at the sign and pondered where he would buy a house when he came to Memphis to live. The St*r-10 launch would ensure that the corporate team at Headquarters would want his expertise in order to market the new project. Being flush with cash from Stellar-Caldmore could open literal doors to better neighborhoods and the right people.

Getting to live in more than dried up small towns was always part of the decision to sell information to a competitor. Roger glanced at the photo of the Memphis skyline that filled the airport ad space. He craved a city that would welcome his ambition.

For a moment, Roger remembered his ex-wife. After eleven years and seven moves to paper mill towns, she left. In the divorce papers, she said that Roger's main problem was that he was more intent on being a good Delta employee than boldly handling his own career. He wondered what she would say if she knew how cunning his aspirations had become.

Exit signs and partitions squeezed the line of arriving passengers into a single file stream. Roger turned on his phone with one hand as he waited in line for the escalator leading to ground transportation.

A text message from Bill Hackman pinged on his phone. Roger swiped across the screen as he stepped on the revolving stairway.

Hope your flight was good. Just to let you know, the police were talking to Starla when I returned to the mill. She said to tell you that she had a special surprise for you after everything you have done the last month. (Don't let on that I spoiled her big plans!) Have a great trip and knock them dead!

Roger looked up as the escalator steps gently floated to the floor. For the first time, he noticed two men, each dressed in black with lanyards around their necks, waiting on either side of the handrails. Something about the two of them reminded him of the detectives in Campton. Their eyes met his.

"Roger McVann? Please step this way."

The men took his elbow insistently. They pulled him to the left.

"But, I–,"

"We need to ask you some questions about John Runar and Calvin Jones," said the older man as his police badge caught the fluorescent lights.

"Wait, you've got this all wrong," started Roger.

"Right this way, sir. We are going to need to take a ride together," he said, pulling out handcuffs.

"Get your hands off me," Roger fumed as he dropped his bags. "Do you know who I am? I just arrived, how dare you!" The cuffs encircled his wrists.

The younger officer tightened his grip on Roger's arm. "Sir, we know exactly who you are," he said, looking at his partner with a smile. "But let me be the first to add, welcome to Memphis."

ACKNOWLEDGEMENTS

Writing a second book is a bit like giving birth to a growing family. After the first novel, or the first baby, you are delighted and relieved. In fact, the you are so happy that you are fairly sure that you won't do it again-until you do! In both cases, the journey and final outcome are well worth the effort.

I have been blessed to receive help from the following people. They have my gratitude and greatest respect.

The story was improved by Amy Miles, a wonderful author in her own right. She has my thanks for coaching so that the first chapters could begin with excitement.

Abbey Suchoski and the team at Palmetto Publishers also have my deepest gratitude for another great cover, formatting and bringing the story to life. They are wonderful advocates for their clients.

Without Chris Peeple, my editor, this book would not exist. Her superb corrections and encouragement were just the wisdom that I needed most for this project.

I am thankful to Rick Miles and Redcoat PR for excellent marketing and helping me reach a wide audience with this most unique murder mystery. Without their help, my readers would not be able to peek into the world of industrial intrigue.

Rounds of applause go to Kimberly Cornett at AT&T for her patience and answers to questions about technology that were so helpful to me. Her "techie" knowledge has my total gratitude!

Johnnie Yancy gave me such thoughtful answers about my "police" questions so that I could frame my story correctly and I am so appreciative.

A huge contribution to this book came from Lieutenant David Townsend. His willingness to read police dialogue and share insights into law enforcement were invaluable to me. I am in debt to him for adding fictional character development to his long list of community services and achievements.

I was also blessed to have Katherine Godoy lend her talent to me as an excellent beta reader. Her careful eye and keen insight were so important to me.

Rick Carter has my love for his repeated reading and excitement of the manuscript. He is the best cheerleader.

Thanks to Will Carter for reading and discussing the Chapters with me. His perceptions were so valuable for the story.

My greatest thanks to Laura Carter Jowers for reading, editing, and critiquing every Chapter, often after long days of teaching. Her support and love mean so much to me.

And finally, to Gray Carter, my heart is full because of his wisdom and faith. I cherish his support. He is the best-always.

ALSO BY BETH KREWSON CARTER

The Nest Keeper

Made in the USA
Coppell, TX
04 October 2021